BOOK REVIEWS

5.0 out of 5 stars ...Wow!

The Cancer Machine is a smart medical thriller that questions motives, greed, virtue, temptation, and friendships. It speaks to a large audience because many people are affected by healthcare and how it's tangled with government affairs and personal aspirations. Anton Thresher's desire to do what's right in order to help others echoes many readers' plight when struggling with all the evils in the world. The story may be fictional, but its realism and intelligent path through the conflict make The Cancer Machine sound as if it were a chilling documentary.

5.0 out of 5 stars ... Well-written and Entertaining

This is an enjoyable story about a brilliant, young doctor who involves himself in a high-risk-high-return clinical test to prove a revolutionary cancer treatment. Author Petteruti's experience as a physician shines through in a storyline that finds the protagonist fighting his way to success only to bump heads with a self-serving, ruthless pharmaceutical company. The story is fast-paced, well-written, and at times eye opening with 'holy cow' moments. It took me two chapters to up my reading game to Petteruti's style, but after that, the story rocked to the end. Well done, doctor. Recommended.

5.0 out of 5 stars ... Medical fictional novel for our times

I praise the author for using the background of our country's current crisis re. Chinese flu, and the competition going on between big pharma companies and the politics of the event. This book was a page turner for me and I found myself reflecting on current events. The novel contains all the necessary genre elements to merit a 5-Star rating.

5.0 out of 5 stars ... Needed info

It's fictional but it's realistic so it's a great way to tell a story about the corruption of the modern medical mafia. It doesn't care about people. It just cares about money. People are choosing money over what is right and because of that everyone suffers. A page turner for sure and a great read!

5.0 out of 5 stars Great book

Reviewed in the United States on October 2, 2020
This is a fascinating story that gives a look on the pharma industry of the modern medical world. I really enjoyed the realism in this fictional book. It is almost like reading nonfiction but a lot more fun. It is a very emotional yet exciting read and the characters are amazing!

5.0 out of 5 stars Wow!

Reviewed in the United States on September 27, 2020
This is highly engaging medical thriller that's sure to get your heart racing!!

To Shannon;
Your belief, enthusiasm, organization and ability brought this book to life.
Your love brought me to life.
-S&S-

THE CANCER MACHINE

A novel

Dr. Stephen Petteruti

ISBN: 0692820914
ISBN 13: 9780692820919

CHAPTER 1

When he was little, Anton Thresher used to dream about flying. With arms outstretched, he would make loops in the backyard, grit his teeth, and make a v-r-r-r sound. He would ascend into the clouds and swoop out again with perfect grace and control, running at top speed. Sometimes he would close his eyes and turn his face toward the sun to see its bright-orange imprint on his closed lids. "V-r-r-r-!" He would block out all other sounds as the sun would blot out all other visions, and the sweet aroma of spring lilacs would completely fill his nose. As he would just about leave the ground, his mother would call to him.

Maybe that's why now, as a medical student, he liked to ride his bike so much, especially along Old Pool Road on a cool summer morning. Who knows how fast he would pedal—forty easily, maybe fifty, probably more. Now, with hands clenched on the handlebars and head bent low to decrease the wind resistance, he churned his legs in a fury. Most people would probably glide down this road, using it to catch a rest while admiring the striking panoramas of the Atlantic coast. But Anton sprinted. His legs began to burn. This was when he liked it the most. He would imagine other riders trying to stay with him and one by one dropping off the pace until only his best friend, Scott Antonelli, was left. Then, with one final surge, he would leave Scott behind as well.

He had only eight more miles to Professor V. T. Roberti's house. The old professor would be expecting him for breakfast, and Mrs. Roberti was probably just finishing the frosting on the breakfast pastries. Anton sometimes thought the only reason that V. T. had invited him to collaborate in his research was so the two of them could enjoy breakfast together. The breakfast would often linger almost until lunch as the two would sit on the front porch drinking hazelnut coffee and discussing religion, philosophy, politics, and occasionally even medicine. But then, as V. T. was wont to say, medicine was simply an amalgam of the former three, so their conversations always had medical applicability.

Old Pool Road leveled out into a flat stretch that paralleled the beach. At the base of the hill was a dip in the road that always collected a veneer of sand, making it particularly dangerous at high speed. From there, Anton could see the small cluster of buildings that marked the university. About the only thing open this early would be Mary's Country Store and Deli. He glanced at his watch, checked the road, and then bowed his head and focused on the white lines as he shifted gears to begin the final sprint to V. T.'s house.

V. T. came out on his porch and greeted Anton. "Well, boy, did you break a record?" He was wearing his tattered, blue, terry cloth bathrobe; sweatpants splotched with gray paint; and worn slippers that exposed most of the toes on his right foot and the heel on his left foot. He sauntered down the crushed-shell driveway, with one hand holding a cup of coffee and the other buried in his robe pocket. The newspaper was tucked under his left arm. Atop his head was a fur hat of the style sported by Muscovites in the winter.

Anton looked up from his stopwatch and smiled at the sight of his old friend. "Yeah, I chopped a full thirty-one seconds off it. Old man, we better get you inside before someone sees you and has you carted away. Dean Handley would love that. It would give him the excuse he needs to bounce you out of the department."

"That's OK. Gives me more time to work on my garden."

Anton put his arm around V. T.'s shoulder. "Tell me, my little friend. Did you shrink anymore since I last saw you?"

"Boy, anyone over five foot seven is a freak. All those extra inches just divert energy from more important functions."

Anton sensed something different in his friend. He looked into his soft, gray eyes for a moment. Was there a hint of sadness there? Did his skin seem somehow less glowing? No, if there were something, it would stand in contrast to his relentlessly positive nature, like tar on snow, not to be missed.

"Well, V. T., what's this breakthrough all about?"

"Boy, don't you know that I can't discuss breakthroughs on an empty stomach? Let's have some breakfast."

The ranch-style house was a modest affair with weather-beaten shingles and jammed full of eccentricities, quite the reflection of its occupants. It was set on a small hill overlooking several acres of land covered with various fruit trees that V. T. tended to as if they were his children. In one corner was his garden, covering a full four hundred square feet. In the other corner was a boccie court, and surrounding the perimeter were sundry varieties of ornamental trees all professionally pruned and richly mulched. Along the back property line were towering sugar maples. In the fall, their brilliant colors were mesmerizing. Anton remembered more than one occasion when he would arrive unannounced to find V. T. staring at that line of trees, lost in thought.

They entered through the front room. A map of the world was plastered on one wall, covering the entire area like wallpaper. Marked in red were all the places where V. T. had traveled. The map was nearly covered with red pins, mostly in Africa. V. T. liked to joke that when he was a kid, his dad had a map of Maine on the wall, with one red mark on it. Maybe that's why V. T. had left home when he was sixteen.

Pictures of children covered the other wall. In one picture was a group of smiling, black faces, with V. T. in the center and holding a child in his arms. Another picture was a candid shot of an African child, legs folded, staring at nothing, with a fly sitting on his eyebrow.

Under a wall of pictures was an old, overstuffed couch that always beckoned Anton to sit in it and disappear into its cushions. In front of it was a wooden coffee table covered with medical journals and magazines. In one corner was a well-worn reclining chair with a floor lamp next to it. Anton suspected that the Robertis may not have bought a new piece of furniture in the past twenty years at least.

Anton and V. T. took their familiar seats in the sunroom while Mrs. Roberti, Pat, served a breakfast of scrambled eggs, bacon, and hash browns.

"Ah yes," said Anton. "Another Roberti artery-clogger special. I think we should be doing research on heart disease instead of cancer."

"Heart attacks are a gift to the old," said V. T. "Now there is a great organ. It works at full speed for your whole life until one day, boom! And you're gone in a few seconds. None of this fading-away nonsense."

"I don't know. The idea of having a little time to prepare and get things in order kind of appeals to me."

"Boy, that's what life is for. If you're not ready after sixty years, what good is a few months? I believe the world would be a better place if people got up each morning and thought about their own death for a few minutes."

"Aren't you men in a cheerful mood this morning," said Pat. "Would you like some OJ with your breakfast, or should I just skip to the arsenic?"

V. T. smiled. "Cheerfulness is a frivolous trait that men cannot indulge themselves with. We are too busy running the world." He waited for his wife's return volley. She only smiled and shook her head, so he continued. "As a matter of fact, I think women are genetically programmed to be cheerful so that they can better entertain men and help take our minds off running the world for a few minutes so we can be sure to propagate the species."

Pat huffed. "If we are born with a natural excess of cheerfulness, it is to withstand the erosion that occurs when we come into contact with the men of the world. Now, if you don't mind, I'll retire to my art studio and let you two men resume running the world. Perhaps you can start a war by lunch."

V. T. turned to Anton. "You know, boy, she may have a point there."

Anton admired the youthful energy that the Robertis displayed around each other. They seemed to enjoy being together. Didn't married couples sort of run out of things to say to each other? Didn't the marriage, regardless of how passionate at the start, ultimately devolve into a business partnership, with each half silently accepting the burden of their role? He thought the Robertis were a bit unusual. Maybe it was because they had no children. Maybe it was because they were Italian. He would have to ask Scott about this when he got back.

"Now my stomach is full," Anton said. "Tell me about the breakthrough."

"Anton, how long has cancer been on the planet?"

"What?" Conversations with V. T. were sometimes akin to being in a boxing match with a wild southpaw. Punches would come from all angles, and Anton was unsure of where the next opening would be.

V. T. continued. "The way I figure it, it's likely to have been here about as long as the planet's been around. I'll bet the dinosaurs had cancer. It probably helped wipe them out. So, I don't guess we need to be in a breathtaking rush to find a cure."

At times, Anton found V. T.'s irreverence annoying. This was one of those times. "People are dying, V. T. We have a responsibility to work in some earnest fashion if we think we are on the right trail."

"And if we are on the wrong trail, then we can dog it?"

"No, then we must work harder so we don't waste so much time."

"Don't worry, Anton. We are on the right trail. I believe we are getting very close now."

"What makes you so sure?"

"First, I have a physiologic tendency toward overwhelming confidence in anything I undertake. Second is the empirical fact that if everyone else is on the wrong path, as proven by the establishment's current cancer-fighting ineptitude, and if our path is in no way related to theirs, then we must be closer to the truth. And third, I believe it was divine intervention that sent you here to figure out what I don't have the ability to decipher. You are the final ingredient in this journey. I'm crazy enough to conceive the concept, but you, Anton, you have the gift to put it all together."

Anton looked into his friend's soft, gray eyes. He had never spoken to Anton in this manner. It all sounded correct. Anton had always felt his life was somehow destined to have a larger impact on the world, that he could not be bound by the normal constraints of humanity, for that might betray his higher calling. Maybe that was why whenever he ran into the guardians of convention, he seemed to instigate conflict in them.

"And I suppose it's my job to create world peace as well?" Anton asked with a joking false modesty.

"Does this role intimidate you? If it does, that would not surprise me. I know you are gifted, and I believe that you have some sense of that gift. Did you ever wonder why you were born with the brilliance that you possess? Was it to become a physician to help people? That is a worthy goal, but there are many less talented people totally capable."

Anton thought of Scott.

V. T. smiled. "I don't believe that God imparts gifts on us so that we can glorify ourselves. I believe he imparts gifts on us so that we can do his work for him on Earth. But, you see, we are given free will so that once the gift has been imparted, we can do with it what we wish. Most people use their gifts to achieve selfish gains. I don't believe you're one of those, Anton."

"I have no interest in making lots of money."

"You can't say that until you're in the position to make lots of money. There are other ambitions that can cloud the divine plan."

Anton grinned. "Are you an angel sent here to outline my divine plan, V. T.? Did God send me here to rid the world of pestilence?"

"Boy, I may be nothing more than a diversion in your life plan. I may be one of those obstacles you have to overcome to get at the truth. That is something you'll have to figure out. I know I am sincere, but I also know that the real threats come at you with heartfelt sincerity. If they were overly malicious, you would ferret them out. Of course, some people can develop sincerity for any interest that advances their aim. They are the kind of folks that can fool a lie detector test."

"Don't worry, V. T. I'll figure it out. Remember, I'm gifted."

"Good. You're going to need your gifts to figure this all out. I've been researching the incidence of cancer throughout the region. I've identified several areas that have a strikingly low incidence of cancer within them. One that stands out is in the foothills of the Longfellow Mountains in a town called Hopedale. I want you to go there and determine if there are any elements in the environment that could explain the absence of cancer."

For the past three years, V. T. and Anton had been doing academic research looking at the origins of cancer, including current theories and treatments. Their focus was on why current treatments were so ineffective and what alternative approaches should be taken. They were both convinced that the answer was hidden somewhere in nature. Their philosophy was that for every problem afflicting people's health was a remedy to be found in nature. The challenge was solving the riddle.

"I know we've looked at leads in the past," said V. T. "But this is the most promising cancer-free zone that we have yet discovered."

Anton studied the map, looking at the surrounding areas and taking note of the topography and the rivers. "Judging from the maps, I suspect it must be a locally grown plant substance. Looking at how the watersheds appear to run, it would be hard to have a water source that would be so isolated. Of course, an airborne agent would likewise be less likely to be so concentrated. This looks promising. I will head up there next weekend."

CHAPTER 2

M uch of the research up to this point had been fairly clandestine. Anton remembered the day four years ago when V. T. had asked him to join the research project. It was after one of V. T.'s anatomy lectures. The old professor had begun the lecture discussing pulmonary anatomy, veered into the politics of tobacco production, darted back into the anatomy of the chest cavity, and then finished on a tangent railing against the "cancer barons" who were making a career out of producing research topics without producing results. Somewhere about halfway through the lecture, some of the students began to drop their pens and roll their eyes in exasperation. Julie Wyckoff, the student council class president, had taken to taping V. T.'s lectures. She hoped to demonstrate to Dean Handley that the professor did not teach in the "appropriate" fashion.

"I can never take coherent notes in his class," Julie said as she and her minions lamented around the water cooler after the lectures. "Hasn't that man ever heard of an outline? This is anatomy class, not philosophy!"

At the same time, Anton and many of the others were enthralled by V. T.'s delivery. Each class was an unpredictable journey, with the essence of human anatomy somehow fitting in neatly with the greater scheme of history, art, science, and religion. Couldn't the others see that the human body was not so much a machine—not just an independent jumble of organs, nerves, and muscles—but rather a central component in the harmonic balance of the universe? This was the approach to medicine that Anton had sought when he first went to medical school.

After that class, he approached V. T. and waited his turn at the podium while his classmates each took a turn asking the professor a question. Some of the others stood around to hear his response. By the time it was Anton's turn, the next class was beginning to form. Dr. Umbercon had arrived to start the next lecture. She was stoop shouldered with mousy, brown hair cut in an uneven pageboy style. Her pale face was adorned by a chronic frown and framed by solid-black horn-rimmed glasses that tilted slightly to the left. Her white lab coat was splotched with the residue of multiple experiments, and her notes were tucked into a folder she carried under her arm. At the beginning of each lecture, she would place her notes on the podium. Then, without ever looking up into the rows of seats where the students sat, she would tap on the microphone, turn to face the blackboard, and begin writing biochemical equations. This was usually the cue for the students to begin an exodus out the back of the classroom, where they would congregate in the library until the end of Dr. Umbercon's lecture. It always amazed Anton that Dr. Umbercon would go about her lecture as though nothing was going on. She would probably lecture to an empty classroom without breaking stride. Sometimes, Anton would stay for one of her lectures out of a sense of pity, invariably gaining little more than a good nap.

"So, this is the famous Anton Thresher." V. T. greeted him while leaning back, as if to take in the whole of his outline. "Now we'll see if your question lives up to your advance billing."

Anton blushed. He knew his background was atypical for the medical school he had chosen, but he preferred not to have that fact so overtly recognized. He couldn't tell if the professor's greeting was amicable or sarcastic.

"Sir, I have some thoughts I would like to discuss with you."

"Well, boy, come by my office at the end of the day. I'll be there."

V. T. left for the anatomy lab. Anton glanced at Dr. Umbercon and accidentally made eye contact with her. He smiled impulsively. She grinned at him before she quickly turned to the blackboard.

Perhaps Dr. Umbercon was less genetically ugly than chronically unkempt. Anton decided to stay. He took a seat in the front row, from where he couldn't help but observe how Dr. Umbercon's skirt made a tight silhouette of her buttock and thigh, showing a smooth contour. He quickly created and then immediately purged many fantasies built around the image of Dr. Umbercon. He strained to re-create her in the asexual image he had always seen her. At the end, he thought that she had once again made eye contact with him.

Later that day, he made his way to the basement level, where the anatomy lab was located. He wasn't sure where V. T.'s office was, so he stood for a moment and glanced at the hallway full of doors, looking for something that would give him a clue. Then, the lonely sound of a trombone floated up through the hall. It was a soft, sensuous tune. Anton followed it to the anatomy lab and silently entered. V. T. was standing at the front of the lab, eyes closed, softly playing this trombone. No lights were on in the room, and the setting sun streaked a red-hued beam through the one window at the far end of the lab. In front of V. T. lay the cadavers, with blue sheets covering their plastic wraps, awaiting another day's work.

The cadaver that his team had nicknamed "Sally" lay in the far corner. Anton had often wondered about her. Where did she come from? How many children did she have? What motivated her to donate her body to science? Or perhaps she was a faceless street person brought here without her consent. Anton had wanted to say a prayer or have a moment of silence before they began to dissect her. After all, he had prayed when his grandmother died. In the lab, his team members had stared at him incredulously.

"Thresher, this is anatomy lab, not a funeral," V. T. had said. "Just read the instructions from the first chapter."

Maybe the professor was right. Anton had read the instructions.

Now, V. T.'s music filled the room with a dignified grace. It occurred to Anton that he might be intruding, so he silently exited the room and then reentered, making an inordinate amount of noise to signal his arrival.

V. T. looked up from his trombone. He seemed uncharacteristically quiet and serious. Then, his face lightened as he greeted Anton.

"When people die, their bodies are handled with reverence. They are laid out by loved ones while prayers are said over them, songs are played, and thoughts turn to the time when our body will have its turn in the solemn procession. Then, their bodies come to us. Did you ever think that these people represent some of the finest elements of mankind? They had a desire to help their fellow man even after their death by donating their body to science. You know, a few years back, I wanted to bring in a priest to say a final prayer before we began the dissection. Then, I was going to play 'Taps,' followed by a moment of silence. It would have been beautiful."

"Why didn't you do it?"

"Handley shot it down. He thought it would be too funereal. Of course, that was precisely what I was trying to achieve. So now I sometimes serenade these volunteers. Pretty strange, don't you think?"

"No, I don't think it's strange."

"Good. Neither do I."

"Sir, I have heard a little about your research in cancer, and I was wondering if you could find some time to discuss it with me."

"Boy, I love to discuss my research. Come to think of it, I love to discuss pretty much anything. Let me ask my audience if they would mind curtailing tonight's performance." He looked out over the row of bodies. "Well, team. What do you say if I pack it in early tonight?"

After a few moments, he turned back to Anton. "There

don't appear to be any objections, Thresher." He then spoke softly, as though the cadavers would hear. "This is a very agreeable crowd. A bit subdued, but agreeable. Must be old blue bloods."

V. T. suggested the two men go to Mary's Country Store and Deli for dinner. Anton had been there once or twice. He remembered asking to see the vegetarian menu. The waitress at the counter had smiled sarcastically and pointed out the door. Anton had vowed not to return, but he did not want to make an issue with the professor.

As they entered the deli, the place didn't appear to have suffered in Anton's absence. It was busy with people, mostly from the school, hanging out in the front section and buying sundry overpriced items that were near their expiration dates.

Mary was standing behind the counter. A food-stained apron covered her blue jeans and blue T-shirt. An unlit cigarette hung in her mouth. Her eyes were fixed in a chronic squint, the kind that seemed to add substance to the things she said. Even the most mundane statements took on a new significance when she would first hesitate, take a long drag on her cigarette, intensify her squint, and then deliver her line. She was a short, full-figured woman. Her facial features were well proportioned. Anton could imagine that at one time she had probably been quite attractive. Even now she seemed to hold court to a gaggle of worn-out, would-be courtiers who would rotate occupancy at the counter's stools throughout the day. The counter was sort of a timeshare for the oversixty lechers. They seemed to compete with each other in a sexual innuendo derby directed at Mary. She was an unblushing partner in their repartee. Anton thought she was calm and self-assured because the men were impotent, or at least uncertain of their capacity to act on their thoughts at any given moment.

Mary greeted her friend. "V. T., where you been hiding?"

Her salutation was followed by a vigorous, hoarse, laughing cough. She had buried her third husband one year ago after he lost his battle with lung cancer. V. T. had been there when he died. After the surgeons had left the room, V. T. remained behind and silently listened while Mary spoke of her love and sorrow. It occurred to him that he might be the only person to have ever seen her cry. The day after the funeral, she was back in the deli, accepting condolences and talking to old friends. Somewhere in the bustle of greeting daily acquaintances was the tonic Mary sought to soothe her life. Even now, whenever he greeted her, there was the silent, mutual understanding of old friends who have a shared sorrow.

"Been working on my trombone," he said. "I'm thinking of heading to New Orleans to see if I can catch on with a jazz group. What do you think, Mary?"

Fred Dankmore was sitting at the center of the counter while nursing a cup of black coffee and trying to get a reaction from Mary. He was a union carpenter who lately had been out of work more than in it. He really didn't seem to mind, since it allowed him time to practice what he truly excelled at—namely, drinking to excess and making loud, rude comments that amused no one as much as himself. His large, abdominal pannus of fat bulged more than ever. His belt buckle was facing nearly parallel to the floor under the pressure from his belly. Strapped to his side was his omnipresent hunting knife, the one he said he used to cut a man's throat when he was in the army. A generous paunch dangled below his chin, covered with gray stubble that partially hid a scar over his left cheek. It was fortunate that he had a stench of stale beer about him, for it acted as a cologne to his more offensive body odor.

Now, he had heard enough of the professor's words to twist them into a leering comment. "Hey, why don't you work on my trombone for a while, Mary?"

He smiled a gap-toothed grin while scanning the crowd for encouraging glances. Finding none, he returned his glance to Mary, hoping she would deign to rescue him.

Mary retorted with a smile. "Dankmore, you pitiful oaf. You know your trombone don't slide no more!" The other patrons who had heard the exchange laughed. Fred gamely smiled along and then turned his attention to his coffee cup, dropping his grin as the attention of the crowd left him.

Mary addressed V. T. again. "Sorry, V. T. It's been like this ever since I quit enforcing the dress code. Never know what is likely to wash up in here."

Over dinner, Anton listened while V. T. discussed his theories and research. Anton was as much energized by the attention he was receiving as he was by the substance of the professor's ideas. Here he was, a first-year medical student, having dinner with the chief of the Department of Anatomy in a student watering hole while discussing the state of cancer research. Surely, this type of thing did not go on at other medical schools. In that moment, Anton felt vindicated by his choice of medical school. He wanted a small school with an unconventional philosophy, a place where he could be a compelling presence rather than just another brilliant student. Now he recognized his plan was beginning to work.

V. T. had been talking for a while. "And so, the cancer-pharmacologic complex has become as entrenched as the military-industrial complex. The drug companies sponsor much of the research and would naturally prefer to see treatments, since they require lifelong therapy, rather than cures, which require one-time therapy and are not as profitable. Of course, the surgeons have a vested interest in maintaining a role for surgery in the treatment. Imagine being a cancer surgeon on the day the great discovery of a cure is made. How many patients do you think will be in your clinic the next day?

"That's why the world needs osteopathic primary care doctors like us to pursue cancer research. Osteopathic doctors have a tradition of believing in the body's ability to heal itself, and our respect for the diversity of therapeutic approaches allows us to consider methods rejected by the mainstream. Since we are not specialists, we have no interest in propagating the disease. Our main interest is in our patients, not in the disease they have."

Anton considered V. T.'s points. "I have known many honorable men who have sincerely pursued cancer research. You make them all sound to be like criminals."

"They are not consciously deceitful. At a subconscious level, they have given up hope for actually curing cancer. Since a few of them believe in their heart they will find the cure, they need some other reason to get out of bed in the morning. Could you imagine how frustrating it would be to spend your entire life looking for a cure and not finding it? Few people would be willing to take that risk. Instead, they play a game where they accumulate research grants from drug companies and the government, and then they sit around publishing useless study results in journals that they have created specifically for that purpose. You see, boy, an entire economy and social culture has been built around cancer research, but somehow the whole game has been separated from the goal of finding a cure." V. T. was building to his final point but, as was his style, broke off his train of thought at the moment he was about to complete it.

"You thirsty, boy? I think I'll order a beer. Not one of those from overseas that's been sitting in the hull of the ship for weeks, but a fresh American draft."

Anton figured that *train of thought* was the wrong expression to use when referring to the professor. Maybe *spasms of thought* would be a more accurate description. V. T.'s attention was wholly diverted to the state of the American beer drinker and the condition of waitresses at Mary's.

Anton was amused but found V. T.'s vernacular style and visceral appreciation of the physical world somewhat inconsistent with the demeanor of a serious researcher. Furthermore, how could a physician patronize a place that so overly promoted unhealthy eating? Anton felt he needed to say something to make his feelings known, but he was afraid such a confrontation might interrupt what he sensed was an opportunity to get involved with the professor's research. Anton wanted to be the first of his class to gain such distinction. His goal was to be published before he was through with medical school. His dad hadn't published his first paper until he was in the last year of his fellowship.

V. T. ordered a Samuel Adams draft. "A beer that hasn't forgotten its mission in life is to taste like a beer, not just a carbonated excuse to consume alcohol. But I may have to change brands again because those boys have begun to advertise too much."

Anton wanted to bring V. T. back to their discussion of cancer research.

"Dr. Roberti, I'd like to get involved with what you're doing."

"Why, boy, nothing could delight me more. But don't you think you would be better off ordering your own beer?"

Anton grinned.

V. T. beamed. "Ah! Finally, I get young Dr. Intensity to smile! Son, I want you to help with finding a cure for cancer. We won't be 'doing research'; rather, we're going after a cure. If anyone asks you what you're doing, that's exactly what you will tell them. We won't publish anything unless it a cure. We won't attend conferences to discuss our research until we have a cure. We will find it or die looking!"

V. T.'s oratory had reached full hurricane force. As he spoke, he had risen out of the chair, less lifted by his legs than levitated by his emotion. His hand gestures had become focused, and his eyes narrowed on Anton. This was a call to arms, and Anton was his willing recruit.

CHAPTER 3

S cott Antonelli explained his plan. "So the way I figure it, Portland Medical Center is my best option for internship because there's a better chance I can catch on there and complete my training. Plus, Ann likes it there, and I don't want to have to drag her around the country."

"So, you and Ann are getting married?" asked Todd Freeze.

"Well, you know, we talk about it. Hey, she's a great girl. We get along great. She'll make a great mom. I know I want to have kids someday—maybe three kids—and before I get too old to play with them. I wouldn't mind starting in residency. We've been dating for three years. I like her family, and her mom aged well."

"Well, drink up, Antonelli, because you sound like a man about to lose his freedom."

Scott drank the last half of his beer in one gulp and then surveyed the room. The party was starting to hit its peak. A beautiful whirl of activity and a blanket of music were covering the dimly lit first floor of the house they were in. It was the kind of atmosphere that afforded freedom of movement in the anonymity f chaos. Most of the graduating class was there, as well as about half the third-year group. Scott had never seen most of these people in such a festive, drunken state.

Scott, Todd, and Brad Sawmiller were clustered in a strategic location by the front door, where they could scan the bulk of the party and view the new arrivals. Brad was tall and heavyset with a full beard and dark-brown hair that hung below his ears. He was headed for a much-coveted residency in orthoped-ics, which he had worked diligently for since entering medical school. He had a winsome smile that he used frequently, and his classmates liked him despite his intensity. Now he stood in a red, plaid flannel shirt; blue jeans; and dirty, white high-top Converse sneakers with the laces undone. He was rhythmically rocking up on his toes and then back on his heels. As people entered, they all congratulated him on getting the position in orthopedics at Philadelphia Osteopathic Medical Center. It was a bit unusual for a student from the small New England Osteo-pathic College to achieve such a prestigious residency, but next to Anton Thresher, Brad was the brightest student in the class. Perhaps such a comparison was misleading, as if saying, "Next to the sun, he was the brightest star in the sky." But to his credit, Brad had a sincere disinterest in comparative assessments, des-pite some of his classmates' attempts to draw him into one.

Tim Beckwith came over to congratulate him. "Hey, Saw! Way to go on the ortho program. You must be pretty pumped. I hear it's between you, Julie Wyckoff, and Thresher for class valedictorian. I hear it's going to come down to the final board exam next Tuesday."

Tim was always "hearing" things, especially things that could come only from school administration sources. Scott sus-pected that Tim was an unwitting lackey for Carol Wolf, the long-time director of student affairs.

"Christ, what a boot-licking dork," said Todd under his breath to Scott.

"Yeah, you got to know that Wolf planted that informa-tion knowing full well that Beckwith would spread it."

Todd glanced around. "I wonder where Wyckoff is. These two travel of the same pack. Hey, Beckwith. Where's your dom-inatrix?"

"My what?" Tim asked.

"Don't be so coy. I've heard all about you and Wyckoff. I'll tell you, the thought of Julie Wyckoff donned in full leather and having you hog-tied while she manipulates your genitals at will gets me a little bit erect. What do you think, Scott?"

"Most definitely." Scott turned to Tim. "As a matter of fact, Beckwith, I respect and envy you for being able to cultivate such a unique and erotic relationship. I mean, who would think that a flathead like you would be able to satisfy the likes of Wyckoff? My hat's off to you, my friend."

Scott then posed with both hands behind his back, thrusted the air with his pelvis, and squealed in a pitched whine remarkably similar to Beckwith's squeal. "Julie! Julie! The ropes are too tight."

Tim sneered. "Both of you guys are jerks." He stormed into the crowd. Scott guessed it was the most potent language Tim could muster.

Todd chuckled. "You know, Scott. I think you got Beckwith all wrong."

"In what way, Todd?"

"I think his real dominatrix is Wolf."

Brad chimed in. "I think you're both wrong. I think our friend Beckwith likes boys. Come to think of it, that might explain why he wants to go into urology."

"God, what a disgusting thought, having your doctor lust for your gherkin while he's giving you an exam." Scott shuddered. "I guess it could be worse; he could have picked proctology."

Someone turned the music up a notch, and the walls began to shake. Wally Proctor, the party's host and future anesthesiology resident, approached them with a plastic bag under his arm. The bag was inflated with nitrous oxide. He was inhaling deeply from a tube running to it. "Care for some laughing gas, boys?"

"Proctor, you're out of control," said Scott. He turned to Todd. "Can you picture this slob as an anesthesiologist? His patient would be lying there screaming in pain while he sucks down all their medication."

Todd shook his head. "All I can say, Proctor, is that it's a good thing you don't have any brain cells left to kill."

"Lighten up, boys. You forget that I'm a highly trained physician and pharmacist by trade. I know the chemical structure for everything that I ingest. Indeed, can you say the same for the food you eat? I can guarantee that a harmless whiff of laughing gas will not cause cancer and is a lot more fun at a party than brussels sprouts." Wally reared his head back and let out a full-throttle scream. He then turned to face the mass of the party and yelled. "I want to see *dancing* at my party! You stiff-legged white people are making me look bad. Julian, strike up the party ball and cut on the strobes! Argh!"

The mirrored ball hanging from the ceiling began to rotate. Several small blue, green, and red spotlights aimed at the ball began to pulsate with the beat of the bass. People begin to dance, not so much with each other but as a free-form mass in the center of the room.

Scott felt a flutter of excitement in his belly. He looked at the far wall and saw a row of local girls looking a bit young, a bit fresh, and a bit nervous, drinking quickly and keeping beat with the music. He thought of Ann. Beautiful and committed, she would make a fine wife. But she was in Rhode Island, and he was in Maine.

Todd leered at the lineup. "My God, there is something about risking the statutory limits of a girl's age that I find incredibly sexy. What say we strike up a conversation with yon fair maidens, comrade?"

"Methinks not. You forget that I am practically engaged to Ann."

"Well, my virtuous friend, I see no ring on that hand. In my opinion, the only people that should act like married men are married men. Now, Ann is an incredible woman, no doubt. But what if just across the room is the girl of your absolute dreams? And let's just say that you wander over there and meet her and get swept away and realize that *this* is the woman you must have. Wouldn't it be better to find that out now before you are married? On the other hand, if after spending a night of reckless groping with her you awake to realize that, cute and taut though she may be, your vixen is no match for your prechosen Ann, then your love for Ann will be reinforced, and you will be reassured that you are making the correct decision! I see this as a win-win proposition, my friend."

"Hmm, you have a point there, Todd. At times like this, I like to think, What would Thresher do in this situation?"

"Why, so you can do the opposite? Let's face it, at this point, he probably would have cut off his unit for thinking evil thoughts. No, we need a more realistic barometer of moral judgment to help us in this dilemma. Sawmiller, you have heard this conversation, what's ye?"

Brad rocked on his heels and sipped his beer. "Boys, leave me out of this great debate. Your philosophy is too deep for me. Besides, I've been out of circulation for five years." His wife, Lisa, had stayed home so he could go out, since they could not find a babysitter. Scott and the gang thought that she was the near-ideal mate. She was just twenty-four but already the mother of a three-year-old girl and a one-year-old boy. She carried a confidence and maturity beyond her years, yet a soft innocence was still on her face.

Todd sighed. "You see, Antonelli? Brad gets to go home and tag Lisa, I'm about to go over and sweep a townie girl off her feet, while you sit here somewhere between marriage and loneliness not sure what to do! It's a fool's conscience."

"It's not a matter of conscience, Freeze. I've seen those girls in the daylight."

"Another tactical blunder on your part. I have no intention of ever seeing them in the daylight."

With brash confidence, Todd strode toward the group of young locals. Scott saw their smiles as Todd greeted them. Soon after that, they began to laugh. Scott smiled to himself. Todd was an irrepressible rake. He had convinced himself that by adopting a reckless vigor to pursue women, he was doing great things to augment their self-esteem, or at least help them achieve their quota of carnal pleasure. As Scott watched the centrist posturing from the girl Todd had isolated from the

pack, it was easy to see how Todd had developed his percep-
tions. The girl tilted her head to one side, stirred her drink with
a straw, and fixed her eyes on Todd with earnest clarity. She
placed a hand on his shoulder and delayed it just long enough
before sweeping it down his arm. Todd responded in kind.

"It's kind of like watching a mating scene from a show on
Animal Planet," said Brad as he tipped his beer toward Todd.

Scott grinned. "I was thinking it's more like watching
Bambi Meets Godzilla."

"Yeah, but with these townie girls, I'm not sure which
one is Godzilla. Well, it looks like it's time for me to roll out of
here. I've got to head down to Boston in the morning and finish
the last week of my medicine rotation. I can't believe they're
only giving us four days between our final exams and the graduation ceremony."

"Carol Wolf was probably worried that someone might
have some fun if she gave us any more time than that."

Brad left Scott alone to survey the party. Scott looked at
his watch. It was 11:00 p.m., too late for Anton to arrive. If he
were going to come, he would have been there by now. Scott
was not surprised that his friend had not come. In fact, he had
expected it, given the halfhearted response Anton had given
when Scott put pressure on him to come to the party. Being
the type of creature who gained his energy from social contact, Scott couldn't understand how someone could sit at home
knowing that there was a party of this magnitude and finality
taking place.

He took a sip of his beer and scanned the crowd, looking
for a welcoming circle of friends. He would be able to stand
here with his thoughts for only a few more minutes before his
discomfort at standing alone in the midst of the party would
overwhelm him, and he would be forced to seek social refuge in
any quarter he could find. The only unthinkable option would
be to go home early. Damn that Thresher! They used to be an in-
separable duo. Lately, Anton had been withdrawing from many
of their mutual activities. It would be one thing if Anton were

at the house with some vixen, but he was more likely in bed alone or reading. Well, at least they could still play basketball together.

Scott sipped the last of his beer. He nervously shifted from one foot to the other. Realizing that he must appear to be nervous, he became even more ill at ease and instinctively headed for the bar to get another beer. The decision gave him purpose and settled his angst. As he walked toward the bar, he could hear Wally Proctor bellowing above the din of the crowd. "Julian! Julian, you Dominican fuck! We're running low on beer. Restock!"

Wally reached out and slapped Julian on the back of the head forcefully enough to send him lurching forward a step. A bottle fell out from the case of beer that he was carrying and broke on the floor.

"What the fuck, Julian? That's alcohol abuse! Clean that shit up before somebody gets hurt."

Scott felt the blood rise in his temples. He threw back his beer and then grabbed another. He'd always hated Wally. Watching him command Julian about made Scott cringe. Julian was a first-generation medical student. His parents had emigrated from the Dominican Republic when Julian was in grade school. Upon Julian's arrival at campus, Wally had taken him under his wing, thereby making him dependent on his social support.

Wally stood over Julian, sucking in deeply on a cigarette and blowing it out with exaggerated purpose as if to assert his dominance.

Scott clenched his fist in his pocket, threw back his beer, and grabbed yet another. Wally reminded him of somebody. Scott's mind drifted back to a time in his childhood.

When he was ten, Scott received a bicycle for his birthday. It was the best bicycle he had ever had in his life—bright red, shiny, new, and with drop handlebars and a banana seat. Scott's father had been saving for this bike for months. "It's the best!" Scott's parents had said proudly as they presented it to him, complete with a bow on the handlebars, on the morning of his birthday. "This bike, you ride it, and someday you could give it to your little brother," his father had said. "This bike is so good, it will last forever."

Scott remembered visiting his father's garage. He would look at the twelvepenny nail that his father had hanging over his cluttered desk. His father had bent the nail fully in half with his bare hands. Scott had seen him do it. Such a man was his father! Even at the age of ten, Scott cherished the bike, knowing the hours of labor and planning his parents had taken to buy it for him.

Scott had ridden it proudly through the neighborhood. The bike was only two weeks old when he made the decision to take it on a shortcut through the woods behind his house to get to his friend's house. He had put playing cards in the spokes. The flapping sound they would make made him feel as if he were riding a motorcycle. The red bike, the flapping sound, the drop handlebars, and the wind speeding through his hair all made him feel as if he could fly. As he came around the turn in the woods, he saw a group of four teenage boys standing around and smoking cigarettes. A sense of dread came over him. He thought about turning back, but he didn't want to be cowardly, so he pedaled forward. Perhaps if he rode quietly past them, they would leave him alone. As he approached, one of the bigger boys with an army jacket stood in the path in front of him. He stopped Scott's bike by grabbing the handlebars.

"Hey, kid," he said, staring down Scott as he sat on the bike. Army Jacket was about fifteen years old. His friends were probably the same age. Scott knew of them but had never encountered them before. He sat nervously on his bike, not sure what to do.

One of the other boys, Denim Jacket, walked up to the side of the bike.

"Hey, kid. It looks like you got something stuck in your wheels." He began to pull off the playing cards, ripping them in half and throwing them on the ground. "You have to thank me for cleaning up your bike. You wouldn't want people to think you're gay because you have stupid cards on your spokes, would you? And what are these? Tassels? Nobody has fucking tassels on the handlebars." He ripped the tassels off the handlebars and threw them on the ground, *too. Scott had loved the tassels, the way they would flap in the wind. He looked at them lying on the ground and felt helpless. He was trying to fight back tears, but his lip was trembling, and he could sense them starting to form.*

"Aw, look at the baby, he's getting upset," said Army Jacket. "I'll tell you what, kid. If you let me take your bike for a ride, we will let you go on your way."

"You promise?" asked Scott hopefully.

"You have my word on it."

Scott stepped off the bike and haltingly handed it over as Army Jacket straddled it and started pedaling furiously down the path. He stopped, made a U-turn, and started pedaling back toward the group. As he approached them, he veered off the path and headed toward a ravine full of huge boulders. "Ramming speed!" The bike went faster and faster. At the last minute, he jumped off the bike. It careened over the edge of the ravine and smashed into the rocks below.

"Oops, it looks like I slipped."

Two of the other kids ran down and retrieved the bicycle. They brought it back up to Army Jacket, who inspected it. "Look at what you did to your bike, kid! The front wheels are bent. For Chrissake, the whole frame is bent! You really need to take care of your equipment. What are you going to tell your mom and dad?"

Tears streamed down Scott's face while the thugs handed him his ruined bicycle. As he slowly walked it out of the path, he could hear them laughing behind him. He would be grounded for weeks, too ashamed of himself to tell his parents what had happened.

The flashback, the alcohol, the strobe light, and Wally's bulging eyes conjured a dark cloud in Scott's mind. He walked up to Wally and stared directly into his eyes. "Julian, don't let this fat fuck boss you around. He's a fucking coward."

The crowd of revelers was starting to take notice of Wally and Scott standing square shouldered and staring at each other.

From across the room, Julie Wyckoff saw Scott. She remembered seeing him like this once before at the Harborview Inn. She had been there with some friends, and when a group of locals had tried hard to impose themselves on her, Scott had intervened, sending two of them to the hospital. She remembered that look in his eye. She could see it again tonight.

"I'll be right back," she said to her friends as she hurried toward Scott.

Wally inhaled deeply from his cigarette. A group of his friends watched closely as he menacingly blew the smoke into Scott's face.

"And just what the fuck are you going to do to me? You lay a fucking hand on me, and you'll be changing fucking flat tires like your grease monkey, Guinea old man back in Rhode Island." He leaned in closer. "You're a greasy wop just like your old man."

Scott's eyes glossed over in a blind rage. "Fuck you, Army Jacket."

In an instant, Scott's left hand struck Wally's face, followed by a crushing right hand that sent him reeling to the floor, unconscious. Julie arrived a second too late. She grabbed both of Scott's hands and pushed him away from Wally.

"Scott, stop! This isn't the Harborview!"

Julie's voice pierced through Scott's daze. A group had gathered around Wally, who was starting to come to and was now sitting up. Julie turned to Scott. "You better get out of here now." She followed him outside. Scott was dumbstruck.

Julie came up to him.

"You heard what he said to Julian," Scott said. "He deserved what he got. You have to admit he deserved that. You heard what he said to me, how he spoke about my father. I had no choice."

"Listen, Scott. Here's what's going to happen. There will be a convening of the discipline committee. You will have the power to choose one of the representatives on the committee. They may try to expel you. Remember, the college hates bad publicity. If you stand firm, you can get away with probation. Now we are even. But I won't be able to talk to you after tonight. You're on your own."

Julie disappeared. The next thing Scott new, Todd was standing by his side.

"Listen, Scott, it's not all that bad. Medicine's not as great as it's cracked up to be. Look, this could open up new vistas of opportunity. You can be 'Antonelli the Brawling Doc.' I'll be your manager. We will make millions."

Scott knew his friend was trying to lighten the mood. "I can't believe it. That pompous asshole, he deserved that. He had it coming to him. I had no choice. Now I'm the one that's going to go down."

CHAPTER 4

With his back to the shore, Anton closed his eyes to the morning sun and felt the orange warmth on his lids. The tide was gentle this morning, as though it were waking up with him, nudging the sand with caressing waves that enchanted him with their soothing mantra. Tanned and lean, he stood on the sand, legs apart, leaning first to the right and then to the left as he gradually limbered up his thighs. He liked to study the ripples in his calves as he stretched. Lean and defined, he felt a sense of pride as their owner. He took off his shirt. Clad in only his running shorts, he began to jog in place. He turned to watch his shadow, noting the square-cut image his shoulders created on the sand. There might be other people with shoulders like his, but few had the legs to match, and fewer still could run a five-minute mile, and none were destined to discover a cure for cancer. He smiled at his private conceit. Then, feeling shame for his lapse of humility, he began to run harder until he was glistening with sweat. He took off to run three miles of shore.

He prayed outloud as he ran. "God, forgive me for betraying the gift you have bestowed upon me. Bless me and guide me in your path. Make clear to me your will so that I may follow you." He began to feel better as the pain from the run was on him. He had never run faster than today. At the end of his run, he turned into the water and began to swim the three miles back to his home. The cold water was invigorating after his run. He could feel his shoulders cut through the water with each powerful stroke.

He had been one of the best swimmers at the Longwood

Country Club in his home of East Greenwich, Rhode Island. When he was thirteen, he had won every event he entered at the annual swim meet, setting three pool records. His dad had been playing golf that day and didn't see the meet, but he had been able to attend the awards ceremony that evening when Anton received all his medals.

Now Anton was off the shore from the house he lived in. He emerged from the water and, feeling a bit tired and reflective, sat on the hard sand and let the last remnant of an ocean wave run over his legs as he looked out to the horizon. One more week and he would graduate. Damn! He was going to have to think of something to say at the graduation ceremony, since he would clearly be the valedictorian. Hmm, it would be a good chance to see how red he could make Dean Handley's face get. Anton could start by praising Dr. Roberti and then build from there. Maybe he could induce a coronary in the volatile despot. It might be just the right combination of provocation in a setting of forced restraint. Of course, the moment Handley keeled over, Carol Wolf would jump out of her seat and have Anton arrested for murder. He thought about being in prison. The concept was somewhat tolerable, as long as they let him work out and read. He laughed at his own bizarre thoughts and then leaned his head back as though to turn a page in his mind.

Dr. Umbercon crept into his thoughts. There she was in his mind's eye, with a tight skirt hugging her thighs. He placed her in a sheer blouse with cutaway sleeves exposing her arms and a deep V-cut in the back exposing her graceful shoulders. He imagined her hair teasingly combed over one eye, and she glared at him with brooding sexuality. Suddenly, to his great embarrassment, he noticed he had developed an erection that could easily be seen through his wet shorts. It could have been worse; someone else could have been on the beach. Thank God for solitude.

Todd Freeze's voice jolted him. "Hey, Thresher. What are you doing, jerkin' your gherkin out here? For crying out loud, look at that woody in your shorts! What are you, infatuated with jellyfish? Hey, maybe if you came out with your buddies now and then, you could rack a real vixen and quit fantasizing about mermaids."

Damn! How long had Todd been standing there? Anton's mind reeled as he thought of a reasonably graceful way to dodge Todd's commentary. He almost got up to greet his friend, but he was shackled by the pole in his shorts. He had to think of a rapid comeback.

Todd continued. "Hey, wait, let me guess. You were thinking about Julie Wyckoff. At least you would be if you were there last night. My God, she had on a tight shirt that was completely erotic. I swear, every time I would rub against her, her nipples would become erect. I think she wants me. But, Thresh, I'm worried about you. No wonder your soldier jumps to attention every time a splash of cold water hits it. It hasn't been fed for months! You know, as a physician in training, I must advise you that such neglect of a vital organ could have a dire outcome."

Todd had ambled around to face Anton and now looked down on him as he sat there in the sand. Anton's initial horror had completely dissolved, and he restored himself to order. He realized that there was little that could phase "the Freeze." Todd was one of those rare individuals who was so completely without moral umbrage about almost any issue that people couldn't help but feel comfortable around him. After all, nobody could say anything that would make him blush or want to pass judgment. Despite his sexual appetite, this trait left him somewhat devoid of passion. He was merely seeking pleasure out of each day, and if pleasure to him meant a sexual conquest, then so be it. If someone else thought pleasure meant meditating in a cave, then Todd would express a sincere joy that the person found happiness.

Anton stood. "You bacchanal imp. How many fair maidens did you disappoint with your hypophallus last night?"

"I'll have you know that I am quite well endowed, thank you."

"Spare me the details." Anton was determined not to give him an audience for his more despicable transgressions.

"Just as well. If you must know, thanks to your roommate —Scott 'Raging Bull' Antonelli—I was more like Don King last night than Don Juan."

Anton's interest perked up. "You guys were at the Harborview?"

"Hell no. Scott dropped Wally right in the middle of his own party! You should've seen it. Boom! Boom! Wally drops, covered in blood, and Scott had to be pulled away before he killed him. It was beautiful."

"I'll bet when Anderson fell, it registered on the Richter scale in Kennebunkport." Anton smiled. "But I'm sure Scott will get some heat from Dean Handley."

"Heat nothing, Wyckoff says they'll bounce him out of school."

"They won't do that. What does Wyckoff know?"

"Everything."

The two friends walked up to the porch of the house where they and Scott lived. Like many of the students at the seaside college, they were able to find inexpensive rental property right on the ocean. This gentile location prompted Anton's father to dub it "Baby Doc College at Biddeford" during one of their arguments—the one that had convinced Anton to come here. Any institution that could elicit such broiling opposition from his father certainly must be worth attending. His father had vowed not to pay for the tuition. Anton had sent him the bill anyway. Of course, his father paid. Anton knew he would pay to avoid telling his colleagues why his son was home digging clams instead of attending medical school.

By now, it was 8:00 a.m. Mortal people were beginning to populate the beach. Todd went in to make french toast for breakfast while Anton went to wake up Scott.

At the breakfast table, Scott filled in Anton about the details of the fight. "You would have been proud, Thresh. I was never in better form. Proctor will look real pretty at graduation."

"Maybe he'll look beaten," Todd said. "But at least he'll be there. And of course I'll be there, with all my fans in the stands. Hey, that reminds me. If you do get bounced out of school, can I have your graduation tickets? I struck up a conversation with that foxy waitress at Mary's place, and I'm going to invite her to the graduation."

"I suppose she wants you," said Anton in a deadpan tone.

"Very badly," said Todd.

"I've seen that girl," said Scott. "Doesn't she work the breakfast shift? If she's the one I'm thinking of, then she looks to be way out of your league."

"Hey, buddy. The only girls out of my league are the ones I haven't met yet. I'll bet twenty dollars that I have a date with her by Saturday night."

"That's a coward's bet, Freeze. Anyone can lose twenty bucks. I'll take your bet if you make it for one hundred. What about you, Thresh? You in?"

Anton shook his head. Todd took the bet.

Todd donned a chef's hat and began the Sunday-morning ritual of making breakfast for his buddies. The tradition had begun early in their first year after a long night of studying. Scott had started to pour some cold cereal when Todd had literally slapped the bowl off the table in a mock rage.

"Don't you fill your brain with those processed sugar chunks! You must cement last night's lesson in your head with some serious brain food. I am master of all breakfast food, and I will save you." After an order of belgian waffles, bacon, scrambled eggs, and fresh coffee, a tradition was born. Todd had been drafted into duty.

"Well, men, what will it be? Hmm, summer in Maine... feels like blueberry pancakes to me. Yes, and a fresh fruit cup on the side." Todd didn't wait for an answer before retiring to the kitchen.

Anton drifted out to the porch, overlooking the ocean. Scott joined him and sat on the glider rocker next to him, staring straight ahead.

"So, what do you think? Am I screwed or what?"

Anton smiled. Poor Scott, such a victim of his impulses. "Well, I think you're definitely 'or what.' Do you want advice or sympathy?"

"Both."

"OK, but I'll have to charge you extra." They both smiled.

"You know that I love you like a brother," Anton said. "But what you did was just wrong. Just because Proctor may have deserved a beating doesn't mean you were justified in giving it to him. In fact, by winning, you have lost because you have given them enough leverage over you to exact some control over your life. This is a terrible spot for you. They will need to be sure you have felt some pain, some humiliation even. Scott, I think you will have to give them a sense of victory in this one if you want your degree."

Scott was gently sobbing—part with rage, part with sorrow. He had been defending his family's honor. His heritage had been mocked by lard-ass Wally Proctor, and now he had to suffer further humiliation?

"What if I fight it—you know, get a lawyer?"

"You can't afford it, and they can. They win the war of attrition. You go broke while your degree goes stale." Anton looked him in the eyes. "You know what this would do to your father? He'll be up here in one week to see you graduate. You know he called last night to talk to you. He's so proud of you that he can't talk about what you've accomplished without starting to cry. I had to listen to him for thirty minutes tell me old Scott stories, all about what a wonderful son you've been." Now it was Anton's voice that was thick. "He told me he has your picture up in the garage, right over his tool bench. Everybody in Apponaug knows about 'Scott the Doctor.' No, you've got to let this one go."

Scott smiled while Anton wiped away a tear quickly so as not to be seen.

They talked strategy while downing Todd's pancakes.

They were able to agree that Dr. V. T. Roberti should be the guy Scott should pick for his representative when the board met. Anton agreed to talk with the professor later that week.

The boys were headed to Biddeford Sports Center to play basketball with the locals. It had become something of a weekend-morning ritual with them whenever they were in town together. However, this morning, Anton would not be going. He had plans to head up to Hopedale, a small, remote town on the eastern side of Mount Richardson. It was the place where Dr. Roberti had identified in his search as being almost devoid of cancer cases. Only three residents had been diagnosed with cancer in the past ten years, and they were all part-time residents.

V. T. wasn't sure if it was a statistical quirk because the town was so small, or if there was something about the place that imparted immunity to the residents. Anton was going to spend the weekend up there to see what he could find out.

First, Anton would have to bike to V. T.'s house to get the professor's car, for Anton did not own one. It was such a clear morning that he decided he would try to lower his speed record. By the time he hit Old Pool Road, he was twenty seconds ahead of pace. He had a bit of a tailwind and hoped to get a burst of speed as he headed downhill to the place where the road flattened out and a veneer of sand covered it. He had never pedaled as fast before. Now his speed was so great that he could sense himself tightening up, a bit nervous. "A new threshold is always ushered in with anxiety," he thought. "Those who master their fear, master the moment." He began to relax. Fear was conquered. But, as it turned out, gravity and sand were not. The last thing he remembered was panic as his front tire twisted in the sand. He became briefly airborne before slamming to the pavement.

Inside Mary's Country Store and Deli, the waitress, Lisa, gasped. She had been looking out the window and had seen Anton wipe out. "My God, Mary, did you see that? Oh my God, I don't believe he's moving!" She sprinted from the restaurant to where Anton lay.

When she reached him, she cupped his head in her lap and removed his helmet. He looked so young and so at peace. His face had a half smile. Lisa stroked his forehead and cheek. Anton began to move his head and strained to open his eyes. He seemed so helpless. She leaned over and kissed him on the forehead. Now his eyes would not quite open, but he could breathe her in. What was it? Lilac? Jasmine? It was sweet and light, whatever its origin. He inhaled deeply, still not fully there. Now he could feel her hands caressing his head, and slowly he opened his eyes. The morning sun was rising behind Lisa's head and cast her in a silhouette as he strained to make out her face.

"Am I alive?" he asked, not quite sure that he was.

"Yes. Either that, or we both died at the same moment."

He smiled, becoming aware. "So which is it?"

She bent over and kissed him on the lips. He wondered if he was feeling love or delirium. Were they the same? He felt fear again.

Mary arrived with a pitcher of ice water, panting. "A little mouth-to-mouth resuscitation, perhaps?"

Anton was beginning to feel the pain of his fall. Blood was running down his head. His knee was bruised, but nothing was broken. He stayed at Mary's place for about an hour while Lisa cleaned his wounds and dressed them. The head injury made him uncharacteristically talkative, and he shared with Mary and Lisa all his plans for curing cancer, including his need to get to Hopedale to do his research.

"Hey, I thought you were supposed to be the doctor," said Lisa, smiling as she put on the last bandage.

"All I have is a degree. You have the gift. Sometimes, I think that patients will not like me very much as a doctor. Now here I am in your care, and you have no degree, yet you are making me well, and I trust you."

"Do you feel your patients won't trust you?"

"No, I fear I won't connect with them. I have trouble connecting with people."

"Funny, I hadn't noticed."

They smiled warmly at each other. Anton felt so at ease. What was this? Could he still be feeling the effects of his concussion? Maybe it was the circumstances.

"You know, the effects of a concussion can last for days, in some cases weeks," he said.

"Are you still feeling effects now?"

"I don't know."

"Perhaps you should cancel your trip."

"No, this is the only weekend before graduation." Anton started to get up but wobbled and fell on her.

"You can't drive," Lisa said. "I will drive you to the town and help you cure cancer, but you must promise to mention me when you get your Nobel Prize."

CHAPTER 5

Automobile air-conditioning was a superfluous luxury in this part of Maine, designed for those who wanted to avoid the least amount of discomfort. Anton was glad Lisa's car did not have it. The morning breeze was cool as it rushed through the car's open windows. Anton looked out his window and took deep breaths to clear his head.

"Are you OK? Do you want me to pull over?" Lisa asked.

He looked at her. "I'm fine. Just a little light headed from the fall."

She smiled when their eyes met briefly. Her lips were well formed and framed a sincere smile with strong, white teeth, a few of which were slightly misaligned. It was a sign of good genetic endowment unenhanced by orthodontics.

"Well, Anton, if I'm going to be stuck in this car with you for four hours, you can at least tell me something about yourself."

"My favorite color is blue." He grinned.

"That's deep. Thank you for sharing that with me."

Anton had the kind of dominating presence that could be felt even when he was silent. Many people were intimidated when he was around, but he didn't understand why. Todd had said it scared women away. Anton glanced once more at Lisa as his head started to clear. He felt less helpless.

Lisa shifted uncomfortably in her seat as she sensed his stare. He had a quiet, self-assured quality about him. She wondered what he was thinking. Did he think she was pretty? She wished she had time to tend to her hair! Then, she railed at herself for being so shallow. Who really cared about this college boy? It had been merely an impulse that made her run to help him. He had looked so wounded and gentle when she held him. The kiss had been an impulse, too. She was doing him a favor, that's all. She would drop him off in town and then leave. She wouldn't kiss him again and definitely would not sleep with him. When she had kissed him, had he felt like making love to her?

Anton thought she was beautiful. He knew he was looking at her for too long, but he could not help it. Her skin was Mediterranean dark with a few scattered freckles about her cheeks. Her hair was natural and carefree. She was the kind of woman whose beauty was best unadorned. Maybe she was an angel. Lately, Anton had been contemplating the existence of angels and had been evolving toward the conclusion that they did in fact exist. He also thought that they sometimes worked through people on Earth (or was that the Holy Spirit, or Jesus himself who worked through people?). Of course, a belief in angels invited belief in their darker counterparts. Could she be a seductive distraction? He noticed her shifting in her seat. Maybe he should say something, but what? He looked out the window. What would Todd say? Silence was beginning to press in on him.

"Next week, I graduate," he finally said.

"Congratulations. I'll try to remember to send you a card."

Damn! That had probably sounded like bragging. Todd had always said that the best thing to do was to ask women about themselves.

"So, Lisa, tell me about yourself." He liked the sound of her name as it came off his lips.

"My favorite color is red."

They both laughed. Lisa felt the tension leave. She really did want to tell him about herself, but how much to tell, and when? Perhaps just as importantly, what should she not tell? Would he understand?

"I've been working at Mary's for the last three years. She is like a mother to me. She lets me stay in an apartment she owns. Last year, I got my GED."

"What's a GED?"

Lisa felt chastened for her pride. Was he teasing her? She glanced over at him and noticed the innocence on his face.

"To you, I suppose it's nothing. To me, it's like a doctorate." She smiled with resignation and explained. "It's a high school equivalency for people like me who dropped out and never got their diploma. At this rate, I'll make it through medical school when I'm fifty-two." She thought it was probably over now. How could he want to be with a dropout townie? Screw him! Who did he think he was anyway? She was every bit as smart as he was, only she hadn't been born with the same opportunity.

"But let's not forget, Cancer Boy, I'm the one with the car, and you don't get your Nobel Prize without my help. It was no accident that you smashed your gourd in front of Mary's place. I believe in fate. So, don't be so smug about my humble GED. I may not have a lot of letters after my name, but that doesn't mean much. I read a lot." Great, insecurity and bragging, all in one statement. How much longer until she and Anton arrived at their destination? Of course, it hardly mattered, because she didn't like him. Even if she did, they were too different, and they definitely didn't have a future.

Anton saw the passion in her face. He could tell she was bright, caring, and very hurt. He thought they had much in common and wondered if they might have a future.

"I'm glad I crashed my bike. Maybe it was the hand of God. I think he directs our lives." Anton thought God directed his life, at least. "You don't need letters after your name to be brilliant." Their eyes met.

Did he call her brilliant? Maybe he was trying to butter her up. It felt good to hear, so she decided to believe it. She wondered if he was a Jesus freak. Probably not; he sounded too sincere. She remembered Jesus freaks waving a finger at her in judgment. At times, she thought she existed merely so the more virtuous would have a point of contrast to compare themselves to. Hypocrites. They would ridicule her behind her back, but no one would help.

Lisa and Anton were on a typical, long, winding stretch of road that carved through rolling hills of pointed firs. The morning had given way to afternoon and the glorious beauty of early summer unique to Maine. The colors were more intense, and the air was blessed with a crisp, clean feel. It was as though God were thanking the people for keeping this harsh and pristine land inhabited.

"Are you hungry?" asked Lisa. "I packed us a lunch. If you like, we can stop and eat. There probably won't be a place to eat between here and Hopedale, and we've got another two hours to drive."

Lisa knew from the map she had looked at before they had left that a small lake was a bit farther up the road. Upon reaching it, she pulled off at a clearing and gathered the lunch basket she had prepared. After a short walk, they found a clearing by the lake. Anton helped Lisa spread the blanket, and she served from the basket. The air was warm and still—perfect picnic weather. Anton was impressed by Lisa's forethought and preparation. They could have eaten in the car, so she must have planned this moment. Was she sincere and kind? Was he the target of seduction? He wanted to believe her, but he had to be careful. He knew that as he got closer to his destiny, the evil one would seek to derail him. He would need to be wary, lest his mission be subverted. He quietly prayed for a sign.

They ate their lunch in silence. Anton got lost in thought, and Lisa gazed out across the lake, half taken by its beauty and half caught in self-reproach. She felt his silence to be a rejection of her effort. What had she been thinking? She had prepared a lunch as though she were on a drive with a boyfriend rather than on a mission with a stranger. How corny. How pitiful. She was determined not to speak first.

After lunch, Anton took his gaze off the lake for a moment

and looked at Lisa. He felt something quiver deep inside him. Was she truly that beautiful, or were his senses still distorted from the concussion? He had an urge to touch her face and move back a strand of hair that had drifted across her eyes. He restrained himself.

"Thanks," he said. "That was a great lunch."

"Would you like some coffee? I have a fresh brew of hazelnut from Mary's." Without waiting for an answer, Lisa poured. The aroma filled the air and reminded Anton of mornings at Dr. Roberti's. He looked into Lisa's eyes. He thought she must be an angel as he sipped the coffee so the moment would linger. He wondered what it would feel like to hold her.

CHAPTER 6

Dean Handley stroked his ample eyebrows. "I think we should summon the Board of Discipline to review this case," he said gravely. He glanced around the mahogany-paneled meeting room at the faces of the others present to gauge their mood. Dr. Walter Proctor, chairman of the Department of Surgery and father of the victim whose case they were discussing, sat simmering across from the dean under an oil portrait of the hospital's founder. Next to him was Julie Wyckoff. Across from Julie was Carol Fox. The dim light had the effect of airbrushing out her small facial blemishes and made her appear almost attractive.

"Review, my ass!" said Dr. Proctor. "I want the son of a bitch expelled! He's a threat to his fellow students, and he has no business entering medicine!" He was already nearing the peak of his red-faced anger. Soon, his facial hue would shade purple, and his eyes would bulge, much like his son's had done on the night Scott Antonelli punched him in the face.

Julie felt strangely detached. She observed the color change on Dr. Proctor's face, as though it were made of litmus paper, as it went from pink to purple. She thought he had one of the most enormous heads she had ever seen. With his receding hairline and fleshy temples, its appearance took on almost lunar dimensions.

Dean Handley sighed. "Now, Walter, we must at least have due process or the prick could try to sue us. I've got Bruce McIntee on his way down here to give us some legal advice. You let Bruce work his lawyer's magic, and he'll have Antonelli feeling like Charlie Manson and groveling before us."

As if he had been waiting for his cue, Bruce McIntee waddled into the room. His extremely outwardly pointed toes gave him a distinct duck-like gait. His hair was matted into place with a distinctive sheen. His pockmarked face glistened with a veneer of grease, even in the dimly lit room. As there were no windows, the stale air in the room took on a distinctly malodorous stench when Bruce entered. He placed his briefcase in front of him and sat down.

"Thanks for coming, Bruce," said Dean Handley. He then addressed the others. "I have briefed Bruce on the details of the case, and he has prepared an opinion for us on how to proceed."

"It better start with his expulsion and get worse from there," said Dr. Proctor, still purple faced.

"Don't worry, Walter. I think you'll like this," Bruce said as he opened his briefcase with his wart-covered fingers. "As I see it, this is a pretty clear-cut case. We can bypass the disciplinary board entirely. Not only can we expel him, but we've got a good shot at hanging him with a felony assault-and-battery charge that could block him from matriculating at any other medical school." He hesitated a moment for effect as he sniffed with vibratory fury. "And with his parents completely leveraged to pay for his tuition, it would put the whole Antonelli family into bankruptcy." He finished with a triumphant sneer.

"Game, set, match. Let's do it," said Dr. Proctor.

Dean Handley smiled. Carol smiled behind folded hands. Julie noticed that the rank odor Bruce had brought in with him had subsided. Perhaps she was getting used to it. She shifted in her seat as a furrow creased her brow. She had met Mr. Antonelli once when he was visiting campus. A paper was placed in front of her.

"Sign this," said Bruce as he pushed his pen toward her. She looked at the pen. The cap of it had been thoroughly chewed. She looked up at Bruce, whose yellow-toothed smile glistened against his waxen face. "It's a statement endorsing our actions. We'd like you to sign it as a student council representative."

She felt a knot in her stomach. "But suppose he fights this? I was there that night. There are several witnesses who could testify that Antonelli was provoked by racist insults. That would look bad on Brad. We can't take everything from him. If we leave him with nothing to lose, he becomes more dangerous. Why not just tie his ankles together and wait for him to trip?"

"What do you mean, Julie?" asked Dean Handley as he plucked at his eyebrows with rhythmic compulsion.

"We nail him with a probation. Then, we wait for him to screw up again. Odds are that he'll do it on his own. If he doesn't, then we can create something. This way, Brad escapes any negative publicity since Antonelli will have to sign off on this incident on our terms, and then we will nail him with the second offense."

Dr. Proctor nodded. "You know, Handley, she might have something there."

Dean Handley was working both brows simultaneously as though milking them for insight as he stared into space. The room was quiet and tense. Julie guessed the incident would be forgotten in a few months. Passions would diminish, and she would never have to see the full evil of her plan unfold.

Having sufficiently abused his brow, Dean Handley's hands came to rest in front of him as he spoke. "Wyckoff, you might have a future in administration, or perhaps law." He darted a hard glance at Bruce, who sat back into his leather chair and took a bite out of his pen. "Well, ladies and gentlemen, I believe our course is set."

As the group got up to leave, Dean Handley leaned in toward Julie and firmly squeezed her thigh just above her knee. "Won't you join me at the faculty club for a nightcap?"

Julie could no longer perceive any remnants of the stench that had once clung about her. Perhaps it was gone. Her stomach turned as it had done when she saw Bruce's chewed-up pen. She smiled with resolve. "Why, I'd love to."

CHAPTER 7

S cott shook his head nostalgically as he peeled off his socks while sitting at his locker. "Thresh should have been here. Do you realize this could be the last time we all run together?"

It was Saturday morning at the Biddeford Sports Center. These basketball wars between the townies and the medical students had been raging ever since Todd had befriended the locals and arranged the games. Everyone played with a sportsmanlike intensity, tweaked by an undercurrent of class tension as the mostly blue-collar locals sought to prove their physical superiority over the mostly preppy medical students. The Biddeford boys would readily admit the students' academic superiority but reserved for themselves a presumption of athletic superiority. That's why the outcome of the games took on more importance to the locals, and they usually won, except when Anton Thresher was there. In the aftermath of a loss, they were likely to revert to bragging about their sexual prowess, which was another area of presumed superiority.

"It's hard to believe it's almost over," Scott said as he changed out of his basketball sneakers for the walk home after the game.

"Don't worry, Scott," said Todd. "I hear they have great pickup games at the state penitentiary."

With graduation only a week away, the notion of a criminal action seemed far fetched. Scott shook his head. All this over a little fight. Why hadn't Wally Proctor just taken his beating like a man instead of scurrying to generate a legal counterpunch? What a coward.

"Maybe you should go over and apologize to Proctor," said Todd.

"You know, that's not a bad idea, Freeze. Maybe I could say something like, 'I'm really sorry you're such an ass and I only broke your nose. I wish I had knocked your face off.'"

"That's the problem with you, Scott. You don't grovel well." Todd then turned to the remaining players in the locker room and offered up a general challenge. "You know, next week will be my last game in this hallowed institution. It's hard to believe that the end of an era is at hand. It'll be like Larry Bird's last time at the Garden, or Ted Williams's last time at bat—"

"Or Napoleon's last stand," said Felix Choppin, one of the locals.

"That's Custer," said Scott.

"You mean Custer was at Waterloo?" asked Felix. "No wonder Napoleon lost the battle. Anyhow, it'll be like shooting ducks in a barrel."

"That's fish," said Scott.

"Hey, you can put fish in your barrel if you want. I got ducks in mine. We'll beat you like a red-haired stepchild. I got fifty bucks saying that me and the boys will school you bad next week."

Todd thought for a moment. "Game to twenty-one, win by two, and we get to include Thresher. And you guys can't import some ringer."

"OK, you're on. But we can bring anyone who's played in the past year."

After that arrangement was settled, Todd and Scott walked home. Upon arriving home, Scott nervously sifted through the mail. His jaw tensed when his eyes met the formal-looking envelope from the dean's office. He took it out on the back porch, which overlooked the ocean, and read it while Todd went inside to get lunch ready.

Scott read in numb disbelief. The letter requested a meeting with the dean. It mentioned "assault and battery." Scott shook his head. Defeat a tyrant in a great struggle, and you're a hero; defeat a bully, and it's assault and battery. Wally Proctor was truly scum. He selfishly used his position to further his own pleasure while hurting others and to assert dominance and support his own pathetic ego. Scott felt self-righteous.

"They should be giving me an award for knocking that windbag on his ass!" he shouted to the ocean. If only Anton were here. But Anton wouldn't be back until after the meeting. Scott took a deep breath. Whatever it took, he couldn't get thrown out of school. What would his father think? What would Ann think? This would ruin their wedding plans. Ann planned on marrying Scott the Doctor, not Scott the Med School Dropout. No, there was too much at stake, and too many people were counting on him. He would have to swallow his pride no matter what it took.

He looked out over the ocean and saw the quahoggers in their skiffs heading home after a day on the water. He felt envy —no boss, no time clock, just a beautiful solitude of the water. He wondered what would happen if a quahogger got into a fight. Would they take his rake away? Suspend him from digging clams for a few months for conduct unbecoming to a clamdigger? No, he would get up and go to work the next day, the fight between the two men being over. Medicine wasn't a very manly profession.

Todd stepped out on the porch in his chef's hat and apron. He knew that his outfit looked absurd and that it always made Scott smile. He reached into the pocket of his apron and handed something to him.

"What's this?" Scott looked at the item. It was a piece of cardboard cut into the shape of a medallion. In the center it read, "To Sir Scott, the great defender of the meek and slayer of dragons."

"It's your award," said Todd. "You're the People's Choice hero."

Scott smiled.

"Now, lunch is served. And don't keep it waiting, because the chef is known to be very temperamental and a bit unpredictable when his food is neglected."

"You're a good friend, Todd."

"We'll get through this, Scott."

"You're a good friend."

CHAPTER 8

Anton always thought that sleep was one of God's gifts and that not needing an alarm clock to wake him up was an example of living in the grace of God's plan. As such, the sunbeams filtered through the window of the small Cambridge Inn bed-and-breakfast and nudged him awake. His first thought was of Lisa. He wondered how she would look with her eyes closed, the sun falling on her hair, and her lean legs stretched out. He wondered what she slept in. Then, he felt embarrassed for the thought. He rubbed his eyes, prayed, and contemplated the upcoming day.

He would need samples of water from several of the residents' wells. He would want to talk with the pharmacist, maybe the librarian. Dr. Roberti also wanted him to sample local foods, particularly wild berries, roots, and other things that were produced and consumed locally—anything that could be a plausible reason for this town's apparent immunity to cancer. But first, there must be time for Anton's morning workout and run. He planned to be back before Lisa awoke.

The main street of town cozied up next to a small river that was fed from the surrounding mountains. The Cambridge Inn was the largest building on the street, which also included a couple of restaurants, the library, the post office, a gas station, the pharmacy, and the general store. The town's quaint dimensions made Biddeford metropolitan by comparison. Anton could hear the river all along the street. Other than a few people walking in and out of the breakfast diner, the streets were deserted. The morning air was cool, but Anton could tell from the still air and the clear sky that the day was going to be warm. He walked by the diner and looked in through the window. Several patrons were eating bacon. "So much for that theory," he thought. The restaurant reminded him of Mary's. He thought of Lisa and then started running.

Upon returning, he was surprised to find Lisa awake and in the dining room, sipping coffee with the innkeeper, who talked with her in an animated fashion. Lisa's disarming beauty caused people to act with more alacrity when they were around her, as though her presence radiated energy that they would absorb, instigating a burst of adrenaline in them. There she sat, unadorned by makeup, fresh from her night's sleep. How tender she seemed in her manner toward the innkeeper. He sat in his chair, wearing a freshly starched blue shirt, a red-pattern bow tie, and an apron that had the Cambridge Inn's logo printed on the front. He caught sight of Anton and promptly stood to greet him.

"So, this is the young man who is going to find a cure for cancer," said the innkeeper as he reached out his hand. "Your charming fiancé here has been telling me all about you. Hope you find a cure before I need it."

Anton shook the man's hand. Lisa met Anton's gaze and winked at him, smiling. He smiled back.

"Well, let me get you some breakfast," the innkeeper said as he exited to the kitchen.

"Fiancé?" Anton asked Lisa.

"I decided it wouldn't be proper for us to travel together like this if we weren't at least engaged. Besides, he was telling me all about his wife, who passed away two years ago. He proposed to her in front of this building thirty-seven years ago. When he retired from New York four years ago, they came back to visit and found this old building for sale. He bought it that day, and they decided to convert it into a bed-and-breakfast." Lisa's eyes filled with tears. "She died before they could open it. Lung cancer." She wiped away a tear.

Anton thought the cancer must have been acquired in

New York. It would help to know exactly when it had been diagnosed.

Lisa continued. "Anyway, when I told him you proposed to me last night, his whole face glowed."

"Last night?"

"His name is Mr. Carlisle. Now, don't ruin his joy. You can be unengaged to me when we get back to Biddeford."

Anton sat, wondering how he could have become engaged and then unengaged so quickly, as well as which situation he preferred.

Lisa had acquired a list of local plants and berries from Mr. Carlisle that might be of interest. Anton looked over the list with admiration for her initiative. He felt as if they were working as a team. He imagined this might be how Mrs. Roberti would have acted.

"Does this mean that I have to buy you a diamond?" he asked.

Lisa tilted her head to one side and looked at him for a moment with a touch of melancholy in her eyes before smiling. "Maybe someday I'll let you."

The specimen-collection kits were in the back of Lisa's car. Each bottle had its own piece of color-coded tape to seal it and its own eyedropper or tweezer to collect specimens. Anton and V. T. had agreed that a curative substance was unlikely to be found in the air, since it would drift about and couldn't explain the county's exceptionally low cancer rate when other counties in the area had only slightly below-average rates. Likewise, a water source seemed less likely because the aquifer that fed most of the wells was spread out over a large area encompassing many counties, yet the protection seemed exclusive to Hopedale.

"Maybe it's just a statistical glitch," Lisa said as they drove to their first destination.

"I hope not. This will be the fourth county I've tested like this, but none of the others were quite so promising. I feel this is the right place." He thought for a moment. "No, I know this is the right place."

"How do you know?"

Anton smiled. "God told me."

They spent the morning collecting water specimens throughout the town. Anton had a town map and had randomly located a sampling of houses to ensure proper testing technique. Lisa would knock on the door and explain their project before getting permission for the sampling. Anton tried one house and was squarely rejected. He muttered to Lisa said that they should just take some water right from the spigot. "These people have no respect for what we are trying to do," he said.

"They have a right to say no."

Next, they moved into the field to sample berries, bark, roots, and anything potentially edible that they knew about. Then, they headed back to the Cambridge Inn for dinner.

Upon arriving, they were surprised to find the parking lot overflowing with cars spilled out on the street on both sides. The dining room was likewise packed. In the center of a swirl of people talking in excited voices stood Mr. Carlisle, looking very important in his bow tie and apron. He was pleasantly chubby; with a dash of curly, white hair on his otherwise-bald head, he could pass for the brother of Saint Nick himself. The townsfolk were dressed as though they had been abruptly interrupted and urgently gathered. Hiking boots, jeans, flannel shirts, and overalls dominated the room. The only ties belonged to Mr. Carlisle and Andy Booker, the pharmacist. A wood-burning stove in the corner gave a cozy aroma to the gathering and robbed the air of its chill. Just then, Mr. Carlisle noted Anton's arrival.

"All right, everyone, settle down. The doctor is here and will tell us all about it." Suddenly, all the eyes in the room were on Anton. He froze, looking back at them blankly. What did they want? He noticed the woman who had refused to give them the water was standing in the corner.

"How nice of them to greet us," Lisa whispered into his ear. Anton thought they looked more like a lynching mob than a receiving line. He thought these backcountry, inbred yokels must have been spooked by all his poking around. No telling what superstitions were aroused. But how would he explain this all to them?

An older man, perhaps in his sixties who wore a long-sleeve thermal crewneck shirt under his bib overalls moved to speak as he scratched his chin, which sported a five-day beard. Anton was reminded of Pa Kettle. He leaned over to Lisa and whispered. "I can almost hear the banjo music playing in the background."

Mr. Scraggly Beard spoke up. "Well, Doc. Me and the other folks are really interested in your cancer research. See, we've all felt for some time that there was something special about being up here, something innately healthy. Fact, my own theory is that there is some sort of germ-equivalent trigger to most cancers and that we have sort of bumped into natural penicillin in the environment. Now, Luke over there, he's got more of an environmental theory."

"That's right," said Luke. "It's got to be the water that runs all the impurities out of the system. Ain't nothing like this pure mountain water!"

Another voice shouted from the back. "Hell, Luke. Every town up here has pure mountain water. That theory is bunk."

"Yeah!" said another voice. "You just want to scam people with that bottled-water idea."

Luke had derived some ridicule over the past few years for attempting to sell "mountain fresh" bottled water to unsuspecting tourists who happened by his house on the main route into town.

Luke shouted back. "A little mountain water wouldn't hurt no one. We could use the money up here."

"You mean *you* could use it," someone else said. "I can see it now: 'Luke's Own Bottled Water and Cancer Elixir' with your ugly mug on the label. Hell, I'd rather die of cancer than have to look at you when I drink it!"

The room erupted into laughter and then broke out into clusters of conversations as Anton looked on in amazement.

"All right, everyone, settle down," shouted Mr. Carlisle above the din. "Settle down, and let the doctor talk." The room came to order as all eyes once again came to bear on Anton.

Anton wasn't quite sure what they wanted to hear. "Um, we have a theory. We think there might be something up here that matters. I can't say what it could be."

"How can we help you, Doc?" asked Mr. Scraggly Beard.

"I…I don't know if you can. This is something I have to do by myself."

A quiet melancholy fell across the room. Lisa could almost feel the energy drain out of the people. A log cracked in the stove as a spark jumped out from between the grate and landed harmlessly on the floor, glowing for a moment before going dark. From the back of the room, a chair scratched across the floor as a woman stood up and came forward. She handed Lisa a jar of water. "I'm sorry I didn't give this to you earlier." She walked back to her chair.

Mr. Carlisle sighed. "Well, I guess—"

"You know, Anton," Lisa said, directing her comment at him but in a manner for all to hear. "I bet these people have some valuable leads for your research."

All eyes looked up, smiles returned, feet shuffled, and a murmur of agreement spread.

Lisa continued. "I think we should hear what they all have to say."

Anton smiled stiffly as the crowd seized the suggestion.

"I'll put on a pot of coffee," said Mr. Carlisle, excitedly. "Ben and Jody, why don't you set up an interview table in the parlor so the doc can talk to us one at a time."

The table was set. Lisa took notes while Anton listened to each person's ideas. He heard of favorite recipes, homemade tonics, herbs, and roots. Lisa took control of the interviews while Anton looked on, not so much noting what was being said but watching the way Lisa connected with each person so readily. The small banter that was so tiresome to him interested her, and she returned the interest with caring eyes. All the people mattered to her, even goofy Luke, who prattled on about the profit and virtue of bottled water. "You see, you really don't need to prove that the bottled water cures cancer in order to sell a ton of it. You just have to suggest that it might. Why, the mere fact that you came up here researching this thing is enough to get it started. Look, this could be a gold mine, and I don't mind sharing it with you two. I'll do all the work. All you need to do is leak out the nature of your research."

Luke's eyes darted back and forth between Lisa and Anton, focusing more on Lisa as Anton's stare became harsher. Luke drummed his fingers nervously on the table as he shared his plan. He wondered if he should cut them in or get started on his own. After all, nothing was to stop him from promoting his water without these two. He considered himself pretty generous to offer them a cut. At the same time, he felt scared that someone else would take his idea to market before he could get it there. The time pressure was starting to eat at him now that he had talked about it in front of the entire town.

Anton sat back, folded his arms over his chest, and studied Luke's face. Luke had hollow cheeks and missing teeth in the front. Those that remained were in ill health. It was a lifetime of personal neglect recorded for everyone to see in one smile. Anton was filled with loathing.

"Tell me, Luke," he said. "Is your mother buried up here?"

Luke look puzzled. "Why, yes, sir. She's buried over at Hopedale Cemetery. Why do you ask?"

"Well, Luke, I was wondering if you thought that we should dig up the remains and have them powdered into an elixir: 'Mother of Luke Cancer Cure.' If we put a little in each, we can make your mom last for years and make millions."

"How dare you insult my dead mother!"

"I'm not insulting your dead mama, I'm insulting you, you scheming moron. Quit wasting my time."

Luke stood up with red-faced anger, glared at them both, and left.

"How many more are there?" Anton asked. He wondered

how he had lost control of the process. He was glad Lisa was with him.

"Just one more," called out Mr. Carlisle.

"Thought you might want to save the best for last," said Mr. Scraggly Beard as he walked up to the desk and sat down across from Anton. "So, tell me, Doc. You and Luke going to get rich selling bottled water?"

"Luke is an ass. If you have ideas like his, you better leave now."

"He is an ass, but he's not as dumb as he looks. Anyway, I think I know what you're looking for, Doc. Orange fern." Mr. Scraggly Beard looked at him with intensity.

"Orange fern?"

"Orange fern, I'm telling you. I've only seen it in this valley. In fact, I've only seen it in one place in this valley over on the side of Mount Richardson. There's an area about the size of a football field where the stuff grows wild. Folks pick it and use it for tea. Some folks chop it up and garnish with it."

Anton was interested. "You've never seen it in neighboring counties?"

"Nope. And I've traveled all over here."

"Does everyone in the county consume orange fern?

"Just about."

"What about the children?"

"Most of them chew on it like tobacco. There's a tradition of moms putting it on the nipples of pacifiers to soothe infants. I've got some of the fern right here." He pulled out a bottle that was expertly sealed and labeled as Orange Fern.

"I'm impressed," said Anton. He admired the bottle.

Mr. Scraggly Beard shrugged. "I used to teach botany at the university. Listen, I'm not like Luke. I don't want anything. Money might ruin me, and fame is for the weak in spirit. I'd love to be a part of your work. I think I could help. I would…well, I would take personal satisfaction out of bringing this disease to its knees. It would also be fun to watch all the parasites get off from the carcasses of the disease when we distill a cure."

"What's your name?"

"Ben Able." They shook hands. "God be with you, Dr. Thresher."

"Call me Anton."

"Let me know how I can help, Anton."

"I might need more of this fern. It might be important to learn how to cultivate it."

"I'll work on that."

CHAPTER 9

Now that the crowd was gone, Lisa and Anton sat at the small table, a bit tired but exhilarated. He took her in with a tender look. She smiled. He wondered if his concussion had worn off, and he wanted to hold her hand. She seemed to like him, but did she like him like that? What if he went to hold her hand and she withdrew?

"It looks like we got some good data today," he said.

Lisa had hoped he would take her hand. Maybe she should take his? She worried that she had been too aggressive already. God, was he handsome. He was tall and so strong; she imagined him holding and kissing her. He had an innocence about him. Was this what love felt like? Maybe he was the one she should have waited for, but how could she have known he would come?

"Yes, I think we made great progress," she said. She hesitated for a moment. "I guess you won't need me when we're back at Biddeford."

The thought of being back at Biddeford saddened Anton. He didn't want this to end. It felt like a moment of perfection. A sense of purpose, a feeling of warmth from the town, a feeling from Lisa—what was it? Comfort? Excitement? Intrigue? Love?

He started to answer her. "We won't have any samples to collect. But, Lisa, I'd like—"

Mr. Carlisle entered the room a bit nosily. He was carrying a tray with two steaming cups and some pastries.

"Martha and I used to love ending our day on the back porch with a cup of tea and pastries. There's not a more romantic spot on a summer night in Maine. I tell you, if you weren't already engaged, you would be by the end of the night. Follow me."

They followed him through the meeting room to a back porch that overlooked the river. The peaceful, rushing sound of the water flowing over rocks surrounded them. Mr. Carlisle set the tray down on a small table next to two rocking chairs. He leaned his hands on the rail and looked out into the night toward the river while Anton and Lisa stood near.

"Yeah, this was Martha's favorite spot. Whenever we sat out here, we could feel ourselves fall in love all over again."

No one spoke. The river flowed. Mr. Carlisle turned his head away from them and silently wiped away a tear. Lisa put her arm in Anton's. He took her hand and squeezed it. He felt his heart beating. Mr. Carlisle walked off the porch and into the house. "And remember, I want a date from you two by morning." He closed the door behind him.

The sweet smell of the summer mixed with the steam from the tea and filled their noses. Lisa laid her head on Anton's shoulder. She felt so at ease, so safe. He wondered what would happen if they kissed. Would she pull away? If she didn't, what would happen next? He never had wanted to kiss anyone more. He felt her head on his shoulder and wondered if she could feel his heart beating. He felt fear and excitement. The moment seemed special, but he wasn't sure what to do. He thought a kiss would be perfect, but what if he kissed her and it turned out to be less than that?

Lisa squeezed his hand tightly. "Anton."

"Lisa?"

"Anton, if you don't kiss me soon, I'm going to go into that hotel and smash all your lab samples."

Anton turned to face her, put his arms around the small of her back, and pulled her to him, kissing her with passion full on the lips. The world faded around them. All that mattered was the exhilaration of this touch. The sound of the river wrapped around them, growing louder as their kiss lingered. Then, they leaned back, supported by each other's embrace, looking into each other's eyes. Neither moved. Lisa had never felt like this. Would he ask her up to his room? She wanted to unbutton his shirt and feel his skin on hers. She wanted to be with him now. In the morning, she might be a townie girl again who had outlasted the magic. Right now, she felt...what did she feel? Virtuous? New? Cherished? If this was love, it was something new. It made her uneasy. Maybe he would take her back to familiar ground.

"It's getting late, Lisa."

"Hold me."

He held her. Her mind eased.

Now there was a good-night kiss at the door to her room. Anton pulled her body into his. He wanted to go into her room.

"It's late," he said. "I'll see you in the morning."

"Anton"

"Yes?"

She yearned to hold on to the moment. It felt so good. What to say? She tried to form the words for an invitation, but only two words came out. "Good night."

Damn! After she closed the door, she stood in front of the mirror and undressed to her underwear. She imagined Anton walking up behind her and putting his arms around her. She folded her arms around her chest and smiled. She looked at her body. She thought she could have waited for him if only she had known. She let her hand trace the scar on her right side. The skin there was slightly darker and a bit raised. What would he think if he knew of her scars? They were, after all, quite ugly. And they never went away. People didn't see them because she wouldn't let them. She remembered the feeling she had tonight on the porch, so whole. She figured she had been born with scars, for she couldn't remember a time when they were not there.

She could hear Anton moving down the hallway. She lay down on the bed and closed her eyes.

CHAPTER 10

T he room was illuminated with the brightness of midday. Anton woke up with a startle and turned to look at his clock. It was only 6:00 a.m. He sank back on his pillow. He would need to leave the Cambridge Inn by 7:00 a.m. in order to make it back to Biddeford in time for his last exam. Upon completing the exam, he would secure his status as the valedictorian in his class, thereby ensuring him of the privilege to give the commencement address at graduation.

He looked at the empty space next to him in the bed. He reached out his hand and swept it over the mattress, imagining Lisa was lying there. He could remember how she felt last night —the curve of her lower back, the perfect arc of her behind, her firm breasts pressing up against his chest, the glowing intensity in her eyes. He had wanted to make love to her. Maybe it was better this way. He needed to get back to Biddeford, take his exam, and clear his head. Maybe the concussion wasn't fully gone.

Lisa was already sitting on the porch, waiting for him when he arrived. Mr. Carlisle had noticed him coming down the stairs and brought out a cup of coffee to him.

"Good morning, Doctor," he said cheerfully. "It's a perfect morning fully deserving of my very best breakfast. I want you two to sit back and relax. Remember, time stands still at the Cambridge Inn. This will be a breakfast to remember!"

Anton looked at Lisa as Mr. Carlisle exited the room. "I have to be back in Biddeford this morning to take my last exam. We really don't have time for breakfast. Maybe we can grab something on the way. If we don't leave soon, I'll miss the exam."

Just as he completed speaking, Mr. Carlisle returned with fresh croissants.

"Feast on these while you wait for the main course. Certainly, breakfast is the most underrated of meals. After a weekend like this, you two deserve a sumptuous start to the day. It's not every week a young couple gets engaged." Before Anton could say anything, Mr. Carlisle had cheerfully scampered out of the room again.

"I see," said Lisa. "This exam of yours, if you take it, will that make you a better doctor?"

"No."

"I see. And if you don't take it, will they still let you graduate?"

"Yes."

"I see. So, I don't understand. Explain to me again the significance of getting back in time for this exam."

"Well, I would be the valedictorian. I would get to give an address at graduation."

"Oh. And this address you are to give, would it change medicine? Impact the world? Would it be recorded and sent out to other states or nations? Do you think anybody will remember it a week after it is given?"

"Probably not."

"I see. So, you need to rush back to take an exam that doesn't matter so you can qualify to give a talk that is not relevant. Is that about right?"

The sound of the river filled the silence as Anton looked at Lisa. Last night had not been a mistake or a mirage. Her beauty transcended the revealing light of morning.

"I told you that when we get back to Biddeford you can unengage me," said Lisa. "But we are not back at Biddeford yet. I am your betrothed. I'm requesting the honor of your presence at my official engagement breakfast, brought to you by Mr. Carlisle. Besides, if you tell him you're leaving without eating his breakfast, it might kill him. You wouldn't want that on your conscience, would you?"

Anton smiled and reached across the table, taking Lisa's hands in his.

"Anton, I know you are brilliant. I will think nothing less of you if you come in second or third or whatever in your class."

Mr. Carlisle returned this time with eggs benedict, bacon, and hash browns, all homemade.

"Will you have time for dessert?" he asked.

"Dessert? At breakfast?" asked Anton.

"Of course! It is in engagement-breakfast tradition."

"Well, in that case, we can't miss it. This is our engagement week, after all."

Mr. Carlisle beamed a bit more as he exited the porch and headed into the kitchen.

After breakfast, Anton and Lisa walked down the main street, holding hands and waving to people as they passed by. Several approached them and exchanged pleasant conversations. Anton and Lisa had been here for only two nights but already felt as if they were part of the community. Anton felt strange being connected to people, to a town, to a place, and to Lisa. It all felt so strange and wonderful. Here, there was peace; in Biddeford, conflict awaited. The thought crossed his mind: suppose he stayed here? Suppose he and Lisa stayed here and never went back to Biddeford? Would the world miss him? There would be plenty of other doctors. How sweet it would be to be relieved of his burden! But his destiny would haunt him. He knew the choice was not his but that his fate had already been secured.

It was early afternoon when they finally loaded the samples into the car and headed back toward Biddeford. The exam would have already been completed. In his absence, he would be given a zero on the exam, dropping his grade from an A to a B, just enough to deprive him of the valedictorian status. He smiled to himself. He was exhilarated and relieved from the burden of convention. Who else would abandon the glory willfully? The whole charade, valedictorian, the speech, the con-gratulatory handshakes—it was all ego stroking, all hollow, and ultimately meaningless. Lisa was right. By not taking the exam, by abandoning vain glory, Anton was embracing higher ideals. As the car pulled away from Hopedale, he looked at the town through the back window, watching it fade from his view.

CHAPTER 11

T he commencement ceremony was still six hours away, but Scott Antonelli was already preparing. He laid out all his clothes on his bed and hung his gown on the closet door. His cap with its distinctive tassel color that distinguished "doctor" was hanging on the bedpost. He sat and stared at it. He held the tassel in his hand. He had taken the twelvepenny nail that his father had bent and tied it to the tassel. On the inside of the cap, he had taped a picture of his family. Inside his gown and over his heart was a picture of Ann. He wanted them all with him when he received his degree. "Doctor Antonelli," he thought. What a wonderful sound it made! All his family would be there, including three aunts and two uncles plus Ann's parents and her sister. It's a good thing Anton didn't need his tickets. Otherwise, Scott wouldn't be able to get all his family into the auditorium. Anton had called from some place in Maine to tell him his family wouldn't be coming and that the tickets were available. Scott had been so excited to get the tickets that he didn't think of the fact that Anton would have no one at the graduation.

Todd had pointed that out to him, and he shook his head in disbelief when he thought of it. "Imagine that. A kid like Thresh—every parent dreams of having a kid like that. He's like a legend, like Sir Lancelot or Julius Caesar. He has all the talent, all the gifts, and a heart of gold." Todd actually became angry as he thought of it. "If someday I have a kid like Thresher, I would crawl on my hands and knees on barbed wire to get to be with him. Imagine this moment. Imagine them not being there. Imagine in this entire graduating class that the only kid with nobody there is going to be Thresher. Something is wrong with this picture, I'm telling you. Something is wrong with it."

"Look," said Scott. "Let's make him part of our family."

"Let's make that *your* family. All I have coming is my crazy mom. She will probably go to the wrong building. Anyhow, we need to make sure we help Thresh through the day."

In another part of town, Tim Beckwith and Julie Wyckoff were on their way to commencement. "I hear Thresher is not even showing up for commencement," Tim said as they drove to the ceremony. He always talked fast when he was nervous. "I hear he and Roberti plan on spending the day at Mary's place drinking beer and—"

"Beckwith, will you shut up for a moment?" Julie said. She had been up past midnight the night before trying to finish her commencement address. She had found out at the last minute that she would be giving the address, and she knew it would be a great chance to shine. But she was worried because she did not have a chance to rehearse. Carol Wolf had given her a prewritten address to deliver and told her that it was to help her, seeing that the decision was so last minute. She had told Julie that it was approved by Dean Handley. Julie had tried to write her own speech, but when she read it to Tim, she lost confidence and went back to the prewritten address. She had always imagined what it would be like to give the valedictorian address. All eyes would be on her as the people silently recognized her achievement. She even imagined her mother smiling in the crowd and how great it would feel. Now the moment was about to arrive. She thought about Anton not showing up for the last exam that would have clinched the number-one ranking for him.

"You know, Julie, showing up is part of the test," Tim said. "Did you ever think that maybe Thresher couldn't handle the pressure of being number one? You were born for this role, so enjoy it."

Julie made Tim reassure her several more times before she began to believe him. Eventually, she felt good about her achievement. Now, if Tim could just get her to feel good about the speech.

Lynn Sawmiller had the whole day planned. She would pick up Mark's suit at the dry cleaners, pick up pastries for the party, finish cleaning the apartment, sweep the deck, call Mark's aunt Grace, and call Mark's cousin Billy to remind him to pick up Grace. Lynn's parents would be there at noon, and her younger sister Rachel would watch the kids. Mark was in the bedroom at his desk catching up on his reading. The chief resident from the orthopedic program in Philadelphia had sent him the file of reading material. He was to have read it by the time he arrived. He also had his call schedule. In one week, he was starting residency. Two days later, he would be on call for thirty-six hours. They would have just enough time to pack and move.

The Sawmillers had been married for four years. They had two children, $183 in the bank, and $56,000 in student loans and had not been on their honeymoon yet. Maybe next year. Mark looked at the stack of reading material on pediatric-fracture management. He thought he might like to be chief resident someday.

Lynn knocked on the door. "Mark, it's time to get ready."

Mark was filled with love and warmth for his wife. "Lynn, come here for minute."

Lynn approached him. "I spoke to your aunt Grace, and your cousin Billy said—"

Mark put his fingers to his lips. "Are the kids still sleeping?"

"Yes."

"How long until your parents get here?"

"Two hours," she said as a smile crept over her lips.

"You know, Lynn, I suppose the house is plenty clean."

"I suppose." She folded her arms and tilted her head to one side.

"And I think I have had my fill of setting broken bones for one morning."

"Why don't you move on to other parts of the anatomy," Lynn said. She walked over to the bedroom door, locked it, and dimmed the lights. "Class is in session."

Dr. Charles Thresher, Anton's father, stared out over the lawn from his study. The large bay windows looked out over the rising slope of lawn like an altar at the head of a church. From here, he could see his manicured gardens and their medley of color before him—azaleas in bloom, daylilies, and flowering cherry trees. The room was dark in the morning twilight, with the first rays of sun peeking through the east window. Behind him on the shelves around the fireplace were his achievements, including his trophy for winning the Charles Regatta and his plaque commemorating the year he spent as the president of the Rhode Island Surgical Society. He kept only the best ones in this room; all the others were in the bedroom. Now, he let his eyes rest on all of them, one at a time. Each trophy allowed him to relive a moment and the emotions he had felt—all the pride and joy—when he received the award. As he regarded the award that Anton had received for Athlete of the Year at Compton Prep, memories of that night flooded him. There was his old football coach, now the athletic director, reminiscing with him about their glory days. There was Ed Rooney, a former classmate and offensive guard on the team, now a professor at the school congratulating him on his son's achievement. The local paper had taken a photo of Charles and Anton, arms around each other, each with one hand on the massive trophy. A faded newspaper story was mounted next to the trophy. Thoughts of that time were still with Charles. Anton could have gone anywhere to college. He had been offered a full scholarship in football to Boston College and a track and football scholarship to Stanford. Instead, he had chosen the University of New Hampshire. When Charles had asked him why, he had said it was because he liked the color green. He liked the way the application felt in his hand. Charles had thought Anton was mocking him and turned away in anger.

Anton had pleaded while holding the heavy-stock paper in his hand. "No, really, Dad. Feel this."

Charles had grabbed the paper, crumpled it into a ball, and thrown it back into his face. "Good fucking paper. Maybe you can become a goddamned origami expert. I'll be at the club." He had slammed the door behind him.

His wife, Barbara, as was her custom during Charles's explosions, had hovered at the fringe of conflict, frozen in fear and indecision. Charles had seemed to be a bit harsh on Anton. Then again, Anton should have known his father's temper by now and should not have provoked him. She had bent down and picked up the paper.

"Look, I think I can flatten this out," she had said as she unfolded the application. Out of the corner of her eye, she had thought she could see Anton's eyes fill. "Look, I will put it under a book, and it will be OK. Your dad will come home by dinner. You really shouldn't provoke him like that."

As it turned out, Anton never played any varsity sports at UNH. As a freshman, he had been projected to be the starting varsity tailback. He had torn up yardage in preseason camp but suffered a concussion in a scrimmage, which had landed him in the hospital for three days. Anton never played again. Charles had a neurologist friend forward him his opinion of Anton's CAT scan. The results were normal, and the doctors had cleared him to play. To this day, Charles felt his son was a bit cowardly for not getting back on the horse as he had told him to do. It had been a bitter pill for Charles.

His reflection was interrupted by the distant sound of the phone ringing and then the shuffle of Barbara's feet. He could tell her footsteps; she didn't quite pick up her feet all the way. It was a habit she seemed incapable of breaking. Charles put down the trophy that he had been gazing at.

After a few moments, Barbara entered the study. "That was Anton. He wanted to let us know he won't be giving the valedictorian address."

"W-What?"

"Apparently he missed his final exam, and another student passed him."

"Goddamn it! All he had to do was put his name on the fucking paper. You see, Barbara, that son of a bitch." Charles's face turned red, and his hands twitched nervously as he paced back and forth. He glanced at Anton's trophies.

"No, Charles," said Barbara.

"Do you see what he makes me do? All we do for him, and he can't show up for the goddamned test. But he is right there with his fucking palm up when he needs money. Goddamn it!" He gripped the trophy with both hands until his knuckles turned white and then hurled it to the hardwood floor. The figure at the top bent as the heavy, metal trophy bounced, leaving a divot behind it but not having the sort of shattering explosion that Charles, in his fury, had hoped for. That served only to enrage him further. With his slippered foot, he delivered a mighty kick to the marble base of the trophy.

"Agh! Son of a bitch!" The fury left him as he limped out of the room and passed Barbara in silence. She bent down and picked up the trophy, making a futile attempt to straighten the top. It has been such a great night. Wiping the tears from her eyes, she placed the trophy back on the shelf. She noticed the shelves needed a dusting, so she went to get the dust rag.

The morning of the graduation, Anton left early before anyone awoke. Todd and Scott weren't sure where he went, although they knew he had no plans to go to graduation. They figured he would rather not be around during the preparation for the ceremony. By the time Anton returned, they had left for the commencement. A note was taped to the refrigerator, imploring Anton to meet them there.

Anton walked into his room. His graduation gown had been dry cleaned and laid neatly on the bed, with the cap lying next to it. Next to the cap was a straw with some spitballs and a note: "To be used during Wyckoff's speech. Your friend, Freeze." Anton smiled. It was almost enough to make him want to go to the ceremony. He could imagine Todd smiling as he entered. Maybe he should go. Everyone was so excited by graduation, as if it were a grand achievement. Activity swirled around campus, students were radiant, and parents beamed, all because Junior could now prescribe penicillin for a sore throat. Big deal. Anton expected more. He always knew he would graduate, that was a given. It was nothing to celebrate.

He lay on the bed and looked at the ceiling. He felt alone. He wondered if Julie Wyckoff's parents were proud. He felt paralyzed, and his body was heavy. It was good to lie here.

His mom had always been a bad liar. "Your father has the flu," she had said on the phone. "We will come up later in the week and take you to dinner." Anton wanted to be angry at them but couldn't. He wanted to feel sad, but he couldn't cry. He felt nothing. It was horrible. It was when he was so empty that he felt free, as though gravity had lost its hold on him, and he was able to float in a sea of...what? Pain? Love? Fear? Or was it nothing, the absence of all human feeling and emotion? He wondered what was the first emotion that a new human experienced. Was it love for the comfort of the womb? Maybe it was curiosity for what was beyond. Anton waited for God to speak. "Be still, be still," he thought. "Breathe slowly, empty your mind, stop the hurry. Give God space."

A flash of light surprised him, and a voice called out. "Thresher."

"What? Who is it?" Anton was temporarily blinded by the light in the room.

"Thresher!"

"What?" He still didn't recognize the voice.

"Do you want a beer?"

Anton's vision cleared. "Freeze? What the hell are you doing here? Graduation can't be over yet."

"Well, Wyckoff was about to give her speech, and I thought I might puke. So, I figured I would come back here and grab a can of carbonated fortitude and see how you were doing."

"I don't know, Freeze. Aren't you going to receive your

diploma?"

"Fuck them. I would not want to give Proctor the satisfaction of shaking my hand. They can mail me my damn sheepskin. That's old news. So, I figured, rather than a sheepskin, I would share a can of beer with my buddy to symbolize our achievement. Hey, boy, we did it! We are fucking doctors!"

Anton took a can from his friend and held it up in a toast. "God said, 'Let there be Freeze.' Now I have to figure out if you are a practical joke or if your existence truly has meaning."

"Thanks for figuring that out for me, Thresh. Let me know when you reach a conclusion."

"Don't worry, Freeze. You'll be the third to know."

The two friends sat on the porch overlooking the ocean and drank beer throughout the afternoon. Eventually, the house filled with family and friends. Todd's mom was there. His parents were divorced, and his dad lived in Arizona with his new wife and children. The Antonellis were there, including cousins, aunts, and uncles. After greeting everyone, Anton began to feel out of place. When the attention of the party turned from him, he quietly slipped out the door, hopped on his bicycle, and was away.

"Well, boy, now you are a doctor," said Dr. V. T. Roberti. It was early June, and he sat with his back to Anton as he used a small hand rake to work the soil around his rose garden. "They're like babies, these things," he said, referring to the roses. "Finicky and requiring constant attention." He turned to Anton. "But if you treat them right, they turn out beautiful. Well, you don't look like a doctor. You look like a kid on a bike."

"You don't look like a professor. You look like a patient from an asylum on plant duty."

"I'm afraid, my dear Anton, that we both are a bit closer to that truth than we care to admit. Oh, look at this one." V. T. directed his attention to a rose bush. "Look at its great stalk, the colors of the leaves. Look at the soil it sits in. This plant will produce great flowers. Anyone can notice the flower in full bloom.

The challenge is to pick out the best rose before it blooms. You have to know which plants are worth the effort. In the garden of life, the rich get richer, and the weeds are pulled up by the roots." He turned and pulled a neighboring rose bush out of the ground, exposing its bare roots. "You see, this rose plant appears green and lush. But if you look closely, you will see these black speckles on the stalk. This plant is in trouble. It will never thrive, and it will infect the others."

"Thanks for the horticultural lesson, V. T., but I've only got a few hours. Shouldn't we talk about the research project?"

V. T. smiled as he shook the dirt off the plant. "We just did, boy. Now, let's get some dinner."

The sunroom at V. T.'s house was always filled with the glow of sunlight and the aromas of coffee and smuggled Cuban cigars from Canada ("Nothing like a government ban to enhance the value of a product," V. T. would say). The added aromas of steak and pasta mixed in the air from the adjoining kitchen.

"Morrissey has some good news at the lab," V. T. said between cigar puffs, now looking more serious. "He said he's never seen a more potent kill zone on the cancer plates than he has seen with your orange fern."

"Which cancers has he tested against?"

"So far, breast and lung. He's working on plates for prostate and kidney. He would like to plate out some lymphomas, but that was the most expensive to acquire. So far, he has been able to borrow plates from the general lab stock. We need to make this much bigger. We have enough information to attract major funding. But if we accept drug-company money or government money, we'll lose creative control of our research. Then, it will be a matter of time before they bastardize the results to suit their purpose."

"OK. What's our next step?"

"We need about thirty thousand dollars to purchase the appropriate equipment for the next phase of testing."

"Look," said Anton. "The people in Hopedale have been eating and drinking the stuff for generations. We know it's safe.

Can't we skip right to the human trials?"

"Not legally."

"How about with hopeless cases? You know, patients who are terminal and have no other hope."

"There still is a process we have to follow, and it could take a while." V. T. was calm as he sipped coffee.

Anton got more restless. He hated the thought of following the bureaucratic path. "If Jonas Salk had to deal with the FDA, he would have died before he discovered the immunization for smallpox."

"You might be right, but we have reached a point where we have got to conform our research to the mainstream for it to do any good. It may slow us down, but we will get there."

"Damn it, V. T. People are dying every day. This is no time to go establishment on me. You know what they will do with our research? You know what they will do to our cure? They will bury it in endless research. They will dilute it down from a simple cure to a chronic treatment to fatten profits. Instead of developing a cheap penicillin to cure cancer, they will develop an expensive cocktail of treatments to juice up profits. Let's just distill this product, go to the media, and start curing people."

"How do you know this will work and that it won't hurt people?" V. T. asked.

"I just know. I have no doubt."

"I know you have no doubt, Anton, and that's what scares me. We are sitting on what is potentially one of the great discoveries of our era, and your rash impulsivity could destroy it all. You've got to remember that we are just a couple of docs in the backwaters of Maine. If something goes wrong, they would be able to bury us in the process and destroy this research forever. We can't afford a misstep."

"Then, there won't be a misstep. You have lost your nerve." Anton was pacing across the room, not looking at V. T. "What happened to you? Don't tell me they got to you. They got to you, and now you're backing away. What are you worried about? Did they threaten your pension? I thought you had the guts to pull this off, but you're starting to waste my time."

"I know you weren't at graduation because your parents didn't come."

Anton stopped pacing and stared out the window. "Don't change the subject. That doesn't matter."

"Anton, there were ninety-five graduates, and ninety-four of them used their tickets."

"That doesn't matter. It was just a ceremony. It doesn't matter." Anton stared out to the ocean, noting the quahoggers working the water in the distance.

V. T. got up, walked over to him, and put a hand on his shoulder. "Son, I love you, and I'm proud of you."

Anton lowered his head and turned to face V. T. His eyes fought back tears.

V. T. continued. "Anton, you are the son I never had, and I love you, and I'm proud of you."

Anton cried on V. T.'s shoulder. V. T. cradled his head with his hand. "My son, I love you, and I'm proud of you."

Anton finally composed himself. He wiped away his tears. "Maybe they will come when I win a Nobel Prize."

"You don't have to win anything. You are a beautiful child of God, and I will love you forever. Eternally. Forever. I will love you if you did clams or cure cancer."

The two walked back out to the garden. Between the two of them, they figured they could come up with $15,000. Some creative use of resources would take them through the next phase independently. But they both knew a decision time was fast approaching.

CHAPTER 12

Each morning, Anton awoke to the sound of waves crashing on the shore. Even in the winter, it soothed his body and mind. So it was on this morning, the last day he would be in this house, the last day he would hear these waves and be with friends. He let the sound work its magic as he watched the sunrise. A little while longer, and the pain from these past few days would be gone. He couldn't imagine living without the ocean so near. Portland Medical Center, the hospital where he would be doing his residency, was in the city. He worried about that. Todd had suggested he bring some tape recordings of beach sounds. Scott planned to bring some framed prints.

Later in the morning, Anton would be playing his last basketball game with his friends. It would be the last in a series against the townies. Of course, the townies would continue to play a new batch of medical students in the future, but Anton and his friends would go on to become too busy as medical residents to have time for basketball.

Life was an endless routine punctuated by sudden changes. Anton thought all great changes were sudden, or at least they appeared that way. He could go to bed thinking he would wake up to the same world, but then someone who had helped define his world would suddenly not be there. Or the revolution could come one day and bring an instant cultural change. Or he could punch a professor's son. Or he could discover a cure for cancer. Or he could fall in love.

Anton was sitting on the back porch, looking over the ocean, as was his custom, when he heard a shuffle of footsteps from around the corner.

"Who is that?" he asked.

"Anton?" called a familiar voice. Then, Lisa came into view. It was the first time he had seen her since they left Hopedale. He had feared this moment, thinking everything would have changed. She stepped out on the porch. She had on denim shorts and a crew neck T-shirt with no sleeves. A bandana was wrapped around her head, and she had a backpack slung over her shoulder. She had ridden her bike here. "I remember you told me you liked to sit on this porch early in the morning. I thought I would take a chance and ride out."

Anton smiled, got up, and walked over to her. They hugged. When he kissed her, it all came back—the car drive, the babbling brook, Mr. Carlisle, everything.

Lisa had brought muffins from Mary's place in her backpack. Mary had given Lisa the day off. Actually, after Lisa had told her about the trip, Mary gave her the muffins and a thermos of coffee and all but ordered her to go. "It's his last day in town," Mary had said. "Don't be afraid. You have to find out if it's real."

Lisa and Anton talked as the house's other occupants began to stir. Todd was the first up and staggered out on the porch in his PJs. At a time when most men slept in their boxers, he still wore patterned pajamas with a matching top.

"Good morning, Thresh," he said. Then, noting Lisa, he did a mock stagger. "Good God, Thresh, what apparition is this? A beautiful mermaid sprouted legs! No wonder you are out of bed so quickly."

"Down boy," said Anton. "Lisa, this is Todd Freeze. Freeze, this is Lisa."

Todd shook Lisa's hand with a formal bearing. "I say, you don't happen to have a twin sister with a certain casual moral ambivalence regarding sexual matters, do you?"

"I'm afraid not," said Lisa, charmed already by Todd's easy manner.

Scott followed Todd to the porch. He appeared unshaven and a little hung over.

"Freeze, you disgusting hose bag, leave the poor girl alone," he said. As he introduced himself to Lisa, he could not remember the last time Anton had a female visitor. Of late, Anton's manner had become more reclusive as he focused much of his time on his research.

Scott knew it had always been Ann's hope to fix Anton up with one of her girlfriends. Ann imagined a life of extended friendship and mutual vacations. Invariably, such arrangements ended poorly as the girls became smitten and Anton remained unmoved. Of course, his lack of response baffled her. "What does he want, Scott?" she would ask after Anton had passively broken another heart. Truly, she selected only the most beautiful and most intelligent friends to introduce to Anton. All of them were women like Ann herself; consequently, she felt their rejection was her rejection. So, when Ann walked in on the morning crew, met Lisa, and sensed the change in Anton, she was worried that Lisa might be the one.

Scott turned the conversation to the upcoming basketball game.

"OK, enough sitting around. Time to focus. Let's get our game faces on." His competitive zeal was palpable. From horseshoes to cards, his indomitable will to win changed the air around events like a summer squall blowing over a warm day. At times, he embarrassed Ann. "I have a lot riding on this outcome," he half joked.

As the men left for the gym, Anton gave Ann a friendly hug good-bye and whispered in her ear. "Get to know Lisa." Then, he hugged Lisa good-bye and handed her some papers to deliver to V. T. She would have to pass by his house on her way home. The papers were summaries of biochemical breakdowns of the orange fern. Lisa put them in her backpack.

"Come back after the game," Anton said. "We'll make dinner for you and Ann. It will be our last supper in the old house."

"OK," said Lisa. They stood for a moment and looked at each other before Anton walked out the door. In that moment, they both felt that rush of their time together.

The room was now empty of men. Ann and Lisa were left together. Ann looked at Lisa and tried to figure out what she had that her friends didn't.

"So, Lisa," said Ann. "Where did you go to school?"

"Biddeford High School," Lisa said, not realizing that Ann expected the name of a college.

"Oh. You didn't go to college?"

"No. I didn't graduate high school." She thought about mentioning her GED but decided it didn't matter. She had noticed Ann's manicured nails, well-placed hair, and designer clothing and began to feel self-conscious. When she had left home that morning, she had picked out her finest T-shirt and her newest denim shorts, turned up just enough to highlight her flawless legs to their best advantage. She had done her best to soften her tattered and calloused hands. Years of labor wouldn't wash off in an hour. When she had left her apartment, she felt good. When she saw Anton, she felt great. In the presence of his friends, she felt warmth. Now she was with Ann, soon to be Mrs. Dr. Antonelli. Lisa felt she had to get this over with.

"I work as a waitress at Mary's Country Store and Deli. I live in a second-floor apartment over the hardware store on Main Street. I drive a twelve-year-old car. I never graduated high school and will never go to college. You're right, Ann, I have no business being here. I have no business being with Anton. It was a mistake that we met. You and Scott have a future. I have no right. Maybe that's as good as it gets for me."

"I never said you don't belong with Anton," said Ann.

"No, but you thought it." Lisa's laser insight cut through Ann. Ann felt uneasy and was relieved when Lisa walked away, hopped on her bike, and rode off.

CHAPTER 13

T he smell of a fresh, leather basketball; the squeaking of sneakers on hardwood courts; the moment of weightlessness as players leaped into the air; and, above all else, the beautiful sound of the cords snapping as the ball dropped through with perfect backspin—such was the beauty of basketball games with Anton and his friends. When they moved with synchronicity like the fingers on one hand, it could approach an art form. If it were art, then Anton was its Rembrandt.

"Hey, Thresh," said Scott. "Let's say after the game we go for a little one-on-one."

"Aren't you tired for getting beaten?" asked Brad Sawmiller, who had joined his friends for their epic last battle.

"I'll win this time because I have heart," said Scott, pounding his chest.

Anton chuckled. "You may have heart, but I have a forty-two-inch vertical leap."

"I thought it was forty-one," said Scott.

"That was last month. I've since added an inch."

"I've added two inches since then," said Todd as he punctuated the statement with a rhythmic pelvic thrust in the air. "And it ain't to my vertical lift."

The gang all smiled and shook their heads as Brad hurled a basketball at Todd, striking him square in the ass.

"Hey, don't hurt him," said Scott. "We only have one sub."

Felix Choppin and the townie squad were warming up at the opposite hoop. Felix floated out to midcourt. "Are you boys ready to throw down the goblet?"

"I think he means the *gauntlet*," Brad said to Anton.

"Hey, you throw what you want, and I'll throw what I want," said Felix.

Scott pointed to a tall player who had just entered the gym. The newcomer appeared to be at least six foot six. "Who's that?"

"That's Bobo Pickering," said Felix. Bobo was a player of some local renown. He was the all-time leading scorer in the history of Biddeford High School and had gone on to play college ball at the University of Maine.

Felix continued. "You remember he played with us last September, so he is eligible, technically speaking."

"Damn, I'm just glad I don't have to cover him," said Rob "Legend" Hill, one of the young doctors. No one was quite sure when he had been assigned his nickname or what it referred to, but it seemed to fit. Being of average intellectual ability and short stature and endowed with no particular athletic attributes, the title of "Legend" was certainly unthreatening, if not downright amusing. Over the course of his career at osteopathic medical school, people began calling him by his nickname to the point where they had difficulty remembering his real name. Legend was heading off to Philadelphia in the morning to pursue a career in urology.

The boys played with an edgy intensity. The townies had brought their best players. At the half, they led by eight points, as Bobo had his way with the doctors, scoring at will inside and blanketing Anton with a defense that took him out of the game. Both teams sat on the bleachers near midcourt, drinking Gatorade and swapping stories during halftime. The stories centered on the usual male array of athletic and sexual conquests. Somewhere in the conversation, Lisa's name came up.

"I'm telling you, Legend, this girl walked right out of a magazine," Todd said. "I mean, she's model beautiful and seems to have a brain."

"So, Thresh, how did you meet her?" Legend asked.

Anton was uncomfortable discussing his life, so he looked

down and shook his head.

"Hey, wait," said Felix. "Are you talking about Lisa, the girl that works as a waitress at Mary's? Old 'Lay-Down Lisa'? Hell, if that girl had as many dicks sticking out of her as she had stuck in her, she would look like a porcupine."

The townies all laughed. Anton felt his spine tingle and his hands tighten.

"Fucking girl is a cocaine freak," said Bobo. "In high school, she would fuck anyone for a line. She used to date Andrew Clark. One night, she fucked half the football team for a fix. Fucking dropped out of school the next day. Fuckin' been working at Mary's, a real fucking burnout."

Anton was about to move toward Bobo, but Todd saw him and jumped in first.

"So, Bobo, were you there the night she fucked the team?" Todd asked.

"Hell no, but—"

"Then you feel at liberty to rip this girl's reputation with all this bullshit hearsay."

"What are you, a fucking lawyer? Look, the facts is what they is."

Scott looked at Anton and saw his jaw lock. He knew something was about to happen.

"Fuck all this bullshit," Scott said to redirect attention. "Let's play some ball."

Both teams murmured their agreement and headed out to the court. Scott had seen that jaw lock once before when he was playing on a summer league in North Providence. A player from the opposing team had seen Anton's overweight sister, Polly, watching from the sidelines and pointed at her. "Hey, look! A white orca!" Anton had scored forty-two points in the second half of the game. Toward the end, he had knocked the kid out with a vicious elbow on a drive to the basket.

Scott went over to Felix. "What do you think about a little side wager?"

"What do you have in mind?"

"Say, fifty bucks, straight up, winner takes all."

"You're on."

On the first possession of the second half, Legend brought the ball up the court while Anton set up on the wing and put up his hand to call for the ball. When Legend did not immediately respond, Anton shouted at him. "Just give me the damn ball!" He said it with such authority that Legend immediately responded with a bounce pass to him. With a head fake, Anton blew by the first defender and then headed toward the hoop. He became airborne for a dunk when Bobo met him in midair and put his hand up to the ball as if to block it. But Anton had another gear and continued up and over Bobo, sending the ball through the hoop and sending Bobo's wrist backward over the rim.

"Ah-h-h!" screamed Bobo. "My hand! My fucking hand. He broke my hand!"

Brad stopped and examined the hand. He didn't detect a fracture, just a sprain. He leaned into Bobo. "If I were you, I would quit playing now and go home."

"Fuck you," said Bobo as he ran down the court.

Anton turned his fury at Bobo into production on the court. Legend kept feeding him the ball, and Anton kept embarrassing his opponent. By game's end, the doctors had won by fourteen points.

Bobo shuffled out, slump shouldered, his reputation tattered. In the locker room, Todd sat with Anton, marveling at his abilities. "Incredible. You're just freaking incredible. That was a phenomenal game. Are you sure you want to waste your talent by being a doctor? Why not go to the NBA?"

Anton was not in a chatty mood as he took off his clothes and prepared to shower.

"Hey, Thresh," said Todd. "You know all those things Bobo said are bullshit."

Anton continued to look down.

Todd continued. "You know how it goes. There's not a pretty girl in the world that doesn't have one thousand rumors about her, mostly from guys who wish things on them that never happened. This girl Lisa, she seems real. Don't let that idiot Bobo fog your brain."

"Thanks, Freeze," said Anton as he went into shower.

Later, they all lingered in the parking lot, reflecting on the game and swapping stories. Nobody wanted to leave; they wanted to pretend it was another game. Although they were eager for the next phase of their lives to begin, they knew this was an end. They knew things would never be the same and that their friendships would alter.

In the parking lot outside the gym, the boys stood together for the last time in their lives. "Hey, Saw, drive safe," said Scott. In the morning, Brad would be Philadelphia bound.

"Yeah, man, take care of that cute wife," said Todd with a wink. "Tell her I'm waiting for her."

"I'm sure she'll be glad to hear it," said Brad as he hugged Todd. "And you, boy," Brad said to Anton. "Stay loose, and remember us little people when you become famous."

"Back at you, Saw," said Anton. "Send me a Christmas card with the family's picture."

Legend was next, followed by another round of hugs and promises and taillights fading into the distance.

Back at their house, Scott and Todd left shortly after dinner. They would all see each other next week at orientation, as all three would be starting their medical residency at Portland Medical Center. As usual, Anton had yet to pack and was left behind. Lisa had stayed for dinner and volunteered to help him. She had dropped the papers off at Dr. Roberti's, who, of course, had invited her in. She had subsequently spent two hours in the Robertis' company.

After Anton and Lisa cleared the kitchen, they sat out on the back porch to sip wine as the sun went down. The night was unseasonably warm, almost hot despite the setting sun. The air was still, and the ocean waves meekly rolled up to the sand, as though the mighty Atlantic had been weakened by the sun, too. "You seem quiet," said Lisa.

"Just thinking," said Anton.

Lisa got up, stood behind him, and massaged his shoulders and temples. She then kissed the top of his head. She thought about what a week it had been for him and how his heart must be sad with the parting of his friends. She wrapped her arms around his chest, hugged him, and kissed his neck.

Anton's mind relaxed. Her touch aroused him. He thought of her as she had been on that night in Hopedale.

"Let's go swimming," said Lisa. Before Anton could respond, she walked off the porch and toward the water. The moon glistened off the rippling waves as she pulled her shirt off over her head. She felt an exhilarating rush of desire, comfort, and trust. Anton was like no one else she had ever known. This beautiful man had tenderness in his soul. Tomorrow, he would leave for Portland. Tomorrow, Lisa would go to Mary's, put on her apron, and go to work. But right now, their world consisted of just the two of them.

She stood ankle deep in the water, arms outstretched as if she were to hug the moon. She liked the dark. In the dark, she felt whole and pure. In the dark, she imagined herself flawless, pure in mind and body, free of all her scars, free of fear. Anton looked at her body silhouetted in the shadow of the moonlight. "My God, she is beautiful," he whispered to no one. He moved to go to her, stopping to remove his clothes, and then glanced overhead at the stars. Why had God made her so beautiful? Why had God put them here in this moment together?

Before Anton could reach her, she ran farther into the water and dived headfirst. "Come in, the water feels great!"

Anton dived in after her. They met and embraced.

She felt so good in his arms. His mind became a storm. He fought to let go of all the doubt, and he fought to believe she was like this only for him. In his heart, he felt the purity of their passion. He tried to let the purity of that moment ease his mind. The doubts that kept creeping in called her a cocaine whore, and now his brain whispered back to him: "Cocaine whore." No, not Lisa.

"Cocaine whore," his brain said again. He needed to trust

his heart. But how would he survive if it were all a lie?

Lisa traced her hands down his shoulders to the small of his back and pulled him closer to her. Her lips were parted and inches from his own. He could feel her breath. The moment was almost perfect, and wholesome passion surrounded him. Then came the darkness from within his brain: "Cocaine whore." The words pressed against him, pushing against his skull, pushing their way out. She kissed him deeply on the lips. He felt unsteady. He was determined to trust his heart, for he was in love. Wasn't he?

She kissed him again. He felt his mind going blank. "Cocaine whore," the dark place whispered again. The darkness came over him. He had to know, but how to get it out? He pushed her away slightly and looked into her eyes.

Lisa saw something different and felt the chill. She wanted to run out of the ocean but felt her nakedness. "Not this, not this," her heart screamed.

"Is this how you kissed the others?" Anton asked. The instant those words left his lips, he regretted them.

A shadow descended over Lisa's face. She looked away in stunned silence. She should be used to pain, but this was different from anything before. Her mouth was open, yet she couldn't speak. One thousand thoughts swirled in her mind and stayed in the back of her throat. She ran out of the water, grabbing her clothes from the sand as she left.

Anton couldn't believe he had let the words come out. "Lisa, wait," he called feebly. She was gone, and he was alone. He felt a rage against his friends at the gym, especially Bobo. He felt a rage against himself. He walked up to the shore, knelt on the beach, and lay on his back, exhausted. The waves lapped at his feet. He looked into the heavens. "So, that's how it is for me? Is that the plan? No woman, no earthly love, just you and me and the green horseman to slay? Your will be done." He closed his eyes and fell asleep.

CHAPTER 14

L isa gripped the wheel and sped away into the night, her wet shirt clinging to her body. She wiped the tears away with the back of her hand as she drove faster, as if to drive away from the pain.

But it followed her, filling up the car with hurtful memories, the ones she kept dammed up inside. The place he had touched, the place he had been so near, was the vault of her own pain. It made no sense. How could he approach her scars without her realizing? Why did she let him in? Maybe he wasn't so different. Maybe there was no one to trust—no man, at least. Maybe Mary was the only one.

She thought of driving to Mary's house. She would fall into her arms in a crying heap while Mary brushed away her hair and kissed her forehead. Mary would tell her she loved her and that everything would be OK. Lisa remembered Mary had once said, "Come by anytime, any day. I'll always be there for you." She had sounded sincere. Lisa wanted to believe it, but she had never tested the commitment.

Now she was in her child's body, her mind wandering to another pain. She was walking home after school. Some of the moms picked their children up. Some of them walked their children home. Lisa walked alone. She had on the shirt and leotards she had pulled off the pile of dirty clothes that morning. She had smoothed them with her hands as best she could. In her rusted lunch box was a piece of bread and the stale salami. When her teacher, Ms. Lamothe, saw her lunch, she frowned and offered Lisa half her own. Then, she took Lisa into the girls' restroom and brushed her tangled hair, placing some of her own clips in the side to keep it in place.

"There," she said. "Now you are certainly the prettiest girl in the class."

Lisa beamed in the reflected approval. She loved Ms. Lamothe. As she walked home, she remembered hoping her mother wouldn't be mad at her for letting Ms. Lamothe fix her hair. But her mom was usually asleep when Lisa got home.

The way home took her past the Andersons' house. It made her nervous to walk past there. The boys were usually home alone, sometimes sitting on the front lawn near the street and smoking cigarettes. On this day, it began to rain softly, but the boys were there smoking. Lisa didn't recognize some of them. She glanced at them and made eye contact with one of the new boys. Her heart froze as he made his way to intercept her.

"Hey, girl. Why don't you come in the house and get an umbrella? Your pretty hair is getting all wet." He stood directly in front of her, stopping her from going forward.

"I don't need an umbrella. Let me go home."

"Who's with you?" he asked.

"No one. Now, let me go, please."

The boy glanced at the others. They were sitting on a torn couch that was placed in the middle of the lawn, facing the street as though the whole world was their living room. One of the other boys came down to assist. Now they held her, one on each arm.

"Come inside, we don't want to see you get wet." They pulled her along into the house while a feeble hope emerged in her brain. Maybe they'd simply give her an umbrella and let her go home.

The inside of the house was filthy and rank. Lisa looked for a grown-up or anyone else to help her. The bigger boy pushed her on a couch.

"Let's play a game. You like games, don't you?"

Lisa didn't answer.

"In this game, you have to pull up your dress and pull

down your pants and show us your butt, and then we will let you go home."

Lisa was crying silent tears. "Promise?"

"We promise," the oldest one answered. The others smiled and nodded.

Lisa stood up, pulled up her dress, quickly exposed her butt, and covered it again.

"No, you're cheating," said the oldest one. "You'll have to pull your pants all the way down to your ankles and pull the dress over your head. Boys, help her."

Two of them advanced and pulled her pants to her ankles. Then, they pulled her dress over her head so it covered her face and pinned her arms over her head. She convulsed in silent tears and was frozen in fear as the boys laughed. "Get me a marker," said the oldest. She felt them drawing on her—laughing and drawing.

When she got home, she burst into the house, crying for her mother. Between wrenching sobs, speaking one syllable at a time, Lisa tried to get the words out. In her first-grade brain, the words jumbled into nonsense. Her mother awoke from the couch, bleary eyed. The odors of beer and cigarettes draped over Lisa as her mother moved close to inspect the graffiti on Lisa's butt and around her vagina.

"Jesus Christ!" she hollered as the words came into focus. "Jesus Christ!" Across her butt, the boys had written *whore, fuck me*, and *slut*. They had drawn a picture of an erect penis surrounded by various scribbles.

"Jesus Christ." Her mother now had a fistful of Lisa's hair as she dragged her into the bathroom, occasionally stopping to slap her across the butt.

"I'm sorry, Mommy! I'm sorry, Mommy!" Lisa cried.

"Jesus Christ! Why did you let them do that? Why did you let them do that? I told you not to go in the house!" She grabbed Lisa's face between her hands, her eyes in a wild fury.

"I'm sorry, Mommy!"

"You disgusting tramp!" Her mom's fist came down across

her face. Bleeding from the mouth, Lisa was dragged into the bathroom. When soap and scrubbing didn't remove the stain, Lisa's mom went for some alcohol and her abrasive sponge. Lisa's bottom was raw, some spots oozing blood, but still the stain defied her mother.

"Jesus Christ!" She ran the water in the tub, hotter and hotter. "Goddamn tramp! Can't even walk home from school!"

"I'm sorry, Mommy."

"Goddamn tramp!" Her mother's voice was hoarse from cigarettes.

"No, Mommy!"

"Now look what I have to do because of you!"

"No, Mommy, no!"

"Jesus Christ! Into the water."

Lisa did not quite remember how she got to school the next day. She had trouble walking into class and had trouble sitting in the chair. Ms. Lamothe could tell something was wrong and took her to the girls' restroom to "fix her hair."

"Oh my God, you poor girl," Ms. Lamothe whispered as she saw the wounds, some still oozing blood. She was on her knees, crying.

"I'm sorry, Ms. Lamothe." Lisa began to cry when she saw the tears on her teacher's face. "I'm sorry, Ms. Lamothe. I didn't mean it."

Ms. Lamothe realized that Lisa had misinterpreted her tears.

"Oh, Lisa." she began. All she could do was cry, hold Lisa, stroke her hair, and call her "my little darling."

Lisa felt her teacher's warm tears and smelled her fresh hair. She put her arms around Ms. Lamothe, utterly confused. It would be the last time Lisa would ever see her mother or her teacher again.

It had been a long time since Lisa had thought of those days. Somehow, the code to her vault of pain had been broken, and the door had opened.

While the emotions and memories poured over her, Lisa

robotically drove home. She walked down the alley between the two buildings that led up to her apartment. In her room, she stared at her phone and thought of calling Mary. Then, she fell on her bed, her wet clothes still clinging to her body, and fell asleep.

CHAPTER 15

In a boardroom on the thirty-second floor of the Brewington Building in midtown Manhattan, the research committee of the American Cancer Society was trying to complete its work. Nine members, consisting of seven men and two women, were trying to finalize the financial awards for the upcoming fiscal year in the area of cancer research.

"Members of the board, this meeting is called to order," said Dr. Peter Larchmont, chairman of the research committee. The members sat in high-backed leather chairs around a mahogany table. They had been in town for a week, all staying at the Park Place Hotel together. This was their last day. They had debated throughout the morning about how to distribute the final few research millions. The unspoken deadline was 4:00 p.m. so they would have time to return to their rooms and freshen up for the 8:00 p.m. play of *Man of La Mancha* that was showing on Broadway. Dr. Larchmont spoke in an impressive baritone that commanded immediate attention. He was a retired research oncologist from Loyola of Chicago and had been the committee chairman for six years. His greatest lifetime achievement was likely the development of a protocol to reduce by 50 percent the amount of nausea and vomiting associated with intensive chemotherapy for pancreatic cancer. As with the other physicians on the committee, his research accomplishments could be best described as modest. All the most progressive and dynamic researchers considered this type of committee work beneath them, a waste of their valuable time. The position was considered a plum for politically well-connected physicians who enjoyed the perks of status and frequent travel, as they would periodically visit the sites of some of the active research. The other members were laypeople. One was a full-time secretary, and the other three were serving three-year staggered terms so that each year saw one replacement.

This year, the new layperson was Charlie Smithson, a photographer from Delaware. He was a bespectacled man and slight of build with loose-fitting suit jackets. It was hard to tell if he preferred a loose style or if he had recently lost a large amount of weight. He had been brought to the committee's attention by his provocative photographic essay of cancer victims as they went through their treatment. His work was published in *Life* magazine, and his wife had been one of his subjects. She had died of breast cancer after a three-year struggle with the disease.

"I think we can all agree that Dr. Owen Vanderbilt's proposal is a worthy study," said Dr. Dave Oppenheimer from Cornell.

"Perhaps it is, Dave," said Cindy Blunt from UCLA. "But didn't Dale Lewis from Wisconsin perform practically the same study three years ago?"

"True, but Vanderbilt's study proposes to use the Norwegian breed of mice and to drop the carbon tetrachloride molecule from the isomer. I think it's an innovative twist."

"All right, then," said Dr. Larchmont. "All in favor?"

"Excuse me, Pete," said Charlie. "But what was the objective of that study again?"

"Damn it, Smithson!" said Dr. Lou Edgemont. "We'll never get through this bullshit if you keep asking stupid questions."

Dr. Edgemont was from Sloan Kettering. In addition to its massive independent research fund, it also routinely secured a large chunk of money from the American Cancer Society. At this point in the proceedings, Dr. Edgemont had secured the funding required for all of Sloan Kettering's projects, and he considered this part of the meeting irrelevant.

Dr. Larchmont thumbed through his massive booklet.

"Charlie, the summary is on page number...page number..."

"I believe it's page thirteen twenty-one, sir," said Tasha Smeals, the committee secretary.

"Thank you, Tasha. OK, all those in favor?"

Eight hands went up. Charlie didn't vote. Dr. Larchmont glared at him. "Measure carries, eight to one."

They were down to the last $1.2 million. There was a project they all liked, but at $1.7 million, there was not enough money left to fund it. They would write back to the lead author of the study and encourage him to resubmit it next year.

Dr. Edgemont spoke up. "What about this proposal from Dr. Walter Proctor at New England Osteopathic?" A spontaneous groan filled the room. "No, wait, I know he's a pompous wind bag, almost as bad as I am." He smiled and adjusted his bow tie as polite laughter filled the room. "But Walter's been submitting proposals for ten years, and we have never accepted one."

"So, what are we doing, giving an award for perseverance of stupidity?" asked Andy Blount.

"No, but remember, Walter was instrumental in the New England chapter setting a record for fundraising last year. Besides that, I reviewed his protocol with him, and he let me have some input. He'll be working with patients who are suffering with terminal, end-stage metastatic breast cancer who have failed all treatments, including bone marrow. He can't hurt anyone."

"That may be true, Lou," said Dr. Stephanie Sleva. "But we can't peddle false hope. If these people are dying, it can't be a double-blinded study. It has to be a single-arm study with an open-label treatment. Time of death will be the measurement end point."

"Agreed," said Dr. Edgemont. The proposal was approved, eight to one.

With the meeting now adjourned, the committee milled about the room. Charlie looked out the window overlooking midtown Manhattan. Dr. Sleva approached him. "Your inquisitive passion is a welcome addition to this committee."

"It didn't seem to be welcomed today."

"You'll get the feel for it, Charlie. This committee does important, good work. It, and we, are not perfect, but we all are trying to make things better. Sometimes, if you're too idealistic, it can get in the way."

"I'll try to remember that. Idealism is a hindrance to success, it seems."

"Do you always have to be a horse's ass?"

"Ideally, no. But practically speaking, it seems that I am."

Dr. Sleva stormed out of the room.

Charlie returned his gaze to midtown. He wondered how much cheaper it would be to run this entire operation from, say, a strip mall in Topeka. He wondered who was paying for their theater tickets that night. He wondered how much longer he would last on the committee.

CHAPTER 16

"Good morning, and welcome to Portland Medical Center's residency program in medicine. Many of you know me already, but for those of who don't, my name is Ron James. I am your residency director."

Dr. James continued to read a list of administrative and housekeeping tasks from a prepared script. In the back of the room, Anton, Scott, and Todd sat in their new short, white lab coats and amused themselves by surveying the group and offering comments to each other in hushed whispers.

Scott and Ann had gotten married the week after graduation. They decided to postpone their honeymoon until November, when Scott had a week's vacation scheduled. They had taken residence in an apartment within walking distance from the hospital. Ann had gotten a job in Portland at a department store managing Young Misses.

Todd and Anton had found an apartment in a mostly poor section of town on the southern edge of Portland. The rent was cheap, and although the neighborhood was run down, neither had anything worth stealing. Thus, they felt safe.

Dr. James droned onward. He was a man with few academic or personality attributes. If the medical bylaws didn't require a physician to occupy the role of residency director, a secretary with a high school diploma could have easily replaced him.

"And don't forget to pick up your pagers from Debbie on the way out. Any questions?"

"Thank God it's over," Scott whispered to Todd. "If anyone raises their hand for a question, I'm going to break it off."

A hand went up. "Dr. James," said Linda Walker, a former nurse. She was about ten years older than most of the other residents. Her most distinguishing trait was her striking beauty. It was hard to address her and not appreciate her ample chest and tight curves.

Scott whispered again. "OK, in her case, I'll leave the arms on."

The meeting was dismissed, and the class of twenty-two residents filed past Debbie's office to collect their pagers. Scott would be doing pediatrics in his first rotation, Todd was headed to surgery, and Anton was on internal medicine.

Before they left Debbie's office, Anton's pager went off.

"May I use your phone?" he asked Debbie as he looked at the number on the screen.

"Baptism into the fire," she said as she handed the phone to him.

Anton dialed the number. A brash voice answered. "Hey, rookie, this is Dale Davis. You'll be my slave for the next month. Meet me in the emergency room in five minutes. We've got some sick people to see. Bring your brain, a pen, and a change of underwear."

Before Anton could respond, Dale hung up.

In the ER, Anton met the other residents he'd be working with. Kathy White was from the Chicago College of Osteopathic Medicine. She was married with two children at home. Her husband studied philosophy at night and was home during the day. The other resident was none other than Tim Beckwith.

"Hey, Anton," Tim said nervously. "I hear Dale Davis is the best senior resident here. I hear he's a bit tough. I've got my *Washington Manual of Medical Therapeutics* and my *Sanford Guide to Antimicrobial Therapy* all loaded up on my phone. You can use it if you want to. I also have a laminated copy of all the advanced cardiac life-support protocols for adults and pediatrics." He held the cards out to Anton for his approval. "Julie Wyckoff can get you some if you like them."

Anton smiled. Tim's impish nervousness and impulse to please disarmed him. "Thanks. I'll let you know if I need them."

Dale Davis burst into the room in a flourish with a purposeful stride. His long, white coat was open and flowing behind him, and his stethoscope dangled from his neck.

"Here, put on gloves." He held a box to the other residents. "A forty-five-year-old white male is en route. Remote tracing from the ambulance looks like this." He handed a tracing of a cardiac rhythm to Kathy. "What is it, and what do you do?"

Kathy was caught off guard. She held the strip in one hand and traced the rhythm with the finger of her other hand. "Hmm..."

"Time's up," said Dale. He snatched the strip from her and handed it to Tim.

"I think...maybe it could be...I would go with atrial fibrillation."

"And your treatment doctor?" Dale asked.

"Well, maybe I would do a little IV verapamil."

"Nice," said Dale. "Indecisive and wrong—a lethal combination. Your patient is dead." Before he could pass the strip to Anton, the patient arrived on a stretcher in the CPR room, with EMTs providing chest compressions and ventilation. Dale quickly took control of the code, assigning tasks to all in the room. An overhead monitor recorded the rhythm.

"What is it, Thresher, and what would you do?"

"Course V-tach, defibrillate with two hundred joules," Anton said as he grabbed the paddles.

"Fucking right!" said Dale as he smiled. "Have at it."

"Clear!" Anton yelled. Three shocks later, the abnormal rhythm persisted.

"Damn," said Dale. "Sustained V-tach. Hold chest compressions, check for a pulse."

"No pulse here," Tim said as he checked the groin for a femoral pulse.

"Prepare lidocaine, check dose," said Dale. Tim nervously flipped through his laminated cards.

"Bolus with one hundred milligrams," said Anton. "Estimate eighty-kilogram man, infuse at one-hundred-milligrams bolus, and set drip at two micrograms per minute."

"Fuckin' A," said Dale to no one in particular. "This kid's all right."

Ten minutes and three drugs later, the malignant rhythm persisted. The room has gradually filled with people as word spread throughout the hospital of the efforts to resuscitate the patient. Surgery was called, and Dr. Proctor appeared with Todd in tow to place a central line. Todd's normally irreverent demeanor was altered to pure focus as Dr. Proctor observed him place a flawless central line in the subclavian vein. With the task completed, the surgeons left for the next job. Todd and Anton made brief eye contact, but neither said a word in the intense silence.

"Hey, Suzi," said Dale to the head nurse recording the events. "Are there any next of kin around?"

"Wife, name of Marlene, is out in the family waiting room."

"White!" Dale said. "Go out there and start hanging some crepe."

"What?" Kathy asked.

"You know, go out there and tell her that her cat is stuck on the roof, and we're having trouble getting it down."

"Huh?"

"He means go prepare the wife for the bad outcome," a nurse said. "Come on, I'll go with you."

"Excuse me, Dr. Davis?" Anton asked.

"What is it, Thresher?"

"Have you considered a bolus of intracardiac epi followed by central pacing overdrive?"

Dale nodded. "*JAMA* article, June of last year. Yeah, I thought about it. But why go ruin a perfect code with that experimental bullshit?"

"What else do we have?"

"I'll tell you what else, Thresher. Game up."

"What?"

"Our boy is not going to survive."

"But why not try at least—"

"Game's up, people. Code is called at eight forty-five a.m. Cause of death is cardiac arrest."

The nurses and respiratory technicians who had been doing cardiac massage stopped their activity. The monitor was turned off. People began drifting out of the room. It didn't feel right to Anton. A human life just passed, and it was as if a shift had come to an end—time to punch the clock, talk about the upcoming coffee break. It didn't feel right. There should be something more. A candle? A prayer? Maybe a trombone solo. Anton smiled to himself.

"Hey, rookie, over here," Dale said as he signaled to Anton. "Now, boy, you did some nice work in there. But when I say game up, game is up. You got it?"

"But—"

"No *but*, rookie. I read that article, too. True, thirty percent of the people survived the code, but of those eighty percent died within one week. And of those who survived, most had major neurological damage. You can't stand on experimental treatments, you understand? We're Portland fucking Medical Center, not Mass General. Don't you be the first motherfucker in a foxhole or the last to get out. You got that?"

Anton nodded. Dale was brash and pompous but well read.

Tim came up to Dale. "The cat is stuck on the roof, and we can't get it down?"

"You never heard that old joke? Hell, remind me, and I'll tell it to you sometime when I'm drunk." Dale left the room.

The rest of the day unfolded in a less dramatic fashion. Dale had given Anton eight patients to follow while assigning only four to Kathy and Tim.

"You're an arrogant motherfucker," Dale told Anton. "I'm gonna beat your ass into submission."

So, the learning had begun.

CHAPTER 17

On the weekends, Ann Antonelli would organize her grocery store coupons. Clip and file, clip and file, she would arrange them by category for easy retrieval when she went shopping. She would plan the week's menu, including lunches for Scott so he wouldn't have to buy them in the hospital cafeteria. Scott left the apartment early before Ann was awake. Each morning, she placed his lunch in the refrigerator, with his name written on it. Often, she would include a brief note to Scott with an expression of love. Frequently, the note included some practical request at the end.

"Good morning, Poochie! I love you! Keep learning! Love, Ann. PS: pick up a gallon of skim milk and some folic acid tablets on your way home (five hundred milligrams)."

The apartment was immaculate but retained a warm, welcoming feel. Over the first few months of the residency, the Antonellis' place had become a focal point for social gatherings. At least once a week, Scott would have Todd, Anton, and a couple of the residents whom he was rotating with over for dinner.

At this stage of their training, they would move on to a different service each month. Anton started with medicine, then surgery, pediatrics, and back to medicine. Scott was about to start surgery with Dr. Proctor, and Todd had pediatrics next.

Meanwhile, back at their apartment, Todd and Anton reflected on the day's events.

"Damn, Thresh. Did you see that? I dropped that subclavian line. Boom! First stick!"

They sat out on a fire escape overlooking the street, sipping beer. They hadn't seen each other since the last night in Biddeford.

"So, how did it go for you and Lisa that night?" Todd asked as he arched his eyebrows in anticipation of some erotic details.

"I'd rather not discuss it."

"That good, huh?"

Anton's voice bristled. "I'd rather not talk about it." He got up to leave.

"Oh, that bad, huh? Do you think Lisa needs me to call her and comfort her?" Todd shouted out as Anton walked away.

Now Todd sat in silence on the fire escape. Silence always made him uncomfortable. He could always make Anton laugh. Nothing felt so good as watching him laugh. But tonight was different. Something had happened that night. Todd knew his friend too well not to notice. Lisa was the woman Anton should not let out of his life. Todd could tell. He worried, though, that Anton couldn't.

Two weeks into the first rotation, all the young doctors were quickly falling into a familiar routine. Early morning "pre-rounds" usually began around 5:00 a.m. These quick, cursory overviews of all their patients allowed each first-year resident time to organize his or her thoughts in preparation for the more formal rounding that would occur later that day, first with the senior residents and then with the attending physician.

Around 6:30 a.m., they would meet with the "night call" team for morning check-in. Those were the residents who were responsible for taking care of the patients overnight at the hospital. As with any teaching hospital, medicine was one of the busiest services. Each subspecialty linked direct patient admissions to the general-medicine team. This would allow them to focus on their more limited scope of expertise, while the general-medicine team had to worry about every other detail of the patients' care.

The night-call team was derived from a rotating list of all the residents in the program of a given service. For medicine, all the residents in general medicine would be pulled into a group and then assigned a night to work. They were teamed together, two first-year residents and one senior resident. First, they would complete their regular work for the day. Then, at around 6:00 p.m., they received "checkout" from all the other residents. Checkout could occur in person or on the phone. Information about the patients in the hospital, including issues that the night team may be asked to address, were discussed.

In addition to caring for all the patients in the hospital, the night-call team also admitted patients from the emergency room who required hospitalization. After completing their night duty, the residents would resume the next day's activities without a break.

After the morning check-in, the residents would meet for "morning report" from 7:00 a.m. to 8:00 a.m. During this hour, the night-call team would present the most interesting cases from the night before to the rest of the staff, residents, and attending physicians.

"OK, slaves, report." Dale Davis sipped his coffee, black as usual, while Tim, Kathy, and Anton presented their cases. Dale was widely regarded as the most knowledgeable senior resident, but he also possessed a brash personality wrapped in a confrontational teaching style. Anton was growing to like him.

"You first, Kermit," said Dale, pointing at Tim, whom he had dubbed as Kermit the Frog because of what he said was Tim's striking resemblance to the Muppet character. By extension, Dale had dubbed Julie Wyckoff (who was rotating on another senior resident's service) as Miss Piggy.

"Well, I've got Mrs. Sanders in room four oh six. A seventy-two-year-old white female admitted two days ago with intractable abdominal pain, nausea, and vomiting. She has been NPO on IV fluids. Electrolytes and vital signs were stable this morning. Her abdomen remains tympanitic with diffuse, nonspecific tenderness."

"Differential?" asked Dale without looking at Tim.

"Rule out diverticulitis, consider atonic ileus, consider

obstruction."

"Imaging studies?"

"A CAT scan of the abdomen was done last night."

"Results?"

"Results are pending."

Dale winced. "What do you mean *pending*?"

"Well, radiology hasn't read the films yet."

"Then you go down there, dig out the films, and read them yourself!"

"But—"

"And if you can't interpret the image, then you wake up the sorry-ass radiology resident and make him look at it with you."

"But I did call the radiology fellow. He gave me an earful for waking him up, and then he told me they would get to it in the morning."

"Kermie, maybe I'm not making myself clear. Let's pretend what we do here in our club"—Dale made a sweeping gesture with his hand—"really matters. Let's pretend we have people's lives in our hands. Let's pretend Lady Abdominal Pain is your beloved aunt. It's now nine fifteen a.m. The operating room slots are full up. If you had looked at that film by now, you would know that Mrs. Sanders has a diverticular abscess and should be headed for surgery right now instead of lying around in pain all day, waiting for her abscess to burst and possibly dying from septic shock. Now, if you have half a brain, your ass is starting to pucker up right now, and it's going to pucker up a lot more when I tell you that at two a.m. Mrs. Sanders's temperature went to one hundred one point two. So much for stable fucking vital signs."

"I didn't see it on the temperature graph."

"It wasn't on the temperature graph. It was buried in the nurse's notes. That's right, it should have been charted, but someone didn't do their job well. Does that shock you? People fuck up here all the time, Kermie. I just don't want my residents to be one of them. In short, your performance this morning on behalf of Mrs. Sanders was pitiful, half-hearted, and incompetent. Tim, that was a lousy display of doctoring."

Tim blinked furiously and inhaled deeply as his eyes teared up. Anton and Kathy both looked down. Anton actually felt bad for Tim as he absorbed the withering barrage. Kathy reached out her hand and instinctively patted Tim on the shoulder.

"Now, Mommy, don't you be doing like that," Dale said sharply. "Young Kermie better grow a pair of gonads real fast, or he can just transfer over to dermatology or some other sorry-ass specialty where they don't take care of sick people. I don't cotton to incompetence. Here, you gotta have thick skin and a short memory. Now, Kermie, the next time you hesitate to drag a colleague out of bed, I want you to think of this moment and fear me more than him. If you ever come to morning rounds that ill prepared again I will have you tossed off my team." He turned to Anton. "That goes for you, too, muscle neck."

Dale then looked at Kathy. "I'm not quite sure what to do with you, but I will think of something." He turned his attention back to Tim. "You see, Beckwith, I know everything about your case because I don't trust you, and I checked in on all your patients. Mrs. Sanders is already scheduled for surgery, which is better than a trip to the morgue. I don't mind teaching you deadbeats, but I'm not gonna let you kill my patients."

He then looked at Kathy and Anton. "Yes, I checked yours, too. Remember, don't trust no one until they prove they are trustworthy."

Tim regained his composure and then completed his presentation of patients. Kathy did the same, getting through it without triggering Dale's ire. Anton was next. When Anton was finished, Dale assigned him extra patients. Whenever Anton said something Dale liked, Dale would nod, snap the fingers on his left hand, and say, "Fucking A!" This morning, there were a lot of those directed at Anton. Tim stewed more with each one.

Lunchtime was the one great social moment of the day. Residents clustered into tables, self-segregating by year, and swapped stories about the day. Todd came up to the table where Anton, Tim, Kathy, and the other medicine residents were sitting.

"I only have a few minutes. They just added a case to the schedule—a Mrs. Sanders for an emergency laparotomy."

"How did they get that on so quickly?" Tim asked.

"Holy shit! You should've seen it. Dale came busting into the staff lounge in the operating room, went right up to Proctor, and told him to add on Sanders as an emergency. Proctor said she should go with IV antibiotics and wait until morning. Then, Dale said, 'I bet dollars to donuts she's got ischemic bowel in there. You wait, and she could wake up dead.' Proctor still wouldn't budge, so Dale threatened to transfer the patient to Proctor's service so she won't die on his watch."

"Man," said Kathy. "He's got some guts. Imagine talking to Proctor like that."

"Well, it worked. Proctor put her on in the middle of the schedule."

The rest of the day passed uneventfully. That night, it was Anton's turn to be on call. He would be teamed with Vince Grodin, who was a fellow first-year resident, and Cindy Neuhause, who was a senior resident. After receiving all the information on the patients, Dale handed the on-call pager to Anton.

"Good luck, Thresher." A sign of Dale's growing respect for Anton was that he hadn't nicknamed him. "You've got Big Tits Neuhause as your senior resident. Maybe you can cop a feel in the on-call room, because that's about all she's good for. And you've got James as your attending. I've forgotten more medicine that those two will ever know. See you in the morning. Or, as the saying goes, 'AMF YOYO'—Adios, motherfucker, you're on your own!'"

Anton liked being on call at night. He liked the solitude. When it was quiet, he liked to go up on the roof, where the residents had cobbled together a makeshift sundeck with some chairs, lounges, and tables. It was there he could lie back, take in the stars, and think. He owed V. T. a call. They spoke on the phone several times a week. Morrissey was having some trouble breaking down the orange fern into its constituent components. They were trying to determine which specific chemical in the fern was responsible for its clinical effects. They would be needing more orange fern soon. Anton wondered why he hadn't heard from Ben Able. Thinking of Ben made him think of Mr. Carlisle and then Lisa. He imagined her as she had been in Hopedale—so cool, so beautiful. It was hard to believe she was only nineteen. What a great mind, though, what a great woman. He imagined how she had felt in his arms the last night they were together. He became aroused thinking about her. He couldn't believe what he had said, and he couldn't believe he had watched her walk away. Maybe it was for the best. For the journey to go on, he would have to make it on his own. If he were called to sacrifice love for the mission, so be it. He could accept his fate. Personal pleasure was not important if it interfered with fulfilling his destiny. He had no doubt that the answer was near. He was pretty certain that, in some way, the price of success was likely to end his life as he knew it. It was better to be alone.

His pager went off, startling him out of his reflection. He recognized the number to the emergency room and called immediately.

"Anton, this is Cindy. We've got a possible subarachnoid bleed down here. Looks like she might need a spinal tap. I remember you said you like doing procedures."

"I'm on my way."

Anton had studied every aspect of the most frequently performed procedures, including spinal taps. Although he had not performed any yet, he felt supremely confident that he could do so successfully.

Before he entered the emergency room, he could hear the woman's screams. "Oh my God! Oh my God! Just cut it out! Make it stop!"

She was sitting on the gurney, rocking back and forth, and pressing a towel to the right side of her face.

"Mrs. Denton, you've got to be still so we can do this," said Cindy Neuhause in a nervous voice. She signaled to the staff. "You may need to pin her down."

"What's going on?" asked Anton upon entering the room.

"CAT scan of the brain was normal," said Vince Grodin. "Cindy called Ron James, and he said to do a spinal tap to rule out a bleed."

"Oh good, Anton is here," said Cindy. "You can help us. Have you ever done one of these before?" She held the needle in her shaky hand.

Anton didn't answer. He was intently watching the patient. "Ma'am? Is your headache only on the right side?"

"Yes."

"Do you feel nauseous?"

"No."

"Are your nose and eye on the right side running?"

"Yes." The one-word answers were all the patient could muster between sobbing and rocking in pain. Anton turned to the nurse. "Get her one hundred percent oxygen with a non-rebreather mask."

"What are you doing?" asked Cindy. "We need to complete this spinal. Her oxygen saturation is fine."

"She doesn't need a spinal tap." Anton put the oxygen mask over the patient's nose and mouth. "That's it," he said to her. "Nice, slow, deep breaths."

The patient complied. After a few deep breaths, her face began to relax.

"It's a classic cluster-type headache," Anton said. "Sometimes, one hundred percent oxygen will stop it right in its tracks."

The patient had put the towel down. She stopped rocking and sat upright.

"Thank you," she said, reaching out and squeezing Anton's forearm for emphasis.

"Wow!" said Cindy. "Nice work."

"James wanted her admitted overnight for observation

after the spinal tap," said Vince.

"She can go home. She'll be fine," Anton said. In an instant, all the authority had shifted to him. Cindy had no ego and was only too glad to have a resident of his ability working on her watch.

At morning report, Anton proudly presented the headache case. The room murmured approval. Dr. Ron James sat in uncomfortable silence, darting his eyes around the room like a nervous bird and gauging the other doctors' responses. Did they all know Anton had defied his orders? Were they silently looking down on him? Anton walked from the podium to admiring glances. The crowd dispersed, and a new day began.

CHAPTER 18

U ncle George was safe to go to. If God had placed a gentler man on Earth, Lisa couldn't imagine it. It was hard to believe he was her mother's brother. Maybe it was because he was twenty years older than her mom, or maybe it was because he had a different father. Certainly, his small stature gave Lisa comfort. He was an even five feet tall, and Lisa towered over him by eight inches. When she greeted him, she would rub his bald dome and kiss his forehead. That always made him blush and smile. Whereas Lisa's mom hardly knew a sober day, Uncle George never drank. And whereas Lisa's mother uttered a stream of venomous phrases, Uncle George spoke a simple language of praise.

When Lisa had run away from her third foster home in Chicago, she made her way to this remote town of Biddeford, which was the home of the only other living relative she knew. Like a third-world fugitive, she was motivated out of pure desperation, unsure of what lay ahead but certain of the horror she left behind. Uncle George and his wife, Ann, had taken her in. They asked no questions, not one. They greeted her with joy as though she were an expected visitor. They made her a bed on the couch in the TV room. Lisa was fourteen at the time. That fall, she would enter Biddeford High School. She would live on that couch for the next three years. In the spring of that first year, when she came home and announced she was dropping out of high school, they asked no questions. Lisa had been making straight As at the time she dropped out. When she spent the next four weeks barely leaving the house and barely eating, they asked no questions. One day, her aunt sat on the edge of the couch and talked with her. "Lisa, your uncle George and I are worried about you."

Lisa looked at her aunt's face, saw the pain etched in the furrow on her forehead, and resolved to get up each morning and eat. She swore she wouldn't bring these people any pain.

Uncle George was a retired deli clerk. He and Aunty Ann had lived in their three-room shack five miles north of Biddeford for their entire married lives. It was on a bluff overlooking a small inlet where the local quahoggers and lobsterman kept their boats. One year after Lisa arrived, Aunty Ann died from complications of her diabetes. Uncle George's small world shrank. After a time of mourning, he returned to his routine of a morning walk to get the paper, a trip to the VFW post to play cards, and then an afternoon with this pipe in his favorite rocking chair on the porch overlooking the cove. He spent Saturday mornings at Mary's for breakfast and spent Sundays at church. He had introduced Lisa to Mary when she first arrived at their house. Shortly after that, Mary offered Lisa a waitress job, and she had been working there ever since. The job enabled her to move out of Uncle George's house and get her own apartment by the time she was seventeen. Lisa was working full time and maintaining her apartment, but she always made time to visit Uncle George.

"Nice to see you, Lisa," he said. "Come in. Let me make you some tea."

"Thanks, Uncle George."

Lisa had ridden her bike over, as usual. It was early September. The leaves were turning, approaching their peak color. Lisa sat next to the old woodburning stove to warm up.

"So, what's new?" Uncle George asked. "Have you met any nice, young doctors yet?"

Lisa hesitated at this familiar question. She thought of Anton, and her eyes misted over.

"Hey," said Uncle George. "I think that might be a yes."

Lisa refocused. "No, no, stop trying to marry me off. I'm

thinking of taking some courses at the junior college."

"That's nice." Uncle George had used the most enthusiastic affirmation he could muster. What could he say about something he couldn't grasp? "Whatever makes you happy."

Lisa ate stale cookies, drank weak tea, and made Uncle George smile. It was a good visit.

Lisa returned to her apartment to prepare for work. She washed her face, grabbed a shirt from the dirty-laundry pile, pulled on yesterday's jeans, pulled back her hair into a ponytail, and hopped into her car.

A fresh crop of new medical students hung out at Mary's Country Store and Deli these days. Lisa put her apron on over her plain clothing. She wore no makeup and hadn't been washing her hair for days at a time. She avoided eye contact and rarely smiled. It seemed to be working. After the first few weeks, the new boys stopped asking her out. Her tips diminished. The rejected preppies had to rationalize their failure. How could the townie girl turn them down? They speculated that she was a lesbian. This made them feel better.

Lisa moved about her job with stern purpose under Mary's watchful eye. A man entered the restaurant, made an inquiry at the front, and then sat in Lisa's section, alone. Lisa approached him, with her head bent over an open pad and pen in hand.

"What can I get you this afternoon?"

"Hi, Lisa. Remember me?"

Lisa looked up. She smiled in spite of herself. "Ben Able!" She leaned over and kissed his cheek. Ben blushed.

"Lisa, I need to talk to you. Can you spare a few minutes?"

Lisa called out to Mary. "Can you cover me for fifteen minutes?"

"Got you covered. Take your time."

Lisa and Ben walked out the back door and across the seashell-covered parking lot, where she sat on the top of the picnic table.

"How are things up in Hopedale?" Lisa asked with genuine

interest.

"Fine, fine. Listen, I'm trying to find Anton. I developed a new technique for growing orange fern. I figured out how to cultivate it indoors. I can re-create the microenvironment on the hillside and produce what I think is the identical plant. Do you know what this means, Lisa?"

Lisa gazed into the distance. "Unlimited supply for pennies. Perfect."

"That's right, Lisa. Perfect. But I haven't been able to reach Anton—no forwarding address, no phone number."

"I know how to get him." She then hollered in the back door. "Mary, got to punch out. I'll catch up with you later."

"OK, I'll cover for you."

"Ben, we better take your car. I'll take you up to Professor Roberti's."

When they arrived, V. T. was in his backyard, piling horse manure over his roses to prepare them for the cold weather.

"Nature doesn't waste of thing, not a thing," he said. "It's all here. It all has a purpose. It all fits together perfectly. Heaven on Earth, Lisa. Heaven on Earth. We just need to figure it all out." As usual, he had dispensed with any formal greeting and welcomed his guests by letting them in on his stream of consciousness.

"Name's Roberti," he said finally, acknowledging Ben's presence. "But I've been up to my elbows in horseshit."

"V. T., this is Ben Able. He's the one I told you about. Ben is a botanist. He's discovered a way to cultivate orange fern."

"Well, boy, now you got my interest."

In the sunroom, Ben told V. T. and Lisa about his new cultivating technique. "If the fern tests out, we will need to develop a large-enough harvest to meet projected demand. It's a bit early to gauge the exact amount. We don't know the potency of our formula or how many plants will be required to produce it, but I expect it to be substantial."

"Will it grow in other climates?" asked Lisa.

"It may. But so far, I have only found it in our county. I

think we need to consider this a regional plant with a limited habitat. The indoor technology may expand our base of operation, however."

"Well, Morrissey has had a bit of a problem down at the lab," V. T. said. "So far, he has broken the plant down to all its constituent components, and they just haven't had any effect. Only the whole plant had a reasonable kill zone against cancer."

Ben nodded. "That would be a challenge not only for production but also for approval. The FDA will want to see a molecular reaction to support the clinical effect. This is going to require a more ambitious research approach."

The three sat in silence.

"We need Anton here," said Lisa. "This is his time."

In the silence of the room, they felt the project growing, taking on a life of its own, and starting to run away from them.

"I'll call him," said V. T.

Later that evening, V. T. walked around the backyard. The branches from the expanse of maples swayed in the breeze, casting an outline against the purple sky of late dusk. V. T. took a sip of his brandy. He thought of Anton's youthful exuberance in those early days and of his own zeal. Did ambition blind him? Had he used Anton's idealism to form him into a weapon for his own purpose? Did he sacrifice Anton's personal happiness to infect him with this crazy dream he carried? Who could have thought it would come this far. V. T. knew that the French said that all beginnings are beautiful. Left unsaid was that all middles are confused, and all endings are tragic.

"My boy, my son, what have I done to you?" he said. He knew it was too late to turn back. In the morning, he would call Anton. "And now, I—and we—are tools in your hands." He tipped his glass to the sky.

"Honey, who are you talking to?" asked Pat.

"The sky, my darling. But it's being very rude. It won't talk back."

"If I know you, it's because you don't give it a chance to speak." She wrapped her arms around his waist and lowered her head on his shoulder. "What troubles you, love?"

"Anton."

"You love him like a son, don't you?"

The words struck V. T. "My son," he whispered. "I do love him."

Pat reached up and wiped a tear from his face. "And you worry about him as things grow. But V. T., this is no time to show him fear. You must be strong and steady. You will be there to lead him, and I will be there for you no matter what. You can't quit. The only thing worse than a deed undone is a deed half-done."

V. T. smiled and shook his head. He breathed in deeply and stood a little more erect. The tears had vanished.

CHAPTER 19

Anton sat across from Dr. Mark Epperly, the hospital medical director. Dr. Epperly was an energetic and athletic man, widely respected for his clinical and administrative skill. He was a rising star in academic circles and the primary reason why Portland Medical Center had such a strong residency class. In addition to wanting to be close to Biddeford to continue his research, Anton, like the others, had been strongly influenced to apply to the medical center because of Dr. Epperly.

Sitting to Dr. Epperly's right was Dr. Ron James, looking nervous and uncomfortable in his chair. He would glance briefly at Anton and then stare at the floor, his mouth twitching into an impulsive frown. To Dr. Epperly's left was Dale Davis, who winked at Anton as Anton entered the room.

"Good morning, Anton," said Dr. Epperly. "Do you know why you were called to my office?"

Anton could tell from the room's mood that something was wrong, but he was truly at a loss to speculate what it could be.

"Let me guess," he said. "You want to tell me I've been nominated for the Resident of the Year Award."

Dale smirked.

Dr. James twisted in his chair. "You see, Mark? You see the arrogance?"

"Ron, calm down," said Dr. Epperly. "Anton, tell me about the headache case in the emergency room from the other night."

Anton recounted the events of the evening, still not clear where this was leading or what he had done wrong. When he completed his summary of the events, Dr. James jump in. "What about the spinal tap I ordered? What about admitting the patient as I ordered?"

"Dr. James, she didn't need a spinal tap. She was fine," said Anton.

"Oh no? What if that had been a bleed, mister? You can play fast and loose with your own license but not with mine. When I give an order, I expect it to be followed." Dr. James's eyes bulged out of his head as his glance darted from Anton to Davis to Dr. Epperly and then back to the floor.

Anton directed his response to Dr. Epperly. He had to clench his jaw to compose himself. "There was no chance, zero percent, that she suffered from a bleed. It was a classic cluster headache, and my treatment made her well. I would never put a patient at risk. Under those circumstances, it would have been malpractice to perform a spinal tap."

Dr. Epperly studied him. "Your clinical judgment, Anton, is not in question. But you should have called Dr. James to explain your plan and get his approval."

Anton felt bewildered and betrayed.

Dr. Epperly held up a paper. "Now, look, I don't want to make this out to be more than it is. Anton, this is a private reprimand." Anton felt the blood leave his face. Dr. Epperly continued. "I want you to sign it. It cites you for failure to properly consult with your attending physician. It will sit in my drawer and not become part of your permanent file, and it will be destroyed in one year, as long as there are no other infractions."

Anton took the paper. He didn't read it. He couldn't believe this was happening. He signed the paper.

"Sir," Dale said.

"Yes, Dale?" Dr. Epperly said.

"I want to go on record as saying that Thresher is without doubt the finest damn rookie I've ever had to waste my time on."

"So noted."

Dale reached over and took the paper from Anton.

"What are you doing?" Dr. James asked.

"He's my rookie, and I accept full responsibility for whatever he does. I'm signing my name right under his." Dale completed his signature and then handed the paper to Dr. Epperly.

"You are dismissed, Anton," said Dr. Epperly. Anton got up and left the room.

Dr. James turned to Dale. "What the hell was that all about?"

"Ron," said Dr. Epperly before Dale could respond. "Shut the fuck up and get out of here."

Dr. James did a head-lurching double take, opened his mouth as if to speak, and then got up and shuffled out the door, head cocked to one side.

Dr. Epperly closed his eyes and grimaced. "Sometimes, I hate this job."

Kathy White approached Anton. "I heard what happened." She, Anton, and Tim Beckwith were waiting for Dale Davis to start the morning rounds. "Sounds like you got screwed."

Anton shrugged. "It happens."

Dale arrived and jumped into his work. "Kermie, you've got two hits in the ER: a fifty-two-year-old male with chest pain needing a medical bed, name of Gomes, and an eighty-one-year-old LOLTBF."

"Huh?"

"Little old lady, total body failure. Head out, and I'll meet you down there." Dale then turned to Kathy. "Cinderella, you got medical consults today on obstetrics: two diabetics and an asthmatic." He handed her the cards with corresponding names on them. "Go ahead and write up a consult, and I'll be there to review it." The two residents left for their work.

Dale then turned to Anton. "Well, how you feeling?"

"Like shit."

"James is a prick, but he's a fool we gotta suffer. I'll tell you, it may not have seemed like it, but Epperly's got your back.

James wanted you suspended and threatened to go to the medical board, but Epperly slapped him down."

"I don't think I can work with Dr. James."

"Boy, if he serves you up a shit sandwich, you better eat it and ask for another with a smile. I have it from pretty good sources that he won't be back next year. But for now, you better do a little butt kissing. Listen, it's been a tough day for you. Why don't you go do some H-and-Ps over on surgery." History-and-physicals for the preoperative cases was considered a bit of a break. It was easy work, no heavy thinking.

Anton got up to go but then stopped and turned to Dale. "Thanks for what you did back there."

"Fuckin' A. We smart dudes gotta stick together or else the morons will run the planet."

H-and-Ps consisted of interviewing patients to gain all the key elements of their personal and medical history. Anton was assigned to surgical oncology, where he would be screening the patients to be enrolled in Dr. Proctor's study.

The awarding of the study grant to Dr. Proctor was big news around the hospital. Indeed, he had seen to it that a press release followed. He had even gotten on the evening news. In Portland, Maine, the award counted as a big story. The hospital loved the PR and planned on featuring him in the next ad campaign promoting Portland Medical Center as being "cutting edge for cancer care."

Anton thought something was off about a not-for-profit hospital trying to drum up business. He had also read Dr. Proctor's research protocol. He thought it was destined to fail because it was theoretically weak and was almost identical to a failed study from ten years ago done in Spain. Anton doubted Dr. Proctor was even aware of the older study. V. T. had also read the study protocol and agreed with Anton. They both agreed celebrating the awarding of the grant was a case of misplaced enthusiasm. It was further proof that the game had devolved into a lottery for research dollars, with the outcome not about producing tangible results but getting more dollars.

Now, here Anton was, feeling like an accomplice in this game of creating false hope. Well, at least he would get home early.

Three women were on his schedule. As per the study protocol, they were all between forty-five and sixty-five years old and had stage-four metastatic breast cancer. They had all failed established conventional treatments.

The first woman, Liz Ammons, arrived in a wheelchair pushed by her husband, Kevin. Before she had become ill, she had been a third-grade schoolteacher. Aside from the cancer, she was a healthy woman of forty-six. She had three children: a son who was an electrician, a daughter in high school, and a twelve-year-old sixth grader. Anton could tell she had been a beautiful woman. High cheekbones and a flawless nose highlighted a complexion that belied her years. Her symmetrically shaped scalp had new growth showing black hair with a few strands of gray.

Liz had been an expert equestrian rider, and her legs retained their sinewy tone despite the atrophy from her disease. She had felt the lump when she was thirty-eight. A lumpectomy, radiation, and chemotherapy had seemingly knocked the disease out. At forty-three, six months after the imaginary five-year interval for a "cure," she developed sudden back pain. Studies revealed her worst fear: metastatic disease to the bone. Subsequent rounds of chemotherapy followed. A brief window of hope came crashing closed one morning two months ago when she awoke again with intense bone pain. This time, it wasn't just in her back; it had scattered everywhere, like dandelion seeds in a summer breeze.

Doctors had told her and Kevin to enjoy the time they had left and enroll in hospice care. She had taught at Saint Kevin's Catholic school, a suburban school just outside of Portland, and they held a day in her honor. She was a passionate teacher whom her students would remember for the rest of their lives.

One night, Kevin began an online search for other treatment options. The Internet revealed several studies, and all were experimental protocols. One of them was originating out of Sloan Kettering. He had noticed that it was a multicenter study, with one of the centers being at Portland Medical Center, and had resolved to call them the next day. It was their last hope.

Anton reviewed the waiver that all participants were required to sign. "You understand, Mrs. Ammons, that the treatment is experimental, and it may not help. Further, you understand and accept all potential risks." He felt like a fraud. He wanted to tell Liz that this protocol was a bogus waste of her time. It occurred to Anton that she could be home with her family instead of checking into the hospital for a week of fruitless chemotherapy.

"I understand, Doctor." She smiled at him, perhaps reading the concern in his face.

The protocol called for four cycles of chemotherapy, with each cycle consisting of daily treatments lasting one week, followed by a one-week rest cycle. The chemo required the subject to remain in the hospital to receive the intravenous medicine and to allow for close monitoring.

Anton's day was brief as he quickly processed each of the three patients. Checkout rounds were quick and easy for him that evening. After he arrived back at his apartment, he felt the need for a cleansing, intense bicycle ride. The cold air whipped his face as he sprinted to South Portland on his bike. He rode faster until his face was nearly numb. It felt purifying. He rode faster. By the time he was back at the apartment, it was dark. The apartment was empty. Todd usually got in around 8:00 p.m. The surgical service was notorious for long days, but with today being Friday, Anton expected him home a bit earlier.

He checked his phone and noticed a series of new messages. The first was marked at 3:45 p.m. "Yeah, Anton, this is your father. Just calling to see how you're doing. I'm at the office."

The second message had come at 4:15 p.m. "Hey, roomie. It is I, God's gift to surgery, calling to put in my dinner order."

Anton could hear Todd put the phone down as he said to someone standing next to him, "You're not a vegetarian or anything weird like that, are you?" Todd got back on the phone. "OK, boy, that'll be fresh steak on the grill, a bottle of red wine—make it two bottles—and whatever else you like. Oh, and I'll be bringing a guest. Say hi to Anton, Gwen."

A woman's voice came on. "Hello, Anton. I like mine medium rare."

"OK, give me the phone. Anton, I love you, brother! Got to go cut someone up."

The next message was from 5:12 p.m. Anton recognized the sound of trombone music, which was V. T.'s signature introduction whenever he left a message. "Call me in the morning, boy." It was V. T.'s habit not to answer the phone after dinner. Often, he just unplugged it.

Anton smiled. It was 6:35 p.m., so he planned dinner for 9:00 p.m. He figured he should eat something now, so he took a loaf of Italian bread and a bottle of water and sat out on the fire escape. The October night still held some warmth. The air was still. He heard cars from the highway overpass in the background, but here they blended into an appealing rush of white noise, almost like the sound of a turbulent river. He closed his eyes and felt the texture of food in his mouth. He savored it. Suppose he never ate again? Supposed tomorrow his mouth didn't work? The bread felt good in his hands. Peace descended on him. A squeal of laughter came up from the street below. He saw children down there, and their faces beamed with unmitigated joy. He wondered how that would feel. Had he ever felt a sensation like the one he imagined the children felt at that moment? He reached back in his memory—thinking, thinking. He ate another bite of bread. He thought of his sister's face on Christmas morning and recalled seeing joy in her. Perhaps it was enough to recognize the feeling in others. Certainly, not everyone could expect that type of joy as a birthright. Perhaps some people were meant to revel in joy, and others were meant to sit on the fire escape, eat bread, and think about the meaning of joy.

His watch read 7:15, which meant it was time to get to the meat market. He grabbed his backpack and wallet and headed out the door. It was 1.6-mile run to the market.

Later, Anton set the table for two, placed candles in the center, and turned on some soft music. He already had picked out the movie he was going to go see. He would be Todd's maître d' for the evening and then head out after he served the meal.

The door rattled, and in burst Todd. "Ah, the aroma of fine steak! Has my honey been cooking? And they said you were just a pretty face." He entered ahead of his dinner guest and then waved her in. "Gwen, this is my beloved friend and manservant, Anton Thresher the Great."

Gwen smiled. "Hello, Anton."

Todd winked at Anton, who was tending to the grill on the fire escape. "Gwen is the surgical scrub nurse I've been telling you about."

"Oh...oh yeah. Todd talks about you all the time."

"Oh really? Then he must have told you all about my brothers and sisters."

"Yeah, I seem to remember something—"

"Well, then, it must be the other Gwen that Todd dates, because I am an only child."

"Todd does talk about you. But in all honesty, I don't pay attention to everything he says."

Gwen smiled and slapped Todd playfully on the back of his head. "If you don't stop bullshitting me, white boy, I'm gonna have to deliver some pain to you."

Anton looked up from the grill. In the light from the room, he saw Gwen for the first time. She was about five foot four with a curvaceous figure; ample breasts; and sculpted, lean facial figures. Her skin was a lovely shade of ebony.

Gwen looked at the table, noting the service for two. "I fully expect to be served a meal and not just watch you two eat."

"I'm going to serve you two and then head out to the movies," Anton said.

"What, and leave me here alone with that man? Not on

your life. You put another steak on the grill. Besides, Todd truly doesn't stop talking about you. I don't want to miss the chance to dine with Anton the Great."

Todd happily obliged and set a third plate.

The meal flowed through animated conversation. Gwen was thoughtful, poised, and intelligent—a clear departure from Todd's typical dates. She was an only child. Her father worked at Bath Ironworks, and her mother was a librarian. Gwen had been a nurse for three years, working the entire time at Portland Medical Center on the surgical service. She took courses online and planned on becoming a nurse practitioner.

"Tell me about Dr. Proctor," Anton said to Todd. "How is the research project going?"

"Well, let's just say he's already outlined his next study proposal."

"What do you mean?"

"The patients are all quite sick. Of the first cohort of five patients, two have died, and the other three have not responded to treatment. The cancer has progressed. Proctor needs to complete twenty cases to meet the requirements of his pilot protocol, and then he plans on reassessing the study and going for another grant."

"In other words, he's already planning on this protocol to fail," Anton said.

"That's one way to look at it," said Gwen. "But really it would be a success to complete a quality study and prove Portland Medical is capable of delivering subjects."

"So you could attract more funds," said Anton.

Gwen nodded. "Correct. Besides, I'm helping collect the data. When the study is completed, I'll get credit for participating. That will give me added status in my nurse-practitioner program."

Anton rolled his eyes and prepared to speak, but Todd tried to redirect the conversation.

"So, what do you think about the Patriots' chances this year?"

Anton ignored him. "Gwen, you don't need Proctor or his bogus study."

"What makes you think it's bogus?" Gwen asked.

"I don't *think* it's bogus, I *know* it is."

"And what studies have you done that you can sit here and throw stones? Not even one year out of medical school, and you've got the whole damn thing figured out. At least Dr. Proctor is trying to do something."

"Anybody care for some wine?" Todd asked.

Anton still ignored him. "Yeah, he's trying to puff up his own ego and status."

Gwen arched an eyebrow. "Maybe you're just bitter and jealous because I'm going to get the status from being involved in the study. I'm going to ride that status into my nurse-practitioner program."

"If that's what you need to get into the program, perhaps you're not worthy of the degree."

"Ouch," said Todd. "Foul. Unnecessary roughness." He attempted to lighten the mood.

Gwen got up to leave. "Good night, Todd. Thank you for dinner." Before Todd could react, she was gone.

Todd silently cleared the table. Finally, he broke the tension. "Well, I thought that went nicely for a first date."

"Sorry, buddy. She was too ambitious for you anyhow."

"Spoken from one who should know."

"I don't think I'm going to make it, Todd."

"You OK, Anton?" Despite his irreverence, Todd worried for his friend. Anton had a way of strapping the weight of the world on his shoulders. Lately, Todd noticed that burden seemed to be growing.

"I don't know how long I can put up with this," said Anton as he sipped a glass of wine and looked out the apartment window.

"Put up with what? My cooking? I admit I've not been at the top of my game, but the surgical rotation has me preoccupied."

Anton smiled. "No, Freeze. The internship. This is not what I want to be doing. It doesn't feel right."

"Oh," said Todd, relieved. Then, the implications of Anton's statement hit him. "What happened?"

"It's Proctor's research. It's the mundane scut work of internship, the ridiculous pecking order. I'm watching people die because I don't have the courage to walk away and finish my work in Biddeford."

"Can't Morrissey do the lab work for you? I thought he was helping?"

Anton didn't trust Morrissey, whom he thought was sneaky and couldn't be relied on. "He's lazy. He won't work. He won't put in the time. It will never get done."

"Why don't you just move the lab here? You could work on the research when you're not at the hospital. We don't entertain, we don't watch TV, and whenever I get a date, you scare her away. We could move this junk out of the living room and make it your lab."

"You wouldn't mind? That's a great idea!"

"Whatever makes you happy, Thresh, makes me happy. Plus, I can't afford to pay the rent on my own."

CHAPTER 20

Anton was glad V. T. had called him to Biddeford to get caught up. Right about now, Anton desired nothing more than to be sitting with his old friend over breakfast, talking about their project. He was surprised when he pulled up to the house to see another car there.

"Ben Able!" Anton greeted Ben with an embrace. Over breakfast, Ben told him about the advance in the production capacity of orange fern. V. T. updated Anton regarding Morrissey's frustrations, and Anton filled them in about his ideas to bring the lab up to Portland with him.

"It's entirely doable," said Ben. "Equipment and energy requirements are minimal. I could ship the fern directly to you. Hell, I'll just deliver it. I can even help in the lab if you have a couch for me to sleep on."

V. T. was silent. He felt where this was going. He worried for Anton. "Then what?"

Anton was puzzled. "What do you mean? We then slay the green horseman, that's what." He felt the energy in him rise. He had no doubts.

V. T. elaborated. "I mean, say we have the cure. How do we get it out? We can't just hold a press conference and announce to the world that we've done it."

After a few moments of silence, Ben spoke up. "Well, why not?"

"Look, nothing says this has to be a drug," Anton said. "It could be a nutritional supplement. So far, Morris has tried breaking down the constituent molecules that make up orange fern, and none have worked as well as the sum of the parts."

"A cancer-curing herbal tea?" asked V. T.

"Sort of. If we don't label it as a drug, we can do clinical research without the need for the FDA's approval."

Everyone paused, and then Anton smiled. "They will try to bury us."

Ben smiled in response. "I suppose they will."

"Are you afraid?" asked Anton.

"I'm sixty-five years old. I watched my son die from lymphoma. My wife left me soon after. I guess that happens. I ran off to Maine, and now I've run into you and orange fern. Maybe everything in my life has led me to this. No, I'm in all the way. When they come for me, I'll smile as I take the bullet because I will know we've won."

"V. T.?" Anton asked.

V. T. knew this was about to get bigger than what they could handle. It would consume them. Ben was old, V. T. was older, but what about Anton? Had V. T. inflamed his sense of martyrdom? Was there a gentler way? Would Anton ever know love, fatherhood, or peace? He looked at the determined face of his young charge.

"I will be with you all the way, Anton. Let's see how far we get. When and if the time is right, I have some contacts in the research world whom I can trust."

Ben and Anton winced at this last statement, but they were of one mind, at least for the moment.

"Can you get all the lab gear to Portland?" Anton asked Ben.

"No problem. I'll stay with the team until we gather it all. I'll have it there in a few days."

Anton gave Ben a key to his apartment. Anton's bus would leave for Portland in four hours. It was enough time. He kept an old bike at V. T.'s, so he couldn't resist a ride down his old path from V. T.'s to the college and past Mary's Country Store and Deli.

He took a slower-than-normal pace and rode even more

slowly as he came closer to Mary's. He was afraid he would see Lisa, but then he was afraid he wouldn't. Maybe that was her car? Maybe he should walk right in and say, "Lisa, I love you. I'm sorry I hurt you. I'm having trouble living without you." But hadn't God steered him away from that path? Hadn't God called him to a different purpose? "I might have to hang," Anton thought. "But it's better to hang alone."

He stopped his bike at the spot where he first saw Lisa. There was even a veneer of sand on the road. No cars were around. He got off his bike and walked over to the spot where Lisa had found him.

Anton lay down in the place he had fallen. When he closed his eyes, he could feel the warmth of the setting sun on his eyelids. Maybe she would come. Maybe they could start over. If she came, it was certainly God's will. After an uncertain span of time passed, the road started to feel cold on his back. He sat up and looked over to Mary's. "I need to see her, and then I'll know. One moment looking into her eyes, and I will know everything I need."

He felt good putting his bike in the old bike stand, as if he were home. He floated in a state somewhere between dream and conscious thought as he walked into the restaurant. The door closed behind him, and he stood in the front area, were several patrons sat at the bar. Beyond that was seating for the restaurant. Anton greeted no one but intently surveyed the room.

"She's not here," said Mary.

Her voice had startled him. She smiled. "She left about one hour ago. I'm sure she's at her apartment."

Anton looked away. Mary could read his mood. She stood closer to his ear and whispered. "Go to her. It will be all right."

Anton looked at the clock.

"There will be another bus tomorrow," Mary said.

"Mary, maybe it's just not meant to be."

Mary's face grew stern, and her tobacco-hardened voice tensed. "Don't give me that destiny bullshit. There is love, and next to love, there is nothing. Nothing. Nothing makes sense about you two except love, so that means everything makes sense because all the rest is bullshit. If you let this love through your hands and it dies, you will never recover."

Anton looked at Mary, the restaurant, and the sun hanging low in the sky. "You know I do love you, Mary," he said as he hugged her, and then he left. Mary watched him riding away from the door until she couldn't see him any longer.

Anton loved riding the bus. It was perfectly melancholy. Nobody wanted to be there. If they had money or friends, they would be in a car or a plane. But that's why Anton liked it. The people were plain and unvarnished. He also liked the smell of diesel and looking out the big window, thinking of Lisa. If it were truly God's plan, she would have been there. "God will not take this cup from me," Anton thought as he fell asleep.

Lisa helped V. T. and Ben load Ben's pickup with all the lab equipment that Anton had requested. When Ben's pickup wouldn't start, Lisa volunteered her uncle George and his truck to bail them out. She knew her uncle loved to feel needed.

When Ben, Lisa, and Uncle George arrived at the apartment in Portland, the place was empty, as expected on a Wednesday afternoon. It took about two hours to move all the gear inside. Ben was going to stay until the weekend, when V. T. would come and pick him up. Ben, Uncle George, and Lisa lingered in the apartment, part resting and part taking in the scene.

"I wonder if this is how Louis Pasteur felt," said Ben.

"You think Pasteur had people?" asked Lisa.

"Does this mean that we are Anton's people?" asked Uncle George.

"I like to think so," said Ben. He turned to Lisa. "He's a good man, well worth the effort."

Uncle George chuckled. "Well, when the boy cures cancer, we can all claim a piece of it. But for now, I just want to get home for dinner."

"You two go on back to the truck," Lisa said. "I'll be right out. Just give me a minute."

Alone in the apartment, Lisa walked around, picturing Anton in certain spots, imagining her next to him, and touching his arm. "He has beautiful shoulders," she thought. She stood in his bedroom, sat on his bed, and held his pillow, inhaling its aroma deeply. So close, they had been so close. What was left? Her life would now be divided into two parts: the time before being with Anton, and the time after. How many times in life did the earth tremble when a person held someone? Maybe never. Maybe once. Lisa was certain she would never feel that way again. A warm, pleasant tingle raced over her body. "Suppose I just lie in his bed and imagine his hands on me." But Uncle George was waiting. Overwhelming sadness fell on her. "This could be the closest I'll ever get." Nothing but a sad reflection of what had been was left after a love that intense passed. She had an urge to do something. There! In the kitchen, she found scissors. She stood in front of the bathroom mirror; looked at her long, brown hair; and, with trembling hands, cut it short above the ears. She left the locks on Anton's bed and went out the front door.

CHAPTER 21

D ale Davis sipped his coffee as Kathy White, Tim Beckwith, and Anton sat across from him. "OK, which of you slaves is up for night call?" They were reviewing end-of-day checkout rounds. Anton had not fully recovered from his weekend in Biddeford. His mind was already drifting to the lab that was going to be set up. He had talked to Ben earlier in the evening, who told him Lisa had been there.

"Anton, you with us, boy? I believe it is your distinct pleasure to hold the Code Blue pager. Hey, the good news is you've got Epperly as your backup attending, not that noodle-dick James."

Anton stared blankly ahead. He was aware that Dale was speaking, but in his mind he was lying with Lisa at the Cambridge Inn.

Dale paused. Anton didn't notice.

"White, Beckwith, you all are dismissed. See you at morning report."

"What about checkout?" Tim asked. "We haven't told you about our patients yet."

"I already know about them," Dale said, losing his temper. "Now, get out of here before I change my mind."

Tim and Kathy scrambled out, leaving Dale and Anton alone.

"Boy, you OK?" asked Dale.

"Yeah, just a little tired."

"Tired my ass. Supermen don't get tired. Guys like us get jazzed by this shit! No, that look is clearly woman sick. And you know I never miss a motherfucking diagnosis."

Anton thought maybe he blushed.

"See, boy, I know I am right. Listen good, because I got the cure."

Anton leaned in, expecting homegrown, Arkadelphia wisdom. He was drawn in not so much by the prospect of advice but by the sentiment of caring that Dale expressed in his unique way.

Dale lowered his voice. "You gotta fuck her outta your brain."

"Huh?"

"You know, when your brain gets stuck on one woman who is torturing you, you gotta go fuck another woman to push her out of your brain."

"Wouldn't that put the other girl there in her place?"

"No, boy, you ain't listening to me. You're in love with girl number one, whoever she is. That much is clear. Now you done broke the first rule of a residency: you've fallen in love. See, that takes over your whole body, especially the brain. It's a true neurologic disease. Damn shame. But you shouldn't feel too bad; it happens to the best of us. Hell, it almost happened to me once. You see, the key is to keep girl number two strictly below the waist. Just fuck her. It's very cleansing to the brain. Now, if you're deep in love, you might need more than one session. But remember—and this is important—never more than twice, maybe three times with the same girl. Next thing you know, that girl will be creeping into your brain. Of course, if she gives you a blow job, you can go up to five times. As long as you don't look them in the eyes when you come, it doesn't really count. I would recommend Nurse Gates on Four West—tits out to here, a little chunky, but in a good way. Your buddy Freeze is on surgical call. I'm sure he wouldn't mind leaving the on-call room to you for sexual psychotherapy."

Anton smirked and shook his head, thinking that Dale couldn't be more wrong. Still, he was touched by his sentiment. "OK, Dale. I'll see what I can do."

"That's the spirit!"

Dale got up to leave. But before he left the room, he turned back to Anton. "I want a full report in the morning. If you can't describe the details of Gate's cleavage, you might flunk this rotation."

The hospital had an outdoor concrete deck off the fourth floor, where a basketball hoop had been erected. So far, the night had been quiet. Anton was alone on the deck, dribbling, shooting, and watching the moon rise over the backboard. This was one of the places where he felt at peace. The other places were near the water and when he was sitting across from Lisa. Time flowed. He looked at his watch. It was a shade past midnight, almost time for his meetup with Nurse Gates.

His pager sounded a Code Blue alarm for room 223. When the third repetition sounded, Anton was on the landing to the second floor. The general code would go out to all interns and residents in the building; soon, everyone would be there. Room 223 was on the Oncology wing, home to the patients in Dr. Proctor's study. Anton was the first doctor on the scene. One nurse was applying chest compressions to the female patient while another handled the Ambu bag, used to support breathing.

"Report," Anton said as he entered the room.

"She was fine one minute," said the nurse applying chest compressions. "I was talking to her, and then she clutched her chest and went out."

"What meds is she on?"

"Really nothing, just a little Phenergan IV for nausea. She did receive the protocol drug by infusion this afternoon."

Todd entered the room, hair ruffled and dressed in wrinkled scrubs.

"Damn, Thresh, you didn't have to go to such lengths—"

"I think she has a saddle embolus," Anton said. "We need to take her to the OR. Call the surgical attending. Let's get her down there STAT."

While they continued to perform CPR, the team of doctors and nurses expertly wheeled the bed to the OR waiting area.

"What you got, Thresh?" asked Garron Lamply, a senior resident in anesthesiology.

"We need to prep her for an embolectomy. Let's get her in the OR so the surgical team can start as soon as they get here."

"We're not supposed to bring her into the OR until the surgeon is on the floor."

"Damn it, Lamp, seconds count here!"

Garron relented. He knew Anton was right. As they transferred the patient onto the operating table, Anton looked through the medical record to make sure no detail had been overlooked. For the first time, he noticed the patient's name. It was Liz Ammons, the beloved teacher he had performed the physical on.

"Hey, I think we have a pulse," said a nurse.

"Hold compressions," Anton said as he felt for the pulse. "Weak, but present." The heart monitor showed a regular rhythm.

"Blood pressure is sixty-four over thirty-two," said Garron.

Anton nodded. "She's fighting. She doesn't want to leave. Now if we can just get that clot out of her. Who is the surgeon?"

"Dr. Proctor," Garron said.

"Damn! Where is he? Lamp, I want the fluids wide open. Let's get another line in her." Anton turned to the nurse. "Let's start a dopamine drip."

"Thresh," said Garron. "I think she's trying to open her eyes."

Anton moved from the foot of the table, where he had been giving commands to the head, and looked into Liz's frightened eyes. She seemed aware. While holding her hand, he knelt to her ear and whispered in a reassuring voice. "There is a blood clot in your lungs. In a few minutes, we are going to put you to sleep and take it out. That will stop the pain and let you breathe." Her hand weakly tightened on his.

Anton stood up and looked at the monitor. Liz's blood pressure read fifty-four over twenty-four and was falling. Her heart rate was 152 and rising. Her oxygen saturation was dropping to 86 percent despite her receiving 100 percent oxygen through a mask.

"We can't wait," Anton said to no one in particular. "Lamp, induce anesthesia."

"But Dr. Proctor isn't here yet."

"We don't have time. I'm doing the surgery."

From across the room, the words hit Todd and snapped him out of his flirtatious dialogue with the scrub nurse. "Did I just hear my good friend and first-year resident Anton Thresher say he was going to crack open this woman's chest and perform complex, life-threatening, thoracic surgery when he has not so much as lanced a boil in his illustrious surgical career? Thresh, are you out of your fucking mind?"

"We're losing her. If we don't move now, she will die."

"Dr. Proctor is on his way," Garron said.

"He can take over when he gets here. We can't wait."

Garron was adamant. "Well, I'm not putting her under. You can burn up your own license but not mine."

"Then I don't need you, Lamp. Step aside. I'll do the anesthesia myself."

Todd grabbed Anton by the shoulders. "Anton, look at me. If you do this, you might save her, but she will be the last person you'll ever save." He leaned close to his ear and whispered. "And you have important work in front of you. Let this moment go."

A heavy silence filled the room, broken only by the rapid beeping of the heart monitor. Todd could feel the tension in Anton's shoulders release a bit as he lowered his head. Suddenly, the rapid beeping turned into a steady beep.

"She's coding," Garron said.

Anton checked her femoral pulse as he stared at the monitor. "No pulse. Start compressions. One hundred percent oxygen, ventilate at twenty." He started the resuscitation by rote, but he knew she was gone. Liz Ammons had one shot, and that moment had passed. Courageous and decisive action may have saved her, but Anton thought he had failed to show either.

Dr. Proctor entered the room shortly after the code began. He was prepared to operate should the patient survive the code. He coolly flipped through the patient chart while he waited.

"I can't hold up her oxygen saturation," said a nurse. "She's down to seventy-five percent."

Anton wasn't surprised. The huge clot he could have removed fifteen minutes ago had grown and was choking her.

"Time," Anton said, and all activity stopped. A nurse turned off the monitor.

Dr. Proctor walked up to Anton. "That was well run, Anton," he said with genuine admiration.

Anton nodded.

"Probably a saddle embolus, don't you think?" asked Dr. Proctor.

Anton nodded again.

Dr. Proctor judged the situation. "However, judging from the time of the admission to the hospital and the moment of the event, I don't think we should honestly count this as a treatment-related complication. I think it was likely preexisting."

Stacy, the operating room nurse, approached. "Dr. Proctor, the husband is waiting in the family room. What should we tell him?"

"Tell him we did everything we could."

Anton found solace in South Portland under the lights of the asphalt basketball court. Chain nets adorned the rims. He had learned to scale the pole and turn on the lights so he could play whenever he wanted. He launched from the three-point line, and the ball found the bottom of the net.

"We did everything we could," he said out loud. "The hell we did! I had a chance to save a life, but my inaction killed her." Slam! The ball went harder through the rim.

"I froze. Out of fear for myself, my status, my career, I froze." Slam! His hand struck the metal rim, opening a wound on his palm. After a few more slams, the cut opened further, making it impossible for him to shoot or dunk with his right hand. No problem; he switched to his left hand.

He continued to talk out loud. "I didn't come here to kowtow to conformity. I answer to one master: God alone. It is he who guides my sight. If I see something, and I know it is right, then it is by God that it has been revealed to me. I need no authority to act other than the clarity of my own vision—the vision that comes from God. It takes on the force of a command from him. To not act when a vision is so clear is to defy the very will of God! Calamity would certainly follow!"

Slam! A light rain began to fall.

"His will be done!" Slam! A small cut on his left hand opened as well. He supposed he had only a few more dunks left in him. "Never again will I fail to act when the path is clear."

Slam! His left hand became briefly impaled on a barbed portion of the rim, altering his descent and throwing him off balance. He landed awkwardly while leaning forward and slammed both knees on the court, tearing them open as he fell.

Lying on his back, he could see the rain as it fell from darkness into light, striking his face, hands, and knees and washing away the blood.

For a moment, he imagined Lisa was holding him and kissing his forehead. He felt her warmth all about him. Then, the image was gone, and the cold rain pressed in on him. His hands and knees began to sting. "Purifying pain. Wash me out, let nothing be left. Empty me so you may fill me up again. I must be ready for the task." His body was exhausted, his mind was spent, and his knees and hands were torn and in pain. His penance was almost complete. Or was it just beginning? Would it ever end? Should it end? "If we are eternally sinful, then shouldn't we be eternally punished? Peace comes only with death. There is no peace on Earth, only in the earth."

Todd was wrong. There had been an ordained moment to

act, but Anton had let it pass. Liz Ammons was dead. "God's will be done, the consequences of man will never again deter me."

CHAPTER 22

As a skilled conversationalist, Larry Bello, president of the Rhode Island Academy of Surgeons, knew it was always best to turn the conversation to a topic of interest to his subject, and nothing was better at drawing people out than asking about their children. "So, Charles, how's your boy doing?"

"He's up at Portland Medical Center doing internal medicine," Dr. Charles Thresher said with fake enthusiasm.

"Well, they're lucky to have him. Does he have any interest in surgery? I always thought that with his athletic skills and the way he can play the piano, he would be a natural."

Charles perked up. Larry had wandered into one of his soapbox topics.

"You know, I always felt that way, too," Charles said. With a little too much wine in him and a spark applied to this dry-kindling of an issue, he was off, describing his son's trajectory from the gifted scion of a leading medical family, to his enrolment at a second-rate medical school, and then to a backwater residency at the end of Earth.

From across the room, Barbara Thresher could tell from her husband's body language and hand gestures that he was going off on a topic not suitable for genteel company. She wandered close enough to listen. She knew it was about Anton. A chill crossed her skin as she worried Charles would embarrass them all.

"So instead of valedictorian, he ends up screwing a local girl in a motel and lands in second place," Charles said.

"Sounds like a chip off the old block," said his partner,

Thad Dylan, who had drifted into the story partway through. "Thinking too much with his little head!"

Guffaws went all around—some genuine, some forced.

Barbara became willfully deaf and drifted far enough away so as not to be perceived as capable of hearing anything. She believed that the appearance of ignorance protected her integrity. Knowledge, or the perception that she had knowledge, would force her to take action or be shamed. She liked her life to be balanced, or at least comfortable. After all, she was a forty-eight-year-old woman with no particular job skills. What could she do? She drifted a bit farther from her husband.

"Charles, how goes the practice?" asked Fred Bowdy, president of Warwick General Hospital. He had used his standard introduction to a business conversation.

"Good, Fred. How's the hospital doing?"

Because Charles was on the hospital's executive committee, he had a general sense of how things were. They had been running in the red for the past two years. Everybody was in a mood to cut whatever fat they could. Of course, that term never applied to high-salaried administrators, who made the decisions.

"Well, you know, not so great," Fred said. "We are thinking of closing the Inpatient Pediatric Department. It's hard to keep nursing skills sharp with such low volume. We could assess them in the ER and then refer them to Hasbro Pediatric Hospital if they needed admission."

"What about the elective admissions for surgery? Are we going to stop caring for all pediatric patients?" As a general surgeon, Charles would sometimes operate on adolescents for appendicitis or other issues.

"It would make financial sense..."

Charles had heard rumors that the hospital would like to drop all pediatric services because they were not profitable, and it would be simple to refer them all to the city hospital. Now Fred was probing Charles. Without the support of Dr. Charles Thresher and his surgical group, a change of this magnitude would be difficult. Charles's group accounted for 20 percent of all admissions, 40 percent of all surgeries, and over 30 percent of the hospital's gross revenue, making them by far the most important group within the hospital. Fred was in his second year at Warwick and was charged with making the hospital profitable again. Charles put his arm around Fred's shoulder and walked with him to a more private area of the room.

"Fred, if your arm is broken, do you cut it off to make it better? My grandfather was a barber. He donated money every year he was alive to Warwick so that if someone in his family got sick, the hospital would be there to help him. The last time I checked, children are part of families. This is a community hospital. We have to serve the children, or we will betray our legacy. Fred, I like you"—that was a lie—"and you're a smart guy. I know you will figure out a way to make the hospital solvent, and you can count on our support. But if you cut pediatrics, my group will start moving our best surgical cases to Rhode Island Hospital, and Warwick General will be fucked, and you'll be the one who fucked them." Charles smiled, reveling in his own power, feeling good for doing the right thing.

"Thanks for your input, Charles."

"Anytime, Fred."

Flush with a sense of virtue and power, Charles sought out his wife.

"How is the most beautiful woman at the party?" Charles asked her as he wrapped his arm around her waist and pulled her into him. Her arm went up reflexively, positioning her forearm against her husband's side as she strained her neck to keep her cheek away from his lips. He overpowered her and kissed her anyway, and then passed his hand over her butt, noting to himself with some pride of ownership that it was still pretty tight. He felt longings well up inside him and became hopeful for his chances at the end of the night.

"So, what are you ladies discussing tonight?" Charles tried to charm his way into the circle of women, looking for an opening to present his I-saved-pediatrics-at-Warwick-General story, hoping to curry favor with his wife. Within a short time, he directed the topic toward himself and delivered the story with mock humility, gaining approving nods from all but his wife, who stood with a well-practiced smile as a chill ran down her spine.

"Can I get you ladies anything from the bar?" As Charles had hoped, no one took him up on his offer. He had freedom to exit.

The short ride home seemed longer than usual. Charles hadn't given up hope of the night culminating in physical pleasure and attempted to engage his wife in genial banter. She responded in truncated answers, effectively killing all attempts at conversation. Charles liked to pull slowly into his driveway, allowing himself a moment to take in his impressive house. It was Greek revival with columns lining the front and running the entire height of the building, all three stories. He pulled his Mercedes into the detached four-car garage. After a silent walk from the car, he and Barbara entered the foyer. The TV was on in the kitchen. The Threshers walked in to find Polly, their daughter, sitting on the stool, eating a bowl of frozen yogurt, and watching a late-night talk show.

"Hi guys, how was the party?" she asked in a nervous, high-pitched voice. They were home earlier than she had expected. She hadn't heard the car pull in. By the time she heard the door open, it was too late. Her best hope was that they were a little drunk and in a good mood. At a glance, though, she could tell they were not nearly drunk enough and most certainly not in a good mood. Instinctively, she continued her attempted good humor as a defense mechanism.

"It's been a quiet night here. I did my yoga video in the exercise room earlier, and then I organized all the board games in the game room. I arranged them alphabetically so they would be easier to find. Then, I started working on my college essays..." Her conversational pace was nervous and breathless. Maybe if she didn't pause, they wouldn't be able to speak. Maybe they would drift off to their bedroom and say good night. Polly wished she could disappear. As she spoke, she imagined that she had superpowers, that she could freeze the scene and leave it, and no one would ever know that she was there.

"And I suppose you thought eating ice cream at ten o'clock at night was a great idea," said Charles.

"It's fat-free frozen yogurt," said Polly.

"Why don't you just slap it on your ass? That's where it will end up."

"It's only one scoop." She averted her eyes and put down her spoon.

Barbara brusquely took the bowl and washed the remainder of the frozen yogurt down the sink. She flipped on the garbage disposal with righteous certainty. Polly was afraid to move or speak. Any action could be seen as provocative. Charles was not finished; Barbara's silent collusion emboldened him.

"All the time with the nutritionist and the trainer so you can stuff yourself with junk?" he asked.

Barbara joined in. "Really, Polly. If you don't care, then maybe we shouldn't either. Then, we can stop wasting our money."

"Sorry, Mom."

Charles was not satisfied. "Like I give a damn about the board games! What a waste of time. They haven't been touched in years. Maybe if you had some pride in your appearance, you would get asked out every once in a while like normal people instead of sitting home alone, staring at TV, and stuffing yourself with ice cream."

"Charles!" Barbara said.

"I'm sorry, Daddy." Polly couldn't hold it in. The tears came—a trickle at first, and then a flood. Charles's anger left him, and he hugged his daughter. She buried her face in his chest and gasped out words one at a time between sobs.

"I'll...try...harder...I...am...sorry..."

Barbara stood back, arms folded over her chest.

"You should go to bed now," Charles said. "We can talk about this more tomorrow. I love you."

"I love you, too, Daddy." Polly left the room.

In her bedroom, she stood in her underwear and in front of her full-length mirror, studying her body. Her breasts were too heavy and hug low. Her belly lapped over the elastic on her panties. She grabbed the fat in her hands. It didn't feel as if it belonged to her, as if it weren't part of her body. She felt uncomfortable—not quite sick, but not right. Restlessness was building within her. It was time to sleep, but her brain was energized. She felt bloated, fat, and ugly. She could walk away from the mirror, but she couldn't walk away from herself. The mirror's image burned in her mind's eye and followed her. She pictured the frozen yogurt sitting there in her stomach, sinister and evil. Now she could imagine it oozing into her body and globbing on her already-ample hips. It was growing in her, like a tumor. Her restlessness transformed into near panic. She would have felt hopeless, but she knew the way out. She had promised herself that she would stop, but this was utterly unbearable. No human could withstand these feelings. One more time, and then the slate would be clean. Get it out, and then she could start anew. She listened in the hallway to make sure her parents had gone to bed. All was quiet. Good. One more time, and then peace. The morning would come, and she could start over.

As usual, Charles was out of his bathroom before Barbara was out of hers. He turned down the bed. He turned up the heat a couple of degrees. He didn't want Barbara to complain that it was too cold in the room to get undressed. He poked his head out the bedroom door into the hallway and listened carefully. All was quiet. Polly wasn't rattling about. He sat in bed, opened a book, and waited for Barbara to join him. He thought of the surgical conference he had registered for, which was three weeks from now in New York. Maybe he would ask Barbara if she wanted to go. He had told Jamie, the surgical scrub nurse he was currently seeing, that he might take her. Their relationship thus far consisted of quick trysts when he was on call. This would be their first time away. But maybe he would take only Barbara.

The bathroom door opened. Charles was disappointed to

see that she had on a flannel nightgown.

"I am so-o-o tired," she said as she crawled into bed. She pulled the covers over her shoulders while lying on her side, with her back to her husband. Charles put down his book and turned off the light. He moved across the king-sized bed toward his wife and started to massage her shoulders.

"Not tonight," she said.

"Are you sure?" Charles pressed his erection against the back of her leg in the hope that it might seduce her.

"Yes, I'm sure." She moved slightly away.

Charles rolled to his back and then asked almost rhetorically. "If not tonight, then when?"

"I don't know. Go to sleep, Charles."

Jamie never said no to him. Barbara closed her eyes and faked being asleep. Charles hesitated, perhaps hoping she would change her mind. Then, he threw back the covers, got out of bed, threw on his robe, and stomped off to the study.

Once there, he sat back in his leather chair. The dim light from his cigar cast a shadow over the trophies, awards, and diplomas that filled the room. He took a sip from his brandy snifter and stared out the window into the night. A day that had been full of personal triumphs and affirmations was now ending in frustration and rejection. Sometimes, it seemed as if everybody loved him except his wife. So, it would be Jamie at the conference. He thought Barbara almost preferred it that way. He finished his brandy, put out his cigar, and went back to bed.

CHAPTER 23

The first two attempts had ended in failure, or at least what most people would consider failure. Anton had taken a concentrated form of the orange fern and brewed it into a strong tea. He was able to give it to the patients in Dr. Proctor's cancer study by returning after his usual hours of work and telling the patients it was an essential part of the protocol. So far, there had been no signs of the cancer going into remission.

At night, he would work at the apartment lab he had created. He would concoct new derivatives of the fern, sometimes working until 3:00 a.m. and then napping for two or three hours before he began his day at the hospital. He felt a sense of purity in his isolated routine: research, medicine, run. He rarely made time for any social activity. Todd was concerned about his friend and was diligent in preparing a breakfast for him each day.

"Eat, Thresher. This is all brain food." Todd offered Anton a cheese omelet.

"Thanks, Freeze. I do love you, my brother. But you realize that old pan is full of carcinogens."

"Then you better quit dogging it and cure cancer already so I can enjoy my food without guilt."

The two friends sat on the fire escape that they had converted into a makeshift balcony. It was one of those rare, precious late-February days when unseasonable warmth gave a hint of spring.

"What are you thinking of for your next trial?" Todd asked.

"I don't think I can concentrate the oral delivery system any more. With the last batch, three of four patients vomited, and while the lab samples have had consistent kill zones on the cancer plates, the blood samples haven't had the same effect in the lab."

Lately, Anton had been transporting samples of cancer patients' blood to his lab after the patients had ingested the fern. He would then place the blood on the plates with cultures of cancer cells and see if it developed a kill zone. He hadn't seen any effect.

"I've got some ideas for the next trial. We'll see how it goes." Anton was purposely vague. He knew exactly what he wanted to do next, and he knew Todd would fully object. It was better not to tell him.

"Scott and Ann have invited us to dinner tonight," Todd said. "I told him we could be there."

"Sounds fine, Freeze. That gives you a night off from cooking."

"I plan on bringing Felicia with me. Scott said we could bring a date."

"And here I thought you were my date."

"You know, Thresh, every great researcher had a woman, or several important women, in his life. A good woman can be an inspiration to a researcher, like a muse is to a writer. It could be that the breakthrough you seek will occur at the moment of Shangri-la as you achieve climactic joy in the arms of a woman you believe yourself to be in love with at that moment. Then, instead of screaming out her name in joyful bliss, you'll scream out 'eureka' and dash off to your lab. Not exactly a tingling afterglow, but if a woman is to be in love with you, she'll have to get used your idiosyncrasies."

Ann's dinner had been precise. The timing of the courses had been seamless. Ann had planned the setting and presentation to the last detail. She fussed over the dishes and glasses, reassuring her guests that the Tiffany wineglasses would someday be matched with the Tiffany water glasses. "After Scott finishes residency, it's on my list for year one."

Year one was the first year as a fully employed physician, with no more eighty-hour weeks at minimum wage. Ann enjoyed being a doctor's wife. Anton admired certain aspects of her. He took note of the way she included Todd's date in the conversation. She was thoughtful in the places she was sure people would notice.

Dessert and coffee signaled that the night was winding down.

"Guys, this has been a great night." said Scott in a voice loud enough to pull everyone out of their conversations and draw all eyes toward him. "We can never let life get so busy that we don't take the time to be with each other, even when we start bringing children into the world"—a broad smile burst over his face as he put his arm around his wife—"like Ann and I will be doing in a few months."

Congratulations went all around. Coffee cups touched in a toasting gesture. Later, after the dishes were cleared and Todd was engaged in conversation with Ann and Felicia, Scott touched Anton's elbow. "Hey, Thresh. Come into the garage with me. I want to show you something."

In the center of the garage, Scott approached a tarp that was hiding something large. "I saw it for sale at the garage on the corner of Main and Division. I don't think the guy knew what he had. I practically stole it!" Scott's eyes were flaming with joy and passion as he slowly pulled off the tarp, revealing the prize in tantalizing increments as if he were a good stripteaser. It was a motorcycle. Anton noticed Scott's hands were trembling. Right now, he wasn't sure which baby Scott would pick if he were forced to make a choice. It was a classic BSA. Scott ran his hand over the gas tank. "Let's start her up!" Without waiting for a response, he jumped on the bike, turned the key, and kicked it into a glorious rumble as the engine jumped to life. His eyes sparkled as he let the throttle out.

"That's better than sex!" Scott yelled over the engine's

roar. He then turned it off and sat back, basking in what he perceived to be his friend's envy. Anton wondered if Scott were aware that he had just diminished his wife. He thought of Lisa.

"That's a very cool machine," he said. "But I don't see any motorcycles in my future."

"No problem, Thresh. You can ride mine whenever you want!"

Anton smiled. "Thanks."

Scott walked over to a refrigerator in the corner of the garage, took out two bottles of beer, popped them open, and handed one to his friend.

"That was only part of the reason I brought you down here." Scott's voice dropped an octave to signal the beginning of a serious topic. "Anton, I think you're a great man"—he waved a hand when he saw Anton start to talk—"no, really, just shut up and let me speak. You're loyal, dedicated, virtuous, a little bit on the smart side, and occasionally you don't suck at basketball. I've always admired you and looked up to you. Ann feels the same way. We would like you to be our first baby's godfather."

Anton was stunned. He knew how important this role was to Scott and his family.

"Are you sure? What about your family?"

"I am sure, Anton. I love you, Ann loves you, and someday little Scott will love you. I want him have a great role model, Anton. I can think of no one better than you."

The two friends embraced.

"It will be fun going through life together, Anton." Scott wiped his eyes.

CHAPTER 24

The first step would be to see if it was toxic. That is, would his treatment kill people or make them sicker than they already were? Anton contemplated this challenge as he sat in his lab and reflected on why his treatments hadn't had the desired effect. A long, hard run might open his brain.

In Portland, winter was giving way to spring. Remnants of snow were piled in the corners of parking lots, and streets were damp with runoff from melting snow. In a T-shirt, shorts, and broken-down running shoes, Anton flew through the streets. He had a familiar route. At 7:00 a.m., dawn was just breaking on a Saturday as he ran to the basketball court. He would jump up, grab the rim, and do twenty pull-ups, with his head coming up through the center of the rim while the chain net draped over his shoulders with each repetition. Here, he could see the sun finally break over the horizon. All the majesty and splendor of God in his golden chariot marked the beginning of another day racing across the sky. It was another day full of nothing but potential and another time of precious, limited life. A new thought was coming to him: cowards never achieved greatness. He remembered Liz Ammons, so the time for action was now.

Back at the lab, Anton was renewed. He increased the concentration of the orange fern extract by a factor of ten and stabilized it in a liquid form at a neutral pH. Before he could try it on patients, he needed to test it for toxicity. His notes were meticulous. Todd would be back from the hospital that evening. If things went poorly, it would be easy for Todd to figure everything out. Now it was, as always, in God's hands. Anton put the tourniquet around his upper arm, held up the syringe with his other hand, and carefully injected into his bulging vein.

Back at Biddeford, the last week of anatomy lab had ended. V. T. Roberti sat at the front of the lab. In front of him were the tables with the cadavers covered by blue-green sheets. Underneath the sheets, the bodies had been fully dissected. The students had tagged and labeled all the critical parts in a daunting effort to commit them all to memory.

"My friends, I am one day closer to joining you." V. T. took out his trombone and began to play a final farewell to the souls he had always considered silent heroes, anonymous altruists, and true believers caring not about their bodies but about the greatness of life. Either that, or they were orphaned John and Jane Does; penniless; landless; and without family, regard for their physical well-being, or hopes or plans for their future. In short, they were closer to Christ than most CEOs and suburbanites. V. T. thought they deserved honor more than anyone.

As he played, he imagined himself flying there. Then, he imagined Anton lying next to him, on the next gurney. Who would play for them? Hadn't he started Anton on a messianic journey? Hadn't he encouraged and amplified his ambition? Wasn't he the elder, the wiser, the one accountable for Anton's well-being? V. T. had to stop playing. He could usually get through the entire serenade, but this time he had to stop to catch his breath. He thought it was a change he would have to look into. As he resumed playing, a growing sense of purpose arose within him. It was time to bring his agent in from the cold. It was time to make their circle of trust bigger and to get the support their research required. He would take Anton off his cross and give him back a chance at life.

Portland Medical Center on a Saturday had a very different feel. Things still happened, but the pace was less frenzied. There were fewer staff and more families. Doctors and nurses moved at a slightly less kinetic pace, especially the residents who were obliged to be there throughout the day. Todd Freeze liked these days; they gave him more time to socialize. He was on a first-name basis with nearly all the hospital staff, from nurses to lab techs, from the kitchen help to the cleaning staff. Dale Davis had dubbed him "the Mayor." Today, Todd and Dale would be on call together for a twelve-hour shift. They had already completed the morning rounds and now were having lunch together at the hospital cafeteria.

"Hey, Mayor, would you ever do steroids?" Dale asked, out of the blue.

"D-day, I already have too much muscle and mojo to handle."

"How about if you had Patty Galantic, Margaret Ackerman, and Monique Padur all lined up wanting a piece of you, one right after the other?" Dale had mentioned the two nurses and one doctor who would be in anybody's consensus pick for the hottest women in the building.

"Then I would take it in a wide-open IV bolus and rock on!"

"Fuckin' A! The Mayor flies again! But tell me, Freeze, what's up with your buddy Thresher? He's lost his balance. His work is still brilliant, but he has no interest in being with people. He's turning into a medical monk. Fuckin' guy could get laid every night. Women fall over him, and he is fuckin' inert."

"Thresh is on a mission from God. He is here to rid

the world of disease. He spends his nights researching a cure for cancer in the lab he set up at our apartment. He really believes he can do it. He's probably there now pouring over his notes."

"Freeze, we gotta rescue the boy. After we leave this dump, we're going to kidnap him and take him out for a night of some reckless pleasure. He can go back to saving the world on Sunday. But tonight, I need him to become a normal human. Speaking of becoming a normal human, I need the on-call room between three and five. Nurses are getting off first shift then, and I hope to interest one in a therapeutic massage."

Dale and Todd left lunch and with it any concerns for their friend, Anton.

The bulk of the shift went by without any major incidents. After turning over the care of their patients to the oncoming residents, Dale and Todd headed out. Dale followed Todd because he hadn't been to Todd and Anton's apartment before. As was his habit, Dale had brought a change of clothes with him. His plan was to go to Todd's place, shower and change, and then head out together for a night on the town.

Todd could tell something was not quite right as he approached the apartment. Although it was now dusk, no lights were coming from the apartment windows. Todd supposed Anton was sleeping, even though he had never known Anton to nap.

"Honey, I'm home!" Todd announced from the hallway as he put his key in the door. "And I have a surprise visitor." The hallway light was off. The apartment was quiet.

"Thresh!"

No answer. Todd and Dale approached the kitchen, and Todd turned on its light. The kitchen opened to the dining room area, which Anton had converted into a lab.

Todd went into the room, and Dale followed. Anton was asleep on the couch, lying awkwardly.

Dale whacked Anton's feet. "Wake up, you lazy rookie. Freeze and I are taking you out, and that is not a request."

Todd frowned. "What the...look, Dale, he's not right."

Anton's eyes drifted about aimlessly as he tried to speak but could only murmur. Dried vomit had crusted around his chin and chest, and a small stream of dried blood was visible from the injection site on his arm.

Dale flipped into doctor mode. "His pulse is strong. Color good. Respirations about eighteen and steady." He carefully inspected Anton's scalp, neck, ears, and throat. "No sign of head or neck trauma." He pulled off Anton's shirt and palpated over his abdomen while watching his face. "No palpable tenderness." He gently slapped Anton's face. "Anton, can you hear me?" He held Anton's face in his hands and looked into his eyes. Anton held his gaze for a moment, and then his eyes began to drift again.

"Should I call 911?" asked Freeze.

Dale looked at the needle mark on Anton's arm. "No, we have to take care of him here. If this gets out, he could lose his residency."

Dale called the lab. Beth Rainville was working the overnight. She would run some labs and then call Dale with the results and not record them.

"Freeze, you go to the hospital. When I get the lab results from Beth, I'll call you and tell you what we need from the ER. Talk to Patty Galantic. You can trust her."

Later that evening, Todd and Dale watched over their patient as an IV bag dripped fluids and medication into Anton while he slept in his bed.

"Hepatic encephalopathy," Dale said. "Whatever he

injected nearly cooked his liver. He will recover fully, but it will take a few days, and he can't be left alone."

"Whom can we trust?" Todd asked.

"No one. The hospital is a rumor mill. If word of this gets out, Anton will never get to be a doctor. Do you think your roommate is using drugs? Is he cooking them up in the lab?"

Anton had sworn Todd to secrecy, but these circumstances changed the rules.

"No, not Anton." Todd looked over and noticed the journal on the lab bench. In it, Anton had written all the details of his experiment. As Todd read the entries, events became clear.

"He used himself to test the toxicity of the treatment."

Dale took the lab notes and read them for himself. Then, he took a pen and began to write in the lab book where Anton had left off.

"What are you doing?" Todd asked.

"Got to complete the experiment, Freeze. Thresh would want us to record everything." Dale continued to study the lab notes. "I hate to admit it, but he is one brilliant motherfucker." He snapped a harsh glance at Todd. "But if you ever tell him I said that, I will deny it and see that you suffer."

CHAPTER 25

Dale and Todd lied, manipulated, cut deals, and stole drugs, all to keep Anton's illness and recovery a secret. Had they been discovered, they would have been invited to leave their profession, but they never hesitated. Dale didn't think he'd ever get caught, and Todd simply didn't care. They took turns calling in "sick" so they could monitor Anton. After seven days, his mind had cleared, his body had improved, and the vigil was over. As far as the hospital administration knew, Anton had the flu.

"Time to saddle up, Thresh," Todd said. "Are you ready?"

"Never better."

This month, both Anton and Todd would be on the internal-medicine rotation together, which was considered the most intellectually and physically challenging rotation in the residency. Each rotation generally lasted one month, but on this occasion, Anton and Todd were on two months consecutively. In addition to their daytime hours, they would serve on call overnight at the hospital twice a week.

Another day began. Morning rounds combined all the residents from the various rotations into one place, where they heard some of the most interesting cases presented. Afterward, the intellectual equivalent of a rugby scrum ensued as egos clashed in a battle of one-upmanship. It was in this forum that Anton extended his reputation for brilliance, as well as arrogance. Unknown to him, he created silent enemies as he exposed other doctors' limited knowledge. Nobody was better read than Anton, and his retention was already legendary both for journal articles and for previous cases. Equal to his intellect was his lack of tact. He corrected a fact or opinion with the same sharp analysis, whether it was from a medical student or the chief of the department. Even Dale would shake his head, wince, and then smile in admiration as Anton used laser accuracy and a cool detachment to throw down a lazy thought or a misstated fact.

"Fuckin' A," Dale would whisper under his breath, giving Anton his highest form of praise.

As everyone filed out of morning rounds, Todd approached Anton.

"Hey, buddy. It looks like it's you and me, stomping out disease and creating a path of healing wherever we walk. Did you see that call schedule? Brutal."

Indeed, the next two months promised to be physically daunting. Every third night, Anton would be staying overnight at the hospital. Although residency rules required them to have a certain minimum number of sleep hours, the rules were often ignored, and the sleep time would often prove elusive. Still, Anton had a sense of anticipatory energy about him. He knew this was the moment. Immediately after his recovery, he had jumped back into his experiments. In the lab, he had calculated the half-life of the orange fern down to its most potent and active form. He knew the best cycle would likely be every other day. The duration was uncertain. He would need real patient experience to calculate the final elements. It was time. His first night on call would be Wednesday, May 13. With the dawn of spring, he would turn the tide against death. He was so certain of his outcome that he felt like a fireman racing to a smoldering site that was on the verge of becoming a major conflagration. He was certain he had the remedy.

Anton reviewed the list of patients in Dr. Proctor's breast cancer study. He had enough serum to dose three patients. Six were listed on the service. His plan was to dose only half the patients in the protocol, leaving the other half as a control group. If he dosed them all, it would be hard to prove that his treatment was making a difference in the outcome.

Finally, it was his night on call. As was his habit, he came to the hospital with his overnight bag equipped with his usual supplies: a change of clothing, protein bars, toiletries, and some medical journals. The new items were three carefully prepared bags of clear IV fluid. This was the fruit of his labor. Years of reflection, untold hours of work in his lab, dozens of self-doses —so much of him was in it that it might as well have been his blood in those bags.

He told no one, not even V. T. or Todd. At this most dangerous moment, he knew he must walk alone. His confidence was supreme, but suppose a patient died? Suppose he was discovered? He would be charged with manslaughter at best, and anyone who knew about it would be an accessory. Nevertheless, it was time to walk alone.

CHAPTER 26

"Hey, Thresh, wake up! It's pancake Saturday!" Wearing his chef hat, Todd had been up preparing his traditional morning feast. It was a "Golden Weekend," which was what he called one of those rare moments when neither he nor Anton was on call. It was a time to celebrate that small part of their lives that wasn't about being a doctor.

He hollered again down the hall. "Vanilla-and-walnut pancakes, kiwi fruit, and your favorite: hot lemon tea."

Anton smiled from under the sheets, with his pillow over his face. He usually would have been up by now, but last night had been a "treatment" night. He hadn't returned from the hospital until 3:00 a.m. He had been forced to wait until hospital activity settled before he could get in the room alone. He had time to administer only one bag each night. It took two hours to drip in, and he had to stand and watch. Lately, he had been working on a "bolus" form of treatment that he would be able to push in over one to three minutes, but for now, this would have to do. Each night, he arrived at the hospital after the 11:00 p.m. nursing-shift checkout rounds. He would treat one patient and then head home. The patients in his first group were nearing the end of their first cycle. On Monday, they would get repeat CAT scans to assess treatment progress.

So far, the protocol as administered by Dr. Proctor had disappointing results. A branch of the study that was being performed at a hospital in New Jersey had been terminated because of "no clinical benefit." Dr. Proctor had already anticipated that his study would lose its funding at the end of this cycle. He was busy preparing proposals to acquire funding for other studies. Anton noted the change. It was akin to being on a losing team. People lacked energy and were going through the motions, as if they were preparing for a game they knew they were going to lose.

Anton came out to the kitchen for pancakes.

Todd was already finishing his. "So, I'm heading to Providence tonight with Scott. His mom made ravioli. After that, we're heading out to the Living Room to watch Sawmiller. He put his band together for a one-night show. Why don't you come with me? Give your brain a break."

"No breaks now. I'm too close."

"Oh." Todd knew there was no room for appeal.

"Anton should be here," said Scott Antonelli over the din of voices and music.

Todd sipped on his Narragansett draft beer. "You know how he gets. He's in his zone. What time does Saw go on?"

The Living Room was a comfortable local bar with randomly placed overstuffed couches that gave it its name. Random decor lent to its appealing bohemian feel.

"Saw is back warming up with his group," said Scott.

Earlier, Scott, Todd, Brad, and Rob "Legend" Hill had met at Scott's childhood home. Scott's mother had prepared a magnificent Italian feast. She was not satisfied until she fed the boys to near bursting.

Mrs. Antonelli had also prepared a huge plate of food for the absent Anton, and she had made Todd promise to deliver it.

CHAPTER 27

No one was in the Imaging Department yet, just a few of the X-ray technicians. The radiologists usually started to arrive around 6:00 a.m. or 7:00 a.m., but Anton couldn't wait. The CAT scans had all been completed the day before and were waiting to be read. Anton pulled up each image on the screen, one after the other, closely scrutinizing them and looking for signs of a change in the tumors.

He stared intently, blinked, and then downloaded the pictures and uploaded them again in case there had been some mistake. Three patients and three CAT scans resulted in no tumors. The lymph nodes looked normal. Anton went over the images again. Maybe he wanted it so bad that his vision deceived him. No matter how long he looked, he could draw only one conclusion: these CAT scans were normal. He was certain of his success. Yet for the first time since his quest began, he wasn't sure what to do.

Morning report would convene soon, and Anton would have to be there. For the moment, it would be life as usual. V. T. had called him a few weeks ago, and Anton already had plans to meet with him this weekend at Biddeford for an update.

Anton left the Imaging Department before the other doctors arrived and headed to the cafeteria. He sat alone by the large window that overlooked a field abutting the doctors' parking lot.

"I will need more orange fern. I will need to speed production. I will need bolus therapy." The thoughts clustered. "I will need to take this out of Portland and go national, global. The world needs this now. Fast." A plan began to form in his mind. He would need to keep control of the process. The raw materials were cheap. If he could control the technology, he could give away the results. It would be as cheap as aspirin. Nobody would get rich, and everybody would get well. The plan roused passion within him.

The operator announced overhead that morning report was about to start in the doctors' auditorium. Anton resigned to business as usual for now.

Dr. Proctor called the morning report to order and invited Tim Beckwith up to present a case. While Tim walked to the front of the room, a commotion ensued at the back entrance. Dr. Foreman from radiology made a frantic signal to Dr. Proctor, beckoning him to come at once. After an excited, hushed conversation, the two doctors exited while morning report droned on.

Back in radiology, all eyes were on the monitors as Drs. Proctor and Foreman entered the room.

"It is almost miraculous!" said Dr. Bruezeze as he looked over the films. "It's beyond anything I've ever seen before. The tumors are virtually gone. The lymph nodes are half their prior size. The response is stunning."

Dr. Proctor took it all in as he studied the screens. "This changes everything," he said almost to himself. "This puts Portland Medical Center on the map. If these results are reproducible with the next group, this changes everything. I knew this project was worth the effort."

He turned to Dr. Foreman. "I want no media leaks. We will wait until the next group goes through treatment. If it is real, we will hold a major press conference."

The vexing fact no one could explain was why half the subjects responded so well while the other half had no response. Still, a 50 percent response rate for terminal cancer was an incredible outcome. Dr. Proctor was immediately on the phone to the chairman of the National Cancer Society. He would need a bigger budget and more staff to expand the treatment. When word got out, the demand would be overwhelming. OncogenX Inc., the manufacturer of the primary chemotherapeutic agent in the trial, would need to be notified. Its drug—which the company had thought might have a small, modest benefit—was about to become a multibillion-dollar blockbuster. Dr. Proctor had his secretary cancel all his patients that day. He would need the time to digest and process the implications of this result. He could see himself sitting on the board of OncogenX, flying around the world, giving speeches, and receiving awards. His life was about to get a lot more interesting and lucrative.

CHAPTER 28

O f all the places in the world, this one felt like home. At least, it's how Anton imagined a home should feel. It was warm, comfortable, and peaceful. When he opened the door, there would be no dread or uncertainty about what was on the other side. He was welcomed with tender eyes, smiling faces, and open hands. As was his custom, V. T. greeted him with a hug and a kiss on the cheek. By now, Anton was able to respond in kind.

"Let me look at you, boy," V. T. said. It was only 1:00 p.m. on a Saturday, but he had already lit his afternoon cigar, having removed it only to greet his charge. He stood back and inspected Anton, half-paternal and half-clinical in his gaze. "You been eating enough, boy?"

"Three squares, sir," Anton said with a smile and in a mock military tone. "I would like to report that I am in my physical prime. But you, my diminutive friend, appear to have shrunk yet again."

"Perhaps so, perhaps so. Maybe we can work on some type of geriatric growth serum once we are done curing cancer. Come into to the sunroom. Mrs. Roberti has an afternoon snack waiting for us."

Nostalgic joy flooded Anton as Pat poured the coffee. The late-spring sun streamed through the glass walls of the sunroom, warming the tiled floor. Lisa came into Anton's mind, as if projected there, beyond his ability to control. He remembered her smiling at him from across the table, with Mr. Carlisle blushing in the presence of her overwhelming beauty that was almost beyond comprehension. For a moment, Anton could see her dark eyes looking at him with pensive intensity, her smooth lips framing a perfectly white smile, her breasts—

"Anton? Anton, you with me, boy?" V. T. said. Anton looked about the room as if to reorient himself and then sat down.

"She's still up at Mary's place," V. T. said, and then he held up his hand to silence Anton, who was about to offer some disingenuous expression of disinterest. "No, she hasn't seen anyone else. And yes, she is as beautiful as ever. When your name comes up, I can see she has to catch her breath and steady herself. She's as clearly in love with you as you are with her. Take it from an old man, you don't want that train to leave the station without you on it. Our work has value, but die we must, if not by cancer then by some other means. Yet love is eternal."

Pat entered with fresh-from-the-oven muffins. The aroma filled the room and complemented the coffee. This was home.

V. T. shifted in his chair, squinted, and drew in deep and slowly on his cigar, as he was wont to do before engaging in a topic of importance. "I've been thinking about you, boy, alone up in Portland, working those long days, coming home, and plowing through your research—all alone. Did you ever think you were being selfish?"

The question startled Anton, who considered selfishness a most despicable trait.

V. T. continued. "Anton, your brilliance and effort are unique. But if we don't share our success and pull in the kind of help we need to bring this to the world, then we will fall shy of our destiny. It becomes a form of selfishness to hold so tightly to the process that its full potential is stifled. You see, Anton, it's not important who gets credit for doing good, it's important that good is done. Do you want credit for curing cancer? Or do you want cancer to be cured?"

"But they can't be trusted, V. T. You know that, you said it yourself! They will change it to maximize profit."

"Maybe I was wrong, Anton. There are some good people

in the world besides you and I. I have an old friend, Roger Allard. He's the CEO for Avenger Pharmaceuticals. I've known Roger since we were in medical school together. Good family man, in it for all the right reasons. I think we can trust him. His company has huge resources we could use to reach our goal. Anton, I'm impressed by the results in Portland. Three people were saved. But you know there are millions more."

Anton looked down at his feet. "You don't think I can do it, do you?"

"Anton, nobody could do it but you. You just can't do it alone."

The room grew quiet as the significance of the moment pressed on them. A clock ticked in the corner. V. T. drew in on his cigar. Time passed.

"How long have you known this guy?" Anton finally asked.

"Almost fifty years."

"Have you told him about our research already?"

"Of course I haven't."

More silence.

Anton was thinking about the way it had been at the beginning—the incredible promise; the new energy; a small, happy band of rebels destined to change the world. This felt like creeping conformity. At the moment of success, they would go running into the comfortable arms of the status quo. How could this be right? Once upon a time, Anton had dreamed of giving the cure away. It was a simple remedy that he could toss into the air to let the world inhale. Why would V. T. pull back now? If he did, who was left to help?

V. T. reached out and put his hand on Anton's shoulder. "Son, look at me. We haven't come this far to cut and run. Roger thinks like us. Let me arrange for you to meet him. If after that you don't think this is the correct step to take, then we won't take it."

Anton loved V. T. like a father, and the man had never let him down. Ever "OK, I'll meet him."

"Good. He'll be in town in a few weeks, and we can meet here. I'll let you explain everything to him. I'll just tell him we have an idea to discuss."

Anton exhaled. It was hard for him to trust anyone, but V. T. was exceptional.

V. T. sat back in his chair and blew smoke rings toward the ceiling. "Now, about Lisa. I say we pay a visit for lunch tomorrow over at Mary's. I'll bet she will be there."

Anton looked down. How could he face her after the way he had shamed himself? She could wound him with one look. Besides, he thought this was no time for love. He wanted to be like Saint Paul—that is, virtuously dedicated to his task, no distractions. Love with Lisa must be sacrificed for the greater good.

"Boy, your hands are clenched tight," V. T. said.

Anton became aware of it for the first time.

"She must mean a lot to you to trigger that kind of passion," V. T. said. "Why do you avoid her?"

"We have no future, V. T. It would only lead to pain. Look at me, and look at how I live. I came close to her and hurt her. I don't want to do that again."

"I see. Anton, I admire and respect you, so I want you to know that I say this to you with great love. Before, I thought you were showing signs of selfishness; now, you are talking like a coward."

Anton sat upright. He had been called many things before but never a coward. If V. T. were any other man, Anton would have dropped him on the spot.

"Anton, you have the balls to stare down the world, but you can't stand to face what's in your own heart. You hide behind your celibate-martyr role not because you are called to it but because you are afraid to face what you might feel. Yes, you may hurt her, and she may hurt you. In fact, if you choose love, I guarantee you will both be hurt, but you will both be better for the experience. Anton, you're a great man, but there was only one worthy of his cross. That cross freed us all. Your cross is a false shield to prevent you from living all of life. Our destiny as humans is to have love in abundance, not isolation. So, lunch it will be."

V. T. triumphantly stuck the cigar in his mouth and sat back with his arms crossed over his chest. A small grin crept to the corner of Anton's mouth. He knew it would be good to see her again.

Spring nights in Maine sparkled. The light from the full moon danced over the hills, and the stars jumped out of the black sky. In Maine, senses were brought to full expression. As he looked out the bedroom window of the Robertis' cozy guesthouse, Anton didn't think the stars looked like that in Rhode Island. He lay on his back and let his mind relive the day's events. Roger Allard, Lisa—he had so much to consider. Damn that V. T.! He had an agenda, and Anton had walked right into it without warning. He was starting to feel a bit manipulated. Meeting Roger Allard was one thing, but to face Lisa again? It had nothing to do with courage but everything to do with what was right.

Anton couldn't sleep. He sat up from the bed and went to the dresser, where he wrote a short, polite note. He gathered his belongings, put them into the car he had borrowed from Dale, and headed back to Portland.

CHAPTER 29

Sixteen participants were in the latest round of the research. When Dr. Proctor realized the "success" of the last cycle of patients, he immediately increased the size of the cohort. He realized that if this round had similar results to the first round, they might choose to "fast track" the protocol to make it available to more patients.

Anton knew what this could mean for him. For the next month, he would be on a gastroenterology rotation, nowhere near where the protocol patients would be. He would need to come back in the evening to administer the treatment. Fortunately, he was very near completion of the bolus-infusion delivery method. That would chop precious time off the treatment, taking it from two hours to five minutes. He would have five minutes for each patient, with sixteen patients a night, plus time to continue documenting his results. He also knew what would happen next: sixteen patients and sixteen remissions of cancer. Then, all hell would break loose. He didn't have much time to prepare.

He continued his daily routine in his usual exemplary fashion, but those closest to him could tell his mind was not fully on task. Dale could tell, even though they were not on the same rotation together.

"Hey, Superman, how are you doing?" Dale asked one day when they finally had a moment alone at lunch. "And don't give me that 'I'm fine' bullshit. Let's start out with me saying I know you're not fine and let you pick up the conversation from there."

Anton gave a tired, sincere smile. It was nice to be understood. He looked at Dale, trying to read in his eyes to see if he could be trusted, even after Dale had put his reputation on the line for him. Anton had been up until 4:00 a.m., and his profound fatigue threatened to cause a delusional sense of proportion. He paused in uncertainty.

"Fuckin' A, Thresh, it's me, Dale. I held your head over a toilet bowl with one hand while I held back the wolves with the other. Talk to me, boy."

Something unfamiliar came up from deep inside Anton. He thought he might cry. He needed some deep breaths, a drink of water, and enough adrenaline to get by the fatigue.

"It's getting heavy, Dale. For the first time, maybe ever, I feel a sense of doubt."

"So, you're fucking human, Thresh. I know you're on the doorstep of greatness. I get goosebumps just thinking about it. In a few months, you could have more fame and wealth than you could dream of. You just gotta step through the door."

"But what door? And how do I step through it?"

"You gotta come clean. Let them know that it's your treatment and not their bogus protocol that's working. They will be pissed at first, but they'll get over it."

"What I've done violates all the ethical and professional standards."

"Few things are more malleable than people's ethical standards when a great fortune hangs in the balance. As long as they need you, all will be forgiven. Just don't let anyone else know what you know."

"V. T. has a guy named Allard from Avenger Pharmaceuticals whom he says we can trust."

Dale rolled his eyes as Anton spoke of trust. It was Dale's philosophy that the only thing he could count on people to do was what was in their own best interest. Anything more was romantic fluff.

"Thresh, I will tell you, all business guys are whores. You gotta decide which one you're going to let suck your dick, and get it over with. The medicine part is pure, and the business part is a journey into the dark side. But that's where you gotta go."

The fatigue was starting to creep back into Anton's bones. He feared Dale was right. "Suppose I can't do that."

"Then someone else will, and you will be crushed or by-passed entirely." Dale shrugged and took a sip of his orange juice as he let his words sink in. "See, Thresh, you have the burden. I don't give a fuck either way. This is your baby. But your baby is growing up, and the world beckons. You can't hold your baby back forever."

Dale could see the light dim in Anton's eyes. His discouragement was palpable. Maybe Dale had gone too far with his reality check. "But then again, you are a motherfucking genius, and I'm the son of a chicken farmer from Arkansas. So, what do I know?"

Anton smiled.

Dale continued. "But I do know this. If you want to try to go all cowboy with this and roll the dice that you somehow come out intact, I can understand your motive. If you win, I want a front seat at the Nobel induction. And if you get crushed, I'll take you back to Arkansas and will get you drunk on my moonshine."

CHAPTER 30

Robert McDougall, the CEO of OncogenX, was reviewing the reports out of Portland, Maine. "How do you know this isn't a fluke?"

"Of course, that's a possibility," said the science director, Tara Lidoffi, MD. "But suppose the results are real? It's better for us to prepare than it is for us to be caught flat footed in the face of something so compelling." She had received the e-mail from Dr. Proctor just a day earlier and had talked with him over the phone about the remarkable findings. Normally, this would be a cause for excited optimism. The problem was that the other sites had not reported anything nearly this effective. If OncogenX could not explain the discrepancy, it would be impossible for the company to move forward with full-speed testing and production. On the other hand, a plausible explanation of discrepancy, as well as reproduction at other sites, would likely lead to fast-track status for the drug, with explosive demand worldwide. The stakes were incredibly high.

"What was Proctor's explanation for the discrepancies?" asked Robert.

"Proctor feels his team's superior attention to detail to the protocol is likely the difference."

"Proctor is an egomaniac idiot, and his theory is bullshit. But we should let him believe it for now while we use his center to figure out the real story. A more likely explanation is that they fucked something up in the protocol and accidentally stumbled into a benefit. What does your gut tell you?"

"I think it's real, but something is not right. There's something different going on in Maine. Once we figure out what the difference is, we will have a clear path to fast-track status. We need to move cautiously so we don't end up with egg on our face if this proves to be nonreproducible."

Robert nodded. "We need a contingency plan in the event the next phase of the study goes well. If it goes poorly, that's easy. Success is more challenging. Also, I want you to go up to Maine personally and investigate what's going on. Execute whatever means are necessary to get the information you need. This is an off-the-grid operation. You will be given whatever resources you need and whatever confidentiality is required. Understood?"

OncogenX had enormous resources. As a multibillion-dollar, multinational company, it could buy immunity from any consequence of its actions. The company knew that the worst outcome would be a corporate fine without personal liability. It could, in essence, do whatever it wanted. In this case, the rationalization was that the greater good required action on the company's part. It had a responsibility to the shareholders to find out what was going on. Dr. Lidoffi had been with OncogenX long enough to realize the stakes and to understand how the game was played.

By the next day, Dr. Lidoffi had set up shop at the downtown Marriott in Portland. She brought along with her a team of scientists, including chemistry and pharmacology experts. Dr. Lidoffi's role was simply to use her status as a physician to open doors and manage the process. She had long ago abandoned any illusion of actually being a scientist or a doctor. At this point, she was a useful tool in the hands of the corporate executives.

Dr. Lidoffi's team sat around a conference table in the executive suite at the hotel. She began the discussion. "Let's start out with the presumption that there is an unknown variable—call it the X factor—that needs to be uncovered in order to determine what's happening to the patients at Portland Medical Center. I want this to be a thorough investigation, not merely a review of the study protocol. It is important for our purposes that nobody be aware of the depth of our investigation. As far as they're concerned, this is a routine oversight of the study."

Dr. Lidoffi was overseeing the strategy meeting. With her was Javier Torres, an expert in phlebotomy and chemical analysis. His job would be to take blood specimens from all the patients without being detected by the hospital staff or others involved with the study. The team had brought enough laboratory equipment with them to do some preliminary screening of the blood specimens. The screening would enable them to design higher-order studies to determine if the blood contained anything that could account for the changes noted in the study.

Also at the table was Cliff Doherty. As a former state trooper from Rhode Island, he had a physically imposing presence that often came in handy if needed. He also had a great instinct for human behavior and a depth of experience in criminal investigations. His job was to be the eyes and ears, scouring the facility and the hospital. It was important to OncogenX that information be carefully controlled. Any leak could do the company irreparable financial damage.

"Remember, all minutes are to be written with the expectation that they will be subpoenaed and reviewed at some point," Dr. Lidoffi said. "They must pass the straight-face test so we can have corporate denial of any wrongdoing. Gentlemen, you have wide boundaries. You have been in this situation before. Corporate wants answers. They are not too concerned with how we get them."

She looked at her watch and became visibly agitated.

"OK, gentlemen, that's enough for one day. Let's pick up this conversation tomorrow evening. I believe you all know where to start."

She ushered the men out of the suite, and they headed to their own rooms. Dr. Lidoffi walked over to the bar and poured herself a glass of vodka. Her room was overlooking downtown Portland. She enjoyed staying in executive suites— one of the perks of her job. She looked at her watch again.

Amanda wouldn't be here for another half hour. Perfect timing. Dr. Lidoffi had her flown in from New York City. At $2,000 daily, Amanda was expensive, but her "companionship" was worth the price. The job had certain pressures and certain requirements to compromise the loftier ideals of this profession. "But I do like the perks," Dr. Lidoffi said to herself.

It was starting to become apparent to Anton that he couldn't do it all. Sixteen patients in this phase of the protocol would require hours of direct contact, even with the bolus protocol in place. The alternative was not to treat some of them. He rejected that as being fully unethical, given what he knew about the orange fern's potential impact. But whom could he trust? At this point, nobody knew. Nobody was at risk except for him. He thought about what V. T. had told him in Biddeford. At some point, letting go and opening up would be necessary.

All these thoughts were running through his mind as he sat at the table waiting for Todd to finish preparing dinner. Anton was staring pensively into space as Todd came in with a bowl full of pasta and meatballs.

"Recipe special from the Antonellis," said Todd as he bounced into the room. "And, of course, you cannot have pasta without proper wine. This is a Super Tuscan, one of my favorites." He poured himself and Anton a glass. "Maybe after you've had a couple of glasses, you will tell me what's been on your mind." He bowed his head in mock sorrow. "You know, Anton, you don't talk to me like you used to."

"Actually, Todd, there is something I wanted to ask of you, but I'm afraid that if you say yes, or even merely have knowledge of what I intend to ask, you can be put in serious danger."

"What are you now, double-oh seven? Are we talking danger as in I may contract a rare disease? Hell, I risk that every Saturday night. Or are we talking danger as in I might become a missing person?"

"Think closer to the latter. Think danger as in you lose

your career, maybe face criminal charges."

"Oh, you mean *that* kind of danger. I thought you were talking about something serious. Merely losing my career or criminal charges? You call that danger? I laugh in the face of danger."

"I'm serious, Todd."

"That's a problem with you. You're always serious."

"We're talking potential career-ending stuff here."

"I don't have a career to end. Besides, how do you know what I want for a career? Maybe my career of choice is to create rebellious mischief."

"What about a peaceful life with a nice family? This could deprive you of all that."

"A peaceful life sounds boring. And who's to say that I need that sort of life to have a family? Maybe the type of girl that likes that kind of life is exactly the kind of girl I want no part of. Look, Anton, I'm your best friend. I can read every movement of your body language. I know you're up to your eyeballs with orange fern and the research. I know you're giving it to patients at night. I know you can't keep up by yourself, and you need help. I know all this because I know you. I was just waiting for you to finally ask me. I want to do it for the same reasons you want to do it. It's the right thing to do, and together we can multiply the effort, not just double it. You can't walk this path alone. If this dies because we didn't have the cojones to act, I couldn't live with myself knowing I let you down at a critical moment. Damn it, Thresher, I'm all in! Whatever happens next, we will deal with as a team."

Todd stood up and started marching in place while singing "La Marseillaise," saluting his friend as he did so. "*Allons enfants de la patrie, le jour de glorie est arrivé!*" He then paused, stopped marching, and looked directly at Anton. "I am your faithful lieutenant, *mon capitaine*. I will follow you unto death."

Todd always made Anton smile, but Anton also knew that he meant what he said. "Are you sure you want to do this?"

"I have no doubts. Whether our fate brings us glory or

death, it will assuredly bring us peace. It is the only path to peace that I can think of."

That night, they drank wine, ate pasta, broke bread, and talked into the morning hours of things to come. Todd was full of excitement talking about the future. It was good to smile with his old friend. If Anton tried, he could imagine it was like the early days. Hope, optimism, and wild plans were all merging together into a tonic of glory.

Anton knew what he was doing was against the rules. However, he knew the rules were corrupt. This was his civil disobedience. His commandments came from a higher source. Faith is all that he needed to propel him forward. Armed with the truth, and a small band of committed brothers, he knew he could change the world.

CHAPTER 31

M ary noticed a slight change in Lisa. First, it was in her eyes. Then, as with the changing weather, Lisa was reverting to her typical pattern. She liked to run the two miles from her apartment to Mary's place. She kept her work clothes in a backpack as she alternated sprinting with jogging. She hated the monotony of a single pace. Mary left the sunroom open for her. Lisa would alternate sets of push-ups with sit-ups, along with pull-ups that she would do on a low-hanging oak branch outside the door of the sunroom. She liked to look at her biceps as she pulled her chin over the branch, knowing full well that very few women could do ten of these pull-ups as she could. She would shower at Mary's and then be ready for work. The routine made her feel strong, immune to harm. The intangible luster was back to her organic beauty.

During the dinner rush, the medical students and locals would crowd the restaurant, all trying to be seated in her section. As with any beautiful woman, rumors constantly swirled about her.

One rumor was that she was having an affair with one of the doctors at the medical school. Another rumor had her engaged to a medical school graduate who was out of town doing his residency. Yet another popular rumor was that she had a gay lover in Portland whom she would visit on weekends.

All the rumors were fueled by her solitary lifestyle. She never dated, and no one knew if she had any friends. The mystery added to her allure.

Lisa's affect turned from brooding and standoffish to

affable but somehow still distant. A warm smile covered a depth of uncertain but tantalizing possibilities lying beneath.

Three medical school students—Jackson, Joe, and Sophia —were sitting in one of the booths at Mary's, watching Lisa as she took orders. "I'm telling you, Joe," Jackson said. "Don't even bother. Asking her out is like putting your hand in the chute of a snowblower. It may seem like a good idea at the time, but you will end up being wounded and bloody."

Joe shrugged. "I wouldn't mind wounded and bloody, as long as she was there to bandage me up."

"More like a vampire waiting to suck out your blood, I think," said Jackson.

"Listen," said Sophia. "If one of you guys doesn't ask her out, I will."

"How do you know she likes girls?" asked Joe.

"How do you know she doesn't?" asked Sophia. "We can all sit here and wonder about her forever, or one of us can simply ask her out."

"Sure," said Jackson. "It's that easy. Ask for the check, and ask her out at the same time. I'm sure nobody has ever tried that before. How many times do you think she's shut people down? No, I don't mind taking a risk, but that recipe is certain to invite failure and embarrassment. The fact is, that girl is simply out of league for any of us. I'm an expert on reading body language, and that girl has a closed-for-business sign hanging out front."

The next morning, as Lisa completed her final sprint to Mary's sunroom, she was surprised to see Joe from the medical school. He was sitting against the trunk of the oak tree where she normally did her chin-ups.

"Good morning, Lisa." He smiled at her as she attempted to mask her surprise. He was lean and athletic, maybe about an inch shorter than Anton, and had a warm face and a quick smile. His hair was a couple of shades darker than Anton's. Before Lisa could say anything, he continued. "I thought you could use some postworkout refueling. I was unsure what you liked, so I brought everything: hot coffee, protein bars, yogurt, bagel. I even made a smoothie with organic greens." He gestured to the array of items laid out on the blanket next to him. Lisa couldn't help but smile at the extent of his effort.

"Now, I know that you still have your workout to do, but everything will keep until you're done. I hope I'm not interrupting you. I thought you might like some companionship for a change."

"How did you know I would be here?" asked Lisa.

"Lisa, your routine is legendary and predictable. You run to work, work out in the sunroom, and then do chin-ups. When somebody matters, a bit of effort can uncover much about them."

Lisa didn't know whether to be impressed, flattered, or disturbed. Maybe she was a bit of each.

Joe smiled. "I've completed my own morning run, so I thought it would be fun to finish the workout together."

"Sure." Lisa wasn't sure what else to say.

For some reason, she was capable of doing more push-ups and pull-ups than usual. She and Joe alternated sets. When they finished the workout, they sat up across from one another on the blanket while Lisa sampled each of the offerings. The smoothie Joe had made was particularly good; she could taste blueberries, strawberries, cinnamon, and a hint of turmeric. Joe watched her sip the smoothie. "I found out what your favorite ingredients were. I hope you like the way I mixed them."

"Perfect," Lisa said between sips.

Joe grinned.

"This has been a nice surprise," Lisa said. She was about to say more, but Joe jumped in.

"Lisa, I know you get asked this a lot, but I've admired you for so long that I would love to know you a little better. I was hoping you would let me take you out to lunch or dinner or go for a run together, whatever you're comfortable with."

The thought of Joe's companionship was appealing. He was nice. As he was posing his question, Lisa could see beyond where he was sitting. In the distance was the dip on the street where Anton had fallen a while ago. That day had been similar to this one. She could feel the warm sun on the back of her head, much as she had felt it when she had been holding Anton's head in her hands. A light breeze brought the scent of lilacs to her. She remembered the aroma from that day, which seemed so long ago. She closed her eyes to breathe it in for a moment and felt herself transported to Mr. Carlisle's porch at the Cambridge Inn. Now she was thinking of the morning coffee, the sound of the river, and the warmth of the tiles while looking at Anton across the table. Mr. Carlisle had blushed. Lisa's mind had wandered back to that moment so many times.

"Lisa?" asked Joe.

"But Joe, I'm engaged."

"Oh." Joe tried to regroup himself in light of this unexpected information. He noted she did not have a ring, but he thought it was impolite and strategically unwise to ask about it. For her part, Lisa couldn't believe what she had said. It had just come from somewhere inside of her. But after having said it, she felt at peace with the statement. It seemed emotionally true. In fact, maybe it was actually true.

Joe concluded that the engagement must be tenuous at best—no ring, no evidence of another man's presence. He began to reconsider his tactics.

"Really, I just wanted to get to know you as a friend. It's hard to make friends at medical school. I think you're more interesting than anybody else I have met since I arrived here."

Lisa was sincerely flattered. Months of isolation had left her unfamiliar with the nuance of personal interaction. She was more comfortable in her role as a waitress, where the discourse was predetermined. Maybe having a friend wouldn't be such a bad idea. Mary often said that isolation was bad for the mind. What harm could come from a run? Joe seemed sincere. Besides, Lisa never seemed capable of making friends with men. She looked again at the spot in the road where she and Anton had their fates entangled for the first time. The sand that had collected there had long since been cleaned away. She wondered if he rode his bike in Portland. She wondered why he had never called her, ever.

She turned to Joe. "The corner of Biddeford Road and Pine Street, six a.m. It's two miles from there to Mary's place. You better be able to keep up."

CHAPTER 32

T odd Freeze found it easy to wander about the hospital hallways late at night. He was such a presence that the staff
were used to seeing him at odd hours. He had never thought that
his days as a wandering hospital Casanova would serve as such
great cover for his current task.

He strode about the hospital hallways with confidence.
It occurred to him that attempting to be clandestine would
only bring greater scrutiny to his movements. Slung across the
shoulder was his weekend bag. This had been his habit when
he was hooking up with women in the on-call room. He always
liked to have a change of clothes available. Therefore, nobody
thought twice about the fact that he was carrying a bag with
him.

All the patients in the protocol had an ongoing intravenous infusion. It was simple for Todd to slide into the room, hook
up the orange fern solution, and quickly infuse it over the recommended five-minute time frame. He was currently doing a
dermatology rotation, notoriously leisurely in its work tempo.
This afforded him ample time to get to the hospital and complete his rounds. Both he and Anton had decided that the third
shift was their best space to operate within. At that time, the
hospital was down to a skeletal staff. Most of the patients were
sleeping, and the infusion could be done without them being
aware because the IV was already established. If a patient happened to be awake, a simple reassurance was all that was required. The patients were so used to a wide array of individuals
coming and going that nothing seemed out of the ordinary to

them.

Todd had only two more patients on tonight's rounds. He knew that the phlebotomy team would be coming by at 2:00 a.m. to take the routine blood work that was used to monitor patients in the protocol. He needed to complete his rounds before they started their work so they would not discover him. Third shift started at 11:00 p.m. The nurses spent the first thirty minutes in "report," where they would share information about the patients on their ward. This was the perfect window of opportunity for Todd to operate within.

Todd entered Gloria Canfield's room. She was fifty-four years old and had stage-four breast cancer metastatic to the liver and the bones. Her abdomen was bloated. The muscles in her arms and legs were withered. She looked at Todd silently with eyes that were yellow with jaundice. She tried to form a small smile. Todd put his hand on her shoulder and looked her in the eyes. "This is going to make you better. This disease will not win." Gloria's smile broadened.

As Todd was about to connect the infusion, he heard footsteps outside the door. He quickly put the syringe back into his bag.

Patty Galantic appeared in the doorway. Todd had noticed her at the nurses' station finishing her report and had hoped she didn't see him. Apparently, though, she had. "Todd! What are you doing here? I thought you had dermatology this month."

"Um, I'm just finishing my genograms as part of my behavioral-medicine project."

"Interviewing patients for their family history at one in the morning?"

"Yeah, as long as they're awake, I thought it wouldn't interfere with their daytime treatments." Todd was desperate to change the topic. "I've been thinking about you a lot, Patty. You're looking strikingly delicious tonight."

"Thoughts are cheap, Todd. Why haven't you called?"

"Ah, Patty, the life of a resident is nothing but work."

"Please, who do you think you're kidding? Since when has Todd Freeze let work get in the way of his recreation? That lie might work with somebody else, but not with me."

Noticing that the patient had fallen asleep, Patty walked up next to Todd, reached behind him, and grabbed his butt.

"Hmm, firm as ever. You know, Todd, Stephanie and I are both getting off this shift. The call room is available. We could re-create our winter wonderland from February."

Patty was both refreshingly innocent and intoxicatingly erotic. Todd began calculating how things might work: a quick infusion here, a break with Patty and Stephanie, complete the work, home by two. He would be cutting it close, but he could make it work.

Patty leaned in closer to him, her left hand on his butt, and now her right hand was on his crotch, feeling him get hard.

"I will take that as a yes," she said as she rubbed the front of his surgical scrubs.

"OK, Patty, just give me a few minutes. I'll meet you up there."

"Well, Todd, this is your five-minute warning. If you're not there, we will leave and take our show on the road."

Intense desire warped Todd's perception of time and space. In that moment, he could imagine achieving anything in order to accommodate his desired rendezvous with Patty and Stephanie. They were simply two of his favorite women at the hospital, who were full of life, devoid of judgment, and always open for adventure. Todd thought they were perfect women.

When he arrived at the on-call room, Patty and Stephanie had already started without him. A candle was burning on the end table. They had poured three shots of vodka. The residents kept a small bottle hidden under dirty clothes in the bottom drawer. The common courtesy was that whoever finished the bottle would replace it.

Patty pushed Todd down into the chair next to the bed. She slowly unbuttoned Stephanie's dress, stripped off her bra, and then sensuously cupped her breasts in her hands.

"Really, Todd, have you seen anything so perfect in your life? And they taste better than they look."

Todd felt comfortable in their company. Stephanie was married to the chief orthopedic resident and had a powerful motive to be discreet. Patty had no fear and no need to be discreet. In fact, her validation of the tryst with Todd could only serve to enhance his cover.

Todd thought the night was turning out great. He downed a second shot of vodka.

At some point after the frenzy of carnal bliss came the luxury of sleep. Todd thought that a greater pairing of joy and peace had yet to be created in the scope of human experience. Nothing could more validate that God was in his heaven and all was right with the world. Todd was in this semiconscious state of reflective bliss when a thought jolted him awake.

The study! He had one more patient to infuse. It was 3:00 a.m. The phlebotomy team would be making their rounds. "I should be OK," he said to himself. "I have only one more to do."

Javier Torres had no problem being invisible. He was not only short but also quiet in movement and in voice. Dr. Lidoffi had managed to have him assigned as the third-shift phlebotomist. He would draw all the required blood work and then the extra tubes needed to perform his clandestine studies.

The blood work for the study protocol had to be drawn between 2:00 a.m. and 4:00 a.m. Javier moved quietly and efficiently from room to room.

Todd had just completed the infusion for his last patient. He had packed up his bag and resumed the flow of the normal IV when Javier wandered into the room. It was not at all uncommon to see residents at any hour of the day on the floors or in the patients' rooms, but something struck Javier as a bit odd. Why would this medical student be carrying around a bag with him? And what was he doing at such an unusual hour of the morning?

"Is the patient OK? I have come to take her blood," said Javier.

"Oh yes, she is fine. The nurses called me to check on her. They said she seemed to be breathing funny, but she checks out just fine." Todd shuffled to the door. "Have a good night."

Javier drew the blood and then marked his chart annotating the usual meeting.

CHAPTER 33

T he results wouldn't be available until next week, after the official interpretation of the posttreatment CAT scans, but Anton and Todd already knew the outcome. Gloria Canfield's abdominal distention had improved, as had the color in her eyes. She was eating and sitting up in bed. The entire hospital was buzzing about the changes seen in all the patients receiving Dr. Proctor's protocol.

"We need to stay in front of the process," said Anton. He and Todd had finished their evening meal on their fire escape, enjoying the warm, early evening air.

"What we need to do next is have a toast of champagne to celebrate. We should enjoy this moment, and then we can figure out what to do next." Todd popped the cork on a bottle and poured two glasses.

"To slaying the green horseman," said Anton. He allowed himself a moment of satisfaction. "We did it. We actually did it. At times, it seemed impossible, but we did it. They're all getting better. This is exactly the way I envisioned it happening. Of course, now comes the hard part. We need to figure out what to do next."

"What about V. T.'s friend? We need to find out whom we can trust and how to bring your discovery into daylight. We don't have much time. Once Proctor reviews the results, there's no telling what will happen next."

In a hotel room at the downtown Marriott, Dr. Lidoffi, Javier, and Cliff Doherty sat around a table as they contemplated the same observations while holding a conference call with headquarters in New York City.

"The clinical results are striking," Javier said. "Patients who didn't have the strength to sit up in bed are walking about their rooms. Their energy is better. All their lab testing has improved. I'm certain the CAT scan will show improvement in the tumor burden." Javier had the benefit of watching the patients on a daily basis as he made his hospital rounds. He was keeping his team informed throughout the process. "The rogue molecule I identified is in all the study patients. The degree of its presence varies greatly. It is an organic molecule but nothing I've ever seen before. There was one patient who had a strikingly high level. That was the patient whose blood I took right after that strange encounter with the medical resident I told you about."

Javier had sent samples of the rogue molecule to the corporate lab headquartered in New York when he initially identified it. Robert McDougal, CEO for OncogenX, spoke from the other end of the phone. "We have been attempting to re-create the molecule but without success. We cannot identify its origins, so it is hard to re-create it. Furthermore, when we do succeed, it will be, in essence, a new drug and will require us to start at the beginning with all the preliminary studies. That could delay its launch into the marketplace by ten years. If we could somehow link it to the present protocol, we could bring it to market within the next twelve months. These results would clearly give us fast-track status. With the right price point, the profits would be in the billions."

"The first thing we need to do is prevent this information from being leaked," said Dr. Lidoffi. "Whatever that molecule is, we need to acquire it and infuse it at the other study sites to create a multicentered result. Since nobody knows that this molecule exists, we should have no problem ascribing the results to the original protocol and simply mixing in the new molecule to the old formula. We could very legitimately and safely bring the drug to market by next year."

Cliff spoke up. "I think we should shut down the other arms of the study now. It will be easier to control if we have just one site to deal with. Besides, with the results we are seeing, the fast-track status will be easy to get."

"OK, but where is this molecule coming from?" asked Robert. "Is it a contaminant? How did it get there?"

"Look," said Cliff. "The results are too consistent for this to be a contaminant. We are dealing with a rogue operator who is somehow infusing the patients in our protocol with this substance. It should be simple to identify who the perpetrators are and get the formula from them. That will prevent us from having to rack our brains as we try to re-create a molecule that already exists."

"OK, Cliff, what are you thinking?" asked Robert.

"Wire me two hundred fifty thousand dollars, and I believe I'll have that formula for you within a couple of weeks."

Robert was silent for a few seconds. "What's your plan?"

"I don't think you want to know that. Once I deliver the formula, I believe a robust bonus will be in order. I'm taking a compelling personal risk here. In fact, the entire Portland team will need to become invisible after this operation."

"What are you thinking, Cliff?" Robert asked.

"Ten million for each of us. We need enough to be set for life. This will be our last assignment."

"Are you fucking kidding? Ten million?"

"You will make that back the first week this drug goes to market. You will have twenty years of profit, and our careers will be over. The money will be transferred to an out-of-country bank account in each of our names. The transfer will occur after you receive validation of the formula. Along with it, we will sign nondisclosure contracts. Everybody wins."

"Five million upon delivery, and another five when the study is validated at other centers," Robert said.

"Agreed," Cliff said. He noted Dr. Lidoffi and Javier nodding their agreement. "We are all in."

"Good," said Robert. "The contracts will be e-mailed

today."

CHAPTER 34

S creen after screen, the images came. The group of radiologists looked at them in awed silence. No one spoke. Words were not needed to amplify the magnitude of what they were witnessing. In every case, the tumor size had regressed or disappeared completely.

"Amazing, just amazing," said Dr. Bruezeze in a barely audible voice.

They kept repeating the images, perhaps expecting them to change upon further review. Dr. Proctor joined them, having been notified of the results. He wanted to see the images for himself.

"I knew it. I just knew it. I could tell by how the patients were reacting that these would be good, but I had no idea they would be this good. Who has seen these images besides us?"

"No one," said Dr. Bruezeze.

"Good. Let's keep it that way for now."

"We can't sit on this for very long. The patients are going to be demanding these results."

"I know, but we can at least wait until I have a chance to speak with New York about how to handle what comes next. This is momentous. This will put Portland Medical Center on the map and put us all into the stratosphere. We're going to be playing with the big boys now. I have a meeting with Dr. Lidoffi in my office in about one hour. I'll talk to you after that, and we will decide how to proceed. For now, nobody says anything."

Dr. Proctor walked slowly back to his office. It occurred to him that after today, everything in his life would be different.

For some time now, he had felt trapped at Portland Medical Center. He thought his surgical genius was not adequately displayed to the greater world. Portland Medical was a nice community hospital, but in the grand scheme of things, it was the equivalent to being in Siberia. His leadership of the study was about to jettison him to international acclaim.

As he sat in his office, he looked at the globe that he kept on the table next to his desk. He could imagine himself flying to all the great capitals, being received like a hero, and giving speeches in front of large, appreciative audiences.

He was surprised when Dr. Lidoffi arrived alone.

"We did it," said Dr. Proctor as he stood up excitedly and greeted her. "Results are in, and we did it. This protocol works better than we could've hoped. The responses are unbelievable."

"I know," said Dr. Lidoffi rather blandly. "We have been tracking your branch of the study very closely and have noticed the profound difference between your outcomes and those of the other sites. It actually represents something of a problem for us."

"A problem? How can success be a problem?"

"Your outcomes are so out of line with the other centers that we have launched an investigation trying to determine why there is such a difference. We have identified a contaminant, an organic molecule that is not part of the original protocol that appeared in every one of your patients' blood samples."

"What the hell are you talking about, Lidoffi? Have you been stealing samples from my patients in order to do your own private research? That is outrageous! It's unethical! Hell, it might even be illegal."

"Calm down, Dr. Proctor. We are all in this one together. You know what this could mean if these results are reproduced. All these patients have signed a blanket release. We can do anything we want with their blood. Remember, OncogenX has ultimate control over this study. You've been given the opportunity to participate, but you have no control over it. Look, Dr.

Proctor, we want you onboard, but make no mistake about it." Dr. Lidoffi leaned in closely. "We can cut you out of this in a heartbeat, kick you to the curb, and move forward without you. Now, I don't want that, and corporate doesn't want that, but you have to be a team player if you want to stay with us."

Dr. Proctor's anger quickly vanished and was replaced by fear and insecurity. Everything Dr. Lidoffi said was true. In an instant, he could go from being king of the world to someone watching the parade passing by. He would do whatever it would take to stay in the game.

"You know you can count on me, Tara. I've been on board with OncogenX since the beginning. You can count on me to do whatever it will take to see this thing through. All I ask is to continue being the lead researcher. It's clear that our center has done something special."

"Look, Dr. Proctor, we need a lead researcher, you know that. We can think of nobody better for that role than you."

Feeling at ease, Dr. Proctor sat back and smiled. "What do we do next?"

"First, we have to release something to these patients and to the public at large. We are going to shut down the other branches of the study until we can discern everything that's going on at PortlandMedical. You will hold a press conference, where you will announce favorable preliminary outcomes. You will downplay these results. We don't want an overexuberant public to run away with this until we are ready. Once we figure out what is going on, we will finance you to run a branch of the protocol at two other independent centers. That will create the validation that we need to move forward quickly."

"What about the substance, the molecule that you referred to? Is that the reason why my branch of the study is doing so well?"

"We think so. All the evidence seems to point that way."

"What is it? How did you get the patients' blood?"

"We need to figure that part out, Dr. Proctor. We need your help to do it. We need to run another round of the study at Portland Medical. We will be scrutinizing every step of the process. For now, the only people who know about the other molecule are you and me and a handful at corporate. If you mention a word of this to anybody, we will deny it, discredit you, and destroy your career. This is a big deal to corporate, and they will let nothing interfere with their plan. If things go accordingly, you will have a high-profile position as we bring this to market, complete with all the status and income that you could imagine would come with that."

Dr. Proctor knew he had stumbled into the cave of the beast. He knew that OncogenX and Dr. Lidoffi could back up any threat or any promise that they made. He knew that this was bigger than him and that his fate was now controlled by Dr. Lidoffi and OncogenX.

"You can count on me, Tara."

"I knew I could, Dr. Proctor. That is why we chose you and Portland Medical. I have a document that corporate wants you to sign in order to stay involved with the next phase of the study."

"Fine. Let me have my attorney review it, and I'll get it back to you within a week."

"No. You will read it now and sign it before I leave the room."

Dr. Lidoffi gave the papers to him. It was a simple, two-page document. Dr. Proctor felt numb. He barely read the document before signing it. He let out a heavy sigh as he handed it back.

Dr. Lidoffi placed a hand reassuringly on Dr. Proctor's shoulder. "Don't worry, Walter. You did the right thing. This is going to turn out to be a great thing for you and for OncogenX. The money to be made will be in the billions. Your life is about to change for the better in every way imaginable."

Dr. Proctor took heart in her words, sat up in the chair, and smiled. He thought nobody would ever know what happened in this room on this day. All they would know is what they would be allowed to know. He would still be the head of the study. His fame and fortune would be secure.

CHAPTER 35

The mood at the Antonelli homestead was as festive as always. The aroma of eggplant and pasta filled the air. The sound of the younger Antonelli siblings playing in the adjacent room spilled into the kitchen where Scott, Anton, Todd, and Ann were sitting. Anton was holding Scott and Ann's new baby in his lap.

Scott's mother joined them in the kitchen. "Look at Anton. He is a natural with babies. When are you going to get married? You'll make a good husband, a good father." She took a few pictures of Anton and her grandson.

"How about me, Mrs. Antonelli? Why don't you worry about me getting married?" asked Todd, smiling.

"Not you," said Mrs. Antonelli. "You have too much playboy in your blood. Someday, maybe, but not until you grow up."

"Now, Mom, be nice to him," said Scott from the head of the table. "You'll hurt Todd's feelings."

Mrs. Antonelli waved his statement away. "No, Todd knows I love him. I just don't want my daughter to marry him."

Todd and Anton had made the trip down from Portland to Rhode Island for the baby's first birthday. It would also present an opportunity for Anton to take care of some uncomfortable but important business.

Dr. Proctor, Dr. Lidoffi, and OncogenX had controlled the announcement to the press. They had provided just enough information to drive up the stock prices of the pharmaceutical giant without overheating expectations. Now they had quietly enrolled another thirty patients into the protocol. The other branches of the study had been shut down. OncogenX explained it as a consolidation of resources to better develop their new treatment. Ben Able was having trouble keeping up with harvesting and processing the orange fern. The requirement to meet the demands of thirty patients would easily outstrip the capacity that Anton had created in his apartment/lab.

After dinner, the men sat on the porch, where everyone but Anton smoked cigars.

Scott blew smoke rings into the air. "You don't know what you're missing, Anton. It's hard to explain what makes smoking cigars so pleasurable—the tobacco, or holding it in your hands."

Todd smiled. "Well, did you ever wonder that the whole thing is a huge phallic exercise? Is it an expression of your suppressed homosexuality?"

"Leave it to Freeze to ruin a perfectly good cigar," Scott said. "Do you ever think about anything other than sex, Todd?"

"Rarely. Of course, now I'm wondering if there's some way to fashion a cigar in the shape of a vagina."

"It's truly breathtaking to witness a great mind at work," Scott said. "I'm sure your contribution to the world will be profound, Todd. In the meantime, how's your side job of being a doctor going?"

"You know, Scott, I wander through the hospital, leaving a trail of healing behind me wherever I go. I think my hands have truly been touched by God. In my spare time, I'm working on a cure for cancer." In the dim light, he caught a stern stare from Anton, which he responded to with a wink.

"I thought that was Anton's hobby," Scott said. "How is the research going, Anton?"

Over the past year since the residency began, Scott had not been able to keep up with his good friends. The combination of different rotations, plus his new life as a married man, had moved them into different pathways.

"I've kind of put things on hold," Anton said, lying. "You know, the residency is so busy that I've decided to focus my energy there for a while."

"Good idea," Scott said.

The conversation then turned to anecdotes of family life, caring for infants, and the routine of marriage. Anton could see the pride and content in his friend. He did his best to fake interest in all the topics, regardless of how mundane he found them to be.

Later, after Todd and Anton said good-bye and got into Todd's car to leave, Todd turned to Anton. "That was fucking drill-bit-to-the-temple painful. If I had to listen to another baby story, I might've screamed."

Anton laughed. "Just the pride of parenthood. I guess it's that way with firstborn children. Everything they do is so compelling in the eyes of the parents. It was kind of nice seeing Scott so happy, but I do agree with you. It was a bit much. Scott is a good father. He's a good man. You know he will always be there for his children, just like his father has been there for him." Anton's eyes looked sad. Todd couldn't tell if it was because of the reflection on what had just happened or because of the dread about what was coming next.

Anton and Todd had decided to continue treating all the new patients in the next phase of the study. To ramp up production, they needed money to expand.

"OK," said Todd. "I'll drop you off at your parents' house, cruise around until you call me, and then come back and pick you up. What time is your father expecting you?"

"He knows I'm on my way there now." Before calling his father last week to ask for a meeting with him, Anton had spoken to his father only a few times. The calls had been brief and stilted, and they had always talked superficially about medicine. His father always called from his office at the end of his workday. Anton was pleased because it meant that his mother was not available.

Todd dropped Anton off at the curb so that he wouldn't have to navigate the long, winding driveway. As Anton walked up to his parents' house, he stopped midway and looked at the marvelous structure, trying to figure out what he was feeling, if anything.

His father greeted him at the door. "Anton. You're looking well."

"So are you, Dad," Anton said, and he meant it. Dr. Charles Thresher had been golfing all week and looked tanned and fit.

Anton's mother and sister were not home. This was by design at Anton's request. He had let his father know that he had some serious business to discuss with him, and he would rather not have anyone else present.

"Can I get you anything?" Charles asked. "Water or food?"

"No, thank you. I don't have much time. I need to be back in Portland this evening."

"Sure. I know how intense residency is."

Charles led him into the study and sat at his desk. Anton sat across from him.

"Dad, I'll get right to it. I have some difficult challenges that I need to overcome, and I need some financial help."

Charles tensed. Of all the topics his son could broach, this was one that gave him the greatest stress. He leaned back in his chair and squinted. "Have you been arrested?"

"No."

"Did you get a girl in trouble?"

"No."

"Do you mind telling me what you need the money for?"

"I can't."

"How much do you need?"

"Fifteen thousand dollars."

To Anton, $15,000 was the difference between success and failure. To Charles, that sum of money was nothing. A long silence ensued. As he looked about the room, Anton could see all his old trophies and awards proudly displayed on the shelves, intermixed with those of his father.

"So that's it," Charles said. "That's all I get, a fucking demand for cash with no explanation. You like to look down your nose at me. You think you're better than me. Well, you don't have a fucking pot to piss in, and you have to come crying to me because you fucked up your life and need me to help unfuck it. But you don't have the decency to offer one shred of an explanation."

"You think I like coming here? You think I like asking you for anything?"

"You've got some fucking balls. You can't find your way to my door except when you need cash. And then you don't tell me jack shit about it."

"For some fathers, all they need to know is that their son needs help."

"Great, tell me what a fucking shitty father I've been through your whole life. You're an ungrateful prick, Anton. I don't know where your mother and I went wrong. I gave you the best of everything. What did I do to make you hate me?"

"What did you do to make me love you? You raised me like a prized thoroughbred, beautiful to display. What about Polly? What about the way you tortured her?"

Charles stood up from behind the desk, his face flushed with anger. He instinctively reached to grab the golf club that was leaning next to the desk.

Anton scoffed. "What are you going to do, crack me over the head with your golf club? What, do you think I'm still twelve years old? You raise your hand at me, and I'll fucking kill you." Anton was standing, towering three inches above his father. He grabbed his father's hand that held the golf club. He put his other hand around his father's throat and pulled him in closer to him.

"You are a desperate, selfish, old man." Anton saw something in his father's eyes he had never seen before: fear.

Charles clenched his teeth. "If you don't get out of my house right now, I will call the police."

"The hell you will, and embarrass yourself in front of all your friends?" His grip around his father's neck tightened. He saw the color change in his father's face as his father—eyes now bulging—began to gasp. Anton wondered how often he had fantasized about a moment like this. He knew he could pummel his father right now, overpowering him with superior strength, size, and youth. It would be no match. "How does it feel, Dad? How does it feel? I can fucking crush you! How does that fucking feel?" He tightened his grasp as Charles choked, unable to speak. In the window behind his father, Anton saw his reflection. His face was contorted, his eyes raged, and the veins in his neck were bulging. He looked exactly how he remembered his father appearing so many times.

Anton released Charles and stepped back.

"Don't call me," said Anton.

"Get the fuck out."

"I will be talking to Polly. If you hurt her in any way, you will have me to answer to."

"Get out!"

Anton slammed the door behind him. Charles slumped in his chair, the golf club still in his grip. His whole body was trembling uncontrollably. He was drained. A strange emotion overcame him. Why was he crying? Why couldn't he stop? "I should have given him the fucking money," he said out loud. "Fucking Anton." He yelled to the empty room. "I love you, God damn it. I love you!" His tears flowed. After a few minutes, he took some deep breaths. The moment of sorrow and calm was overcome with a renewed rage. He stood up and gripped the golf club with both hands. His face was crimson, and his arms were shaking. "Son of a bitch!" He screamed to no one, spun around, and swung the golf club. The window shattered. Not satisfied, he smashed another one and then a third. "Son of a fucking bitch!"

Todd picked up Anton and did not have to ask him how the meeting had gone. They drove in silence as they headed north. It was nearing dinnertime as they crossed into Maine.

"Let's stop at Mary's for some food," Todd said.

"I'm not sure, Todd. I don't know if I could take seeing her right now."

"Look, Anton, you can't dodge her forever. If she's there, she's there. Besides, I want to see Mary, and I'm starving."

As they pulled in to Mary's Country Store and Deli, Anton found himself looking around the parking lot and around the outside of the building. He was looking for anything that might give a hint Lisa would be there. His heart raced, and he subconsciously clenched his fist.

"It's going to be OK, Anton," Todd said. "I'm not sure how it will happen, but everything is going to work out the way it's supposed to. Aren't you the one who taught me to walk by faith? Now, let's go in there and have dinner."

The normal dinner rush hour had passed, and the place was beginning to thin out. Mary greeted them at the door.

"Well, what a happy surprise for me to see you guys! I thought you forgot about your old friend Mary."

Todd gave her a big hug. "It's nice to be home."

Mary hugged Anton. "She's not here tonight, Anton. She has the night off." Anton felt both disappointed and relieved at the same time.

Mary smiled. "Let an old gal buy you dinner. I want to hear everything that's going on with you boys up in Portland."

Over burgers, fries, and beer, Todd regaled Mary with some of his more risqué and hilarious escapades during his residency. Mary was a rapt audience. She loved hearing Todd's stories almost as much as he loved telling them. The more she laughed, the more animated he became.

After some time, Mary finally turned to Anton. "What about you, Anton? Are you still carrying the weight of the world on your shoulders?"

Anton smiled sadly and sipped his beer.

"Tough day for us, Mary," said Todd. "It looks like a research project may end up going dry."

"What do you mean? I thought it was going well."

"It was, but the demands are growing. We need to expand, and we have no money. Our only option may be to partner with a big pharmaceutical company."

Mary slammed her open palm down on the table. "The hell you will! You've come all this way on your own. You don't need their money, and you don't need their corruption. You need to stay on your path."

She then got up and hurried away from the table. A few minutes later, she returned with something in her hand. "How much money do you boys need?"

Anton raised his eyebrows. "Are you kidding, Mary? We can't ask you to give us anything. We will find a way."

"For God's sake, Anton, I'm old, and I smoke two packs of cigarettes a day. I have no children. I can think of nothing better to do with my money. Besides that, you need to find a cure before I get lung cancer. Now, tell me how much money you need."

Todd cleared his throat. "Mary, we need fifteen thousand dollars."

Mary wrote a check and handed it to Anton. "There. Now, go back to Portland and finish your work. And don't ever say another word about this. I never want anybody to know that I gave you this money. It's a gift, nothing more."

Anton sat looking at the check. He then folded it in half, put it in his pocket, and kissed Mary on the forehead. "You're right, Mary," he said to her as he looked at Todd. "We will do the right thing."

That night at their apartment, Anton stared out the window of his bedroom, reflecting on the day's events. He thought the providence of God was certainly with him. First, he had to purge himself of the toxic relationships in his life. The divorce from his father was now complete. Only then could he unburden his soul to accept the gift God would give him. Sometimes, the face of God appeared in the most unlikely place. More than ever, Anton believed in his mission. Just when Anton thought he was at the end of this trail, God opened a new path. Anton had no doubt that if he continued to move forward, there would inevitably be more doors opening in front of him. He was more certain that his path was ordained by God. If he simply continued to move forward, he could not help but succeed. It was, after all, the will of God.

CHAPTER 36

Javier Torres pointed out Todd's movements on the surveillance videos. "See? Right there, see what he's doing? He does that in each of the rooms of the study participants."

Cliff Doherty had installed surveillance cameras in all the rooms of all the study patients. He also had their phones bugged. Todd and Anton were on twenty-four-hour surveillance. Cameras were following their actions.

Javier and Cliff were now aware that Anton had set up a lab in a local warehouse, and they had identified Ben Able delivering the product to the lab.

Cliff had done this before, so he knew how to operate. It was almost too easy. He was a professional among amateurs. In a matter of a few weeks, he knew almost everything regarding Anton's operation.

"Why don't we just steal the formula from them?" asked Anthony Sam, a short, scrawny man who wasn't that bright. Cliff had brought him on for his primary traits: blind obedience and an affinity for violence.

Cliff shook his head. "No, if we steal the formula, they still have it. They could make trouble. They could disclose it independent of our research. They could tie us up in litigation for years. They could even uncover our operation if we are not careful." He contemplated his options while pacing about the room.

Anthony ran his hands through his slicked-back, raven hair. "OK, then, why don't I just steal the formula and then kill them both? I can make it look like an accident. They can burn in a warehouse fire, something like that. We will have the formula, and they will not be able to tell anybody."

"No," said Cliff. "When young people die, it creates too much attention. Investigations. We need a more effective way to neutralize them. It's better to make them irrelevant than have them dead. We have to get the formula without them knowing that we have it. Then, all that will be left to do is to marginalize them. Take their voice away. We also need to know the process. If we simply possess a sample of the formula, we may have trouble engineering it. We need to know how it's made. We don't need just the end product, we need the recipe."

Anthony had more ideas to share. "How about if I break into the lab and steal all their notes? Maybe the recipe is there."

"That might be an option, but I expect the notes to been encrypted. Even if we happen to get a hold of the right information, there is a risk of being caught. If they know we're on to them, our mission is in jeopardy. I think we can get what we need through a more elegant approach."

"What about Allard and Roberti?" asked Javier.

Cliff had gotten all of Anton's phone records and had bugged every phone conversation Anton had in the past six months. At the end of each week, Javier would go over the calls and note any useful information.

"That meeting must not occur," said Cliff. "If Allard and his company get ahold of the formula, they will launch a research project and bring this into daylight. We will lose control. We will lose the opportunity. We need to find a way to stop that meeting from happening."

"Want me to take care of Roberti?" asked Anthony.

"Roberti is the linchpin. Without him, the deal with Allard will likely fall apart or at least be delayed significantly. Either way, it will give us time to get things done. When is the meeting scheduled?"

"Two weeks from Saturday," said Javier.

"I want you to be prepared, Anthony. From this point forward, we will not communicate by text, by phone, or in person. I will signal you like we did in the California case. After you get the signal, put the plan into action and then disappear until you're notified."

After Anthony left the room, Javier called for Dr. Lidoffi to meet them. It was important that Anthony and Dr. Lidoffi never see each other.

Cliff addressed the doctor. "We have made arrangements to ensure that the meeting between Thresher, Roberti, and Allard will not take place. Now we need to have the next step ready to go. I think the best way to go is to isolate Thresher and eliminate all his support. Once we have full control of the formula and know how to make it, he will have no recourse. Because what he did is illegal, if he comes forward, he can be arrested. If he goes to the press, we have enough connections to make him seem like a fringe lunatic. I just don't think he or his buddy, Freeze, will be a problem for us once we eliminate his support network and get the formula. In the process, we leave them with nothing."

Dr. Lidoffi knew better than to ask for further details, but she did have one question. "Should we have him kicked out of the profession and have his medical license stripped?"

"I don't think we need to do that. That would create administrative and legal hearings. Who knows what could happen if he gets a good attorney. We're better off letting them sit and rot. In some way, the best thing for us would be if he gets stuck in a nine-to-five job with a mortgage."

"How about if we have him arrested for drug manufacturing?" Javier asked. "It would be real simple to make his lab look like a methamphetamine-manufacturing center and have him raided."

"Interesting option. Not a bad idea to see him sit in prison for about twenty years. Once again, we have the risk of an investigation. As much as I'd like to see the arrogant prick busted, it's better for our objective if we leave him broken on the side of the road." Cliff noted Dr. Lidoffi had become quiet and withdrawn, looking at her hands. "What is it, Tara?"

"It's just that...well...I've been studying this kid's work.

What he has accomplished is pure genius. It is the stuff of Nobel awards. His methods are insane and reckless, but his thought process and results...well...look at what has happened to those patients."

"Don't go soft, Tara. You said it yourself. 'Insane and reckless.' He may have stumbled on something through luck, but we need to get them out of the way, or else it will be nothing. This punk has no respect for due process. He disregards every convention that has been established. Those conventions are meant to protect patients and legitimate companies. Suppose things had gone wrong? He has no regard for people. He is after only his own glory. No, everything that's about to happen to him, he has earned. So, shake off that sorry-ass sympathy. How many times in your life do you have a chance to get ten million? Look, business is always bare knuckled. This kid doesn't belong in the arena."

Dr. Lidoffi knew Cliff was right. It was too late for sympathy. Her career had been formed years ago, and now was its culmination. A $10 million parting gift was not bad.

"Javier, do you have the file on Antonelli?" asked Cliff.

Scott Antonelli had been targeted. He had the right profile: a mixture of vulnerability, access to Anton, and lots to lose. Dr. Proctor had already altered Scott's rotations so that Scott was now at Portland Medical Center and rotating on the same service as Anton. On Monday, Todd Freeze would be transferred to another hospital. The process of isolation had begun.

CHAPTER 37

A s a medical resident, Scott Antonelli had learned not to ask too many questions when things changed administratively. Therefore, he was not shocked when his rotation was redirected to Portland Medical Center. These types of last-minute shifts were not uncommon. Although he was disappointed he would not have the opportunity to rotate in his home state of Rhode Island, he was looking forward to spending some time with his good friend Anton. At first, he was hopeful that Todd would be with them. But at the last minute, Todd had been shifted to the hospital in Rhode Island, originally intended for Scott.

It was Scott's first night on call in his new rotation. As usual, Ann had packed him a bagful of snacks. He set himself up in the on-call room and put the snacks on the table. On the desktop, he placed a picture of him holding his baby. Other residents teased him about it, but Scott liked to say that it reminded him for whom he was working for. In the pocket of the scrubs he wore, he kept a photograph from when he was a child. In it, he was standing next to his father, mimicking his pose. His mother had taken the picture in the garage when Scott was eight years old.

Scott had just settled in when he received a page from the surgical floor.

"What is it?" Scott asked when he called back the nurses' station.

"Dr. Proctor wants you to do a history and physical on the new admission in room four thirty-two," said the nurse.

"Tonight?"

"Yes, he said tonight. They're planning on operating tomorrow morning. Should be a piece a cake—a young, healthy girl with a twisted knee."

Scott thought orthopedic cases were pretty straightforward. At least there wouldn't be a lot of work involved. When he arrived on the floor, Patty Galantic handed him the chart.

"Have fun with this one," she said with a knowing smile. "Let me know if you want any help in there."

Scott couldn't imagine what help he might need. He took the chart and headed for the room.

It was unusual that the patient had a private room. She was sitting up in the bed, legs crossed "Indian style" while reading a magazine. It occurred to him that the posture was a bit unusual for somebody with a knee injury.

"Hello, I'm Dr. Antonelli. I'm here to do your history and physical."

The patient had on scrub bottoms with a patient gown on top, loosely tied at the neck and opened in the front. As Scott approached, she stretched out her legs, put her arms behind her, and looked up at him.

"Hi, my name is Rebecca. Nice of you to come and visit me."

As she put her arms back, the opening in the front expanded, exposing her perfectly flat abs and the inner portion of each breast.

Scott fumbled a bit with the chart, not quite sure where he should put his eyes but having a tough time not noticing her striking physique.

"Well, tell me what happened to your knee," he said.

"I twisted it while I was dancing."

"Is that a hobby of yours?"

"No, more of a profession," she said with a smile. "They tell me I'll be out of work for a few weeks after the surgery. Maybe when I've recovered, you can come and watch me dance?"

Scott smiled and didn't say anything. She seemed nice enough. He thought she seemed innocent, too. After all, she was only twenty-two years old. Scott was able to take her full history. As expected, she was a healthy woman. A former high school athlete, she had moved to Portland from Bangor about two years ago. She lived in an apartment with her roommate.

"Now I just need to examine a few things," said Scott in preparation for the physical.

"You can touch me all you want." Rebecca looked right at him.

He put his hands on her neck, examining her thyroid.

"Your hands are so nice and warm," said Rebecca. "Did I mention that I think I might have a heart murmur?"

This obliged Scott to examine her heart. As he put his stethoscope over her chest, she pulled back her gown, revealing a nipple. Scott glanced at it, noticing it was pink, erect, and perfectly shaped. He felt a bit disoriented. Aroused and intrigued, he nevertheless did his best to remain neutral.

"I've also been having some stomach pain, right down in this area," said Rebecca, pointing to the left-lower quadrant of her abdomen. Scott pressed on her abdomen. "Yes," Rebecca said. "Right down there. When you touch it, it makes it feel better."

As he was leaning over her, she reached her right hand and rubbed his crotch. He knew that he should have pulled away immediately and left the room, but he lingered.

"I thought I could tell you liked me," said Rebecca skillfully.

Scott stepped back and noticed a wet spot in the crotch of his scrubs. He quickly covered it by pulling over his white lab coat.

Scott tried to ignore what had transpired. "Well, I expect you will do well in surgery tomorrow. You seem to be in excellent health." He tried to fashion a clean exit.

Before he could leave, he heard footsteps at the door. Another young woman burst into the room. She looked at Scott and then at Rebecca, who was lying on the bed with her breast still exposed.

"What's going on here?" asked the new woman. She glared at Scott. "What kind of doctor are you? What kind of hospital is this? Why are you here so late? What are you doing to my friend?"

"I'm just doing her physical. I was just leaving." Scott dashed out the door.

The women looked at one another and burst out laughing.

"Oh my God," said Rebecca. "Lindsey, that was perfect! Did you see the look on his face? I think you gave him a heart attack."

"It was kind of perfect timing," said Lindsey. "How did it go with you?"

"Perfect. Couldn't have been better. I even think my knee is miraculously healed. I'll bet I can cancel that surgery and go home tomorrow morning."

Scott paced the hospital's hallways, trying to put distance between him and what had happened. "Never again will I be alone in a room like that," he thought. He couldn't understand why he had felt so paralyzed. Why didn't he leave at the first sign that things were not proper? If he had, he would have been reprimanded for not doing the physical. How was he supposed to know when the patient was crazy? Had he really done anything wrong? After all, he completed the physical. He never responded to any of her flirtations.

Back in the on-call room, he stared at the picture of his family. Everything was so confusing. He hoped Rebecca would be discharged tomorrow, and that would be the end of it.

CHAPTER 38

As he drove into the driveway of his rented house, Anthony Sam noticed the flag was up on the mailbox. Tied to the base of it was a small piece of black fabric.

'Good," he thought. "Finally, some action."

He lived for action. He had gone through high school barely being noticed. Too small to be athletic, too ordinary to be academic, not good-looking enough to be a ladies' man—he had been a plain guy walking invisibly through the halls. After graduating, he had joined the US Army and served in the Middle East. It had been the first time in his life he felt important. He remembered the first time he shot a man. After all his training, he found it rather easy. He had been able to sleep well that night without any reflective thought. He looked forward to his next opportunity.

When he had returned from overseas, no other job satisfied him. All jobs were boring and unimportant. How could anything else in life compare to the significance of sighting an enemy, pulling the trigger, and killing another human? By comparison, everything else was bland. Ending another human's life was the most powerful, thrilling thing he had ever done. His high school counselors had often told him to find his passion. So, he had. He wanted to be the best killer.

He had transplanted his battlefield mentality into his new work. After all, if warfare were an extension of diplomacy, then selective killings were an extension of business negotiation. There were good people, and there were bad people. The good people were the ones who paid him, whereas the bad people were the ones who became his targets. Bad people had earned their fate through their own actions. Their fate was sealed, if not by him then by someone else. Perhaps someone with less skill would take his place.

Anthony looked at the black fabric. He smiled, thinking of the opportunity in front of him. He would be removing an obstacle. Progress would occur. It was not too much unlike tearing down an old building so that a new structure could take its place. First came the demolition and then the reconstruction. In a short period, demolition would be forgotten, and the new structure would be celebrated.

It was a particularly warm spring day in Biddeford as Dr. V. T. Roberti worked in his garden. He figured it was time to plant the summer bulbs so he would have flowers throughout the season. He had a new idea that he kept secret from his wife; it would be a fun surprise.

As he worked, his thoughts turned to Anton Thresher, as they often did. The meeting with Roger Allard from Avenger Pharmaceuticals could not come quickly enough. The new phase of the study had begun, Anton was stretched beyond thin. Because Todd Freeze had been transferred, Anton was doing all the orange fern infusions himself. This madness had to end. V. T. knew Anton had done enough. It was time to take him off his island and bring him home.

He looked up to see his wife bringing him some iced tea. "You should really take a break, V. T. You've been out here for hours."

"Gardening gives me energy. I feel eternally young with my hands in the soil."

"If you don't take a break, your hands will be in the soil along with the rest of you for a very long time."

V. T. stood up and kissed his wife on the cheek. They walked together to the Adirondack chairs placed strategically next to the garden. The spring sun was full on them as they sat next to one another.

"I feel tired, Pat. For the first time, I feel like taking a sabbatical."

"You certainly have earned it, V. T. Where would you like to go?"

"Italy."

"Where in Italy?"

"Southern Italy. A small town near where my family came from. You and I will rent a villa for the entire year. Each morning, we will get up and wander into town for a cup of coffee at the café. There, we will think about what we will have for dinner that evening. We will have nothing but time. Over our morning coffee, we will think about what wine we will have with our evening dinner."

"And what of Anton?"

"It's time to bring him in from the cold. It is my fault he is out there by himself. I should never have launched him in that direction."

"You launched each other. The work you have done together is brilliant and could not have been done any other way. You two have done all you can. Roger Allard is a good man. He will help you complete this project."

V. T. took a sip of his iced tea and then extended his head back toward the sun. He closed his eyes. The orange glow filled his vision behind his eyelids. He remembered when he used to feel full of energy. Those times had been full of excitement and innocence. He thought it was always better to dream of projects than actually do them. Philosophy was a flight of the mind. Putting a vision into action was a grind. Yes, that sabbatical would feel good, but only if Anton were all right.

"I'm going to head into town for a few hours to do the shopping," Pat said. "When I come back, I'll prepare a special meal. Just be sure you haven't gotten too attached to the dirt."

Anthony Sam waited fifteen minutes after he saw the car pull out. He wanted to make sure that Mrs. Roberti didn't happen to forget something and double back. The rental car that he had was sufficiently nondescript.

The greeting was one of the parts he liked best.

"Can I help you?" V. T. asked when he saw Anthony at his door.

Anthony knew this was the most critical moment. He had to win enough confidence to get inside the house. The rest would be easy. Part of this job involved being a good actor and looking innocent and harmless.

"Dr. Roberti? Hi, I'm Anthony Sam. I'm here to talk to you about the research that you and Anton Thresher are doing."

V. T. looked startled and was about to say something.

"It's OK, I know all about it. You see, Anton is in some trouble, and I thought I could help. I have gotten to know him through my work at Portland Medical Center. May I come in?"

V. T. stood at the door for a moment, confused and uncertain about what to do next. Whoever this person was knew a lot of detail about Anton and about the research. He seemed genuine. V. T. needed to know whatever information he had.

"What did you say your name was, boy?"

"Anthony. Anthony Sam. I work in the chemistry lab at Portland Medical Center. That's how I got to know Anton. I know about the research. He told me about it one night when we were both working late. I'm worried about him. Some of the people at the hospital are starting to become suspicious."

"Come in." V. T. looked outside the door after Anthony entered to be sure no one else had observed him. He led his guest into his living room.

Having the knowledge that this would be the last conversation V. T. Roberti would ever have thrilled Anthony. He liked the moment when his target became aware that he was about to die. He liked the look of panic in his target's eyes—the desperation, the fear. It gave him a thrill. He had the power to take life. It was almost godlike.

Anthony fumbled in his pocket for something as V. T. sat down. Just as V. T. sat, Anthony reached out and slapped him forcefully on the shoulder.

"Well, old man, how do you think it's all going to end?" Anthony's polite voice had turned harsh. "Do you think your boy Thresher wins a Nobel Prize and becomes celebrated for his genius? Or do you think he'll go to prison for assault and battery, having violated patients without their knowledge?" His question had a gleeful tone, as if he knew the answer to a riddle and was enjoying watching the other party struggle to figure it out.

V. T. had felt a sting on his shoulder when Anthony had slapped him. Now, he began to feel drowsy.

"That's right, old man. Getting tired, aren't you? You see, I know all about your research project. I've been sent here by OncogenX to make sure that your meeting with Allard and Thresher never takes place. You see, they want that formula for themselves. It turns out that the two of you have actually produced something of value. We just don't think that you should keep it to yourselves, so we're going to take it from you for the good of mankind."

V. T. opened his mouth and attempted to speak, but no words came out.

"That's right, you don't even have the power to scream for help. That thing you felt on your shoulder might be the last sensation you'll have in this life, my friend. Right now, you are losing control of all muscle power. In a few minutes, I will give you a drug that will sclerose the arteries in your heart, giving you a fatal heart attack. When they do your autopsy, if they even bother, you will look like another old man with heart disease dying of natural causes. I will be long gone, and your wife will find you sitting in the chair, dead. The meeting with Allard will never happen. We will get Thresher next, get the formula, and do the right thing. You see, Dr. Roberti, this is the price you pay for going off the grid and doing things your way instead of the proper way."

V. T. noticed he was having difficulty breathing. He tried to move his arms, but they wouldn't respond. He could still think, and he could still pray. There was no drug that could disrupt the most important activities of his life. He knew that his life could now be measured in minutes.

V. T. knew every life on Earth would eventually come to an end at some time, and he knew this was his time. Strangely, he had a deep sense of peace and acceptance. He was even grateful for this brief interlude, a moment of reflection before he left his earthly vessel to take on a greater presence. By virtue of his presence, the mere fact that Anthony Sam had been sent to kill him validated the significance and importance of the work that he and Anton had done together.

He knew that his wife would be OK. They had talked about the phase of life where there would be only one of them. He was glad that he was leaving first. He was reflecting on what heaven would be like. It was almost exciting knowing that he would be there in a few minutes. He felt like a kid on Christmas Eve. A smile came over his face.

"What the fuck are you smiling about, old man? You're about to die. You're about to feel searing pain through your chest. You won't be able to breathe, you will die in your chair, and your wife will be a sad widow. Then, I will see to it that your protégé is destroyed and your research amounts to nothing except for glory for us."

It was as if V. T. could not hear anything Anthony was saying, even though Anthony knew his hearing was perfectly intact. V. T.'s smile deepened, annoying Anthony further.

"Stop smiling at me, you sick bastard." Anthony got up as if to strike him in the face but then realized that he didn't want to leave a mark. "Damn it!" He struggled to contain his anger. "You're about to die. Doesn't that scare you? How about if I told you I could stop it from happening? Would you beg me to spare your life?"

V. T. kept smiling, and utter peace overcame his entire face. Anthony had never seen anything like this. He wanted to crush V. T.'s skull and make him wince in pain. But he could not lay a hand on him. He took the heart attack drug out of his pocket and gave a vigorous spray up V. T.'s nose. There would not even be a needle mark. "It's minutes now, you old fuck! I'm going to watch you gasp for life, and then I'm going to piss on your dead corpse!"

V. T. was in the room and someplace else at the same time. Anticipatory joy swept over him. A strange surge of strength and energy flowed through him. He stood up and looked directly at Anthony. "Everything is happening the way it is supposed to. You don't know it, my friend, but you are a tool in the hands of God. Your service will not go unnoticed."

Anthony backed away from him. He was trembling in fear, not sure if he should run or beat V. T. to death. He couldn't leave any trace.

"What are you, some kind of freak? You're not human! Why aren't you dead?"

"Because I will never die. And you're right, I used to be an Earth human, but that part of my life is over."

V. T. smiled more broadly and leaned in toward Anthony.

"You see, my friend, in my new life, I will not have any limits. I will be given powers beyond your imagination."

Then, V. T. walked over to the sunroom and sat in his favorite chair. "Your work here is finished. I think you best leave now. I have a feeling you'll be seeing me again."

V. T. closed his eyes—no thrashing, no clutching his chest, no sign of pain. Anthony was dumbfounded, wondering if this was all a ruse. Maybe they gave him a placebo. Maybe Cliff had set him up. He never had trusted Cliff.

A few minutes passed. Anthony watched carefully to see if V. T. would move again. He walked carefully toward him and leaned in. There was no sign of breathing. Anthony walked backward out of the room, keeping an eye on V. T., afraid to turn his back on him for fear that he would suddenly spring up from his chair.

He looked down at his own hand and noticed it was trembling and white. His forehead was sweaty. He got into his rental car and drove away.

CHAPTER 39

D r. Proctor dispensed with the formal greetings. "Do you have any idea why you are here?" he asked Scott.

Scott sat uncomfortably in his chair while looking around the room. Dr. Proctor sat at his office desk, with Scott directly across from him. No one else was in the room.

Scott had been pulled from his rotation that morning and asked to go to Dr. Proctor's office. He had no previous warning that a meeting would take place.

"No, sir."

"Does the name 'Rebecca Klinger' mean anything to you?"

Scott felt the blood leave his face. "She's the woman I did a history and physical on the other night."

"Did anything unusual happen during that exam?"

Did the doctor know? What had Rebecca said? Scott's brain was spinning. He had done nothing. All he did was the physical. She was the one who had been out of line. His heart was racing. He thought of Ann. He thought of his father.

"I did her physical, and that's all."

"Was anyone in the room with you during the physical?"

"No."

"Why not? This was a physical on a young woman. Why didn't you ask for a chaperone?"

"It was a routine physical. There was nothing about it that would've required a chaperone."

After a moment of silence, Dr. Proctor continued. "Scott, the patient is threatening to file a formal complaint against you for sexual assault. She claims that you assaulted her by fondling her breasts and pressing your penis against her."

"That's a lie! She's the one who acted out. All I wanted to do was complete her exam and get out of there. She's the one who was making innuendos."

"There was a witness. And there was physical evidence: semen on her underwear. She gave us the underwear. We can have it tested if we need to."

Scott lowered his head, and his eyes filled with tears. "I didn't do it. You have to believe me. She is lying. I didn't touch her."

"Look, Scott, I believe you. I think this girl is a cheap whore looking for a quick buck. But these facts, Scott, are damning. The fact is, you are on probation. You should have been more careful. If this complaint comes forward, your career will be over. Hell, you could face criminal charges. Jail time."

The effect was what Dr. Proctor had been hoping for. Scott's head hung low. He was broken. Every dream he had was vanquished. It was perfect.

"Look, Scott, I think I can help you. The only people who know about this are me and you."

Scott looked up, puzzled. Why would Dr. Proctor want to help him? He thought he hated him after Scott had punched out his son.

"At times like this, we need to stick together," said Dr. Proctor. "These lunatics are trying to do anything they can to tear down doctors and damage medicine as we know it. Look, I think I can help you. But we need your help, too."

"I don't understand. What help do you need from me?"

"The hospital has become aware of the clandestine research that Anton Thresher has been doing. You know, Scott, his methods are unethical. He is violating medical principles and jeopardizing patients. Despite that, the results have been intriguing. We want to help Anton. The problem is...well, you know Anton. I don't think he would let us near him. His research has merit, and we need to bring it into the mainstream, get it out of the shadows. What we need from you is to find out what exactly the formula is that he's putting into our patients. If we can get that information, we can move this research forward in a way to help patients."

"You want me to spy on Anton?"

"Not spy, help us protect patients. Help us get the information we need. Consider it research."

"What happens to Anton?"

"Look, nobody wants to hurt Anton. Quite frankly, we don't care about him. We just need to get the formula and the process he uses to make it. With that information, Anton will not be important. We can leave him alone to go about his business. He keeps his career and his license. No consequence will come to him. He can go about his private business."

Scott felt his fear and shame turning to anger. "So that's what this is all about. You set me up to get at Anton. You think I'm stupid? I'm not going to sell out my friend."

Dr. Proctor had been restraining his temper and trying to act considerate, even though he thought Scott Antonelli was a greasy Guinea with no business being a doctor. His tactic of empathy seemed to be failing.

"Fine," he said. "Go down in flames with your lunatic friend. Maybe the two of you will be cellmates. If this girl comes forward, you're fucked. No career, you will never practice medicine. You'll be facing criminal charges. She has a witness. She has physical evidence. You've got nothing. You got a history of erratic behavior. You're on probation for hitting Wally. Nobody's going to believe you. Go home and convince Ann that you were not dry humping this woman during your physical. Explain away your semen on her underwear. Good luck with all of that. See how long your marriage lasts. See how long your life lasts. And all for what? So you can help Thresher continue his illegal research? Who gets helped by that? Look, Scott, don't be foolish. Your friend is brilliant but is going off the rails. He's on an island. You know his behavior is not normal. You will be doing him a favor. He needs to get off this treadmill, and he doesn't know how. We will not hurt him. I promise you that. The formula will go on to help millions of people. You have a chance to be a hero. Be somebody who makes a difference—a positive difference. Don't be foolish. If you work with me, this can be a life-changing moment. If you don't, your career and your life as you know it will be over."

Scott was staring into space. "Anton doesn't get hurt. He keeps his license. You do him no harm."

"I promise you, nothing happens to Anton."

"I've seen him. He's not the same as he was. He looks tired and worn down. I think you're right. This is getting to him."

"Of course it's getting to him. You're doing him a favor by getting this burden off his back."

"Nobody gets hurt. If I can get this formula for you, my probation goes away. This complaint goes away. Nobody gets hurt."

"Nobody gets hurt, I promise you."

"What if I can't do it? What if I can't get that formula?"

"You must get it. Everything depends on it. I can make this complaint go away, or I can make it come back just as easily. Think of your father. It would kill him to see you go up in flames. Think of him visiting you in prison. This is your only way out. You get to save yourself, you get to help advance medicine, and you get to help your friend get out from under the burden he has created for himself. You will be celebrated for your work in this field. Your future will be one as an honored pioneer in medicine. Scott, don't be stupid. The options are stark: prison, professional shame, or professional glory and all the benefits that go with it. You and Ann will live in luxury. Your father will bask in your glory. You know we will get that formula one way or the other, with or without your help."

Scott closed his eyes and drew in a deep breath. Relief and dread struggled inside him.

At dinner that night, Scott sat quietly across from Ann.

"You seem so pensive," she said.

Scott smiled. "What do you think of Anton?"

"Why, he's one of your best friends."

"I know, but what do you think of him?"

"He's a bit...unusual. You know, I wondered about him as Scott Junior's godfather. He doesn't seem very religious."

"Do you think he's a good man?"

"Well, he certainly is brilliant. And I've never known him to do anything bad. He's just hard to figure out. So quiet. I just wish he were more—I don't know—normal. You know what I mean? I mean, why can't he be happy being a doctor? Find a girl? I mean, a normal girl, not that odd waitress friend of his. I don't know. He's your friend and all, but he's so strange."

"Strange. Yes, I suppose he is."

"Your father called and was wondering if we could go down there Sunday for an afternoon meal."

Right now, nothing seemed better than that. Scott liked nothing more than basking in the admiration of Ann and his father.

He reached across the table and held Ann's hand. "You know, I will do anything to keep this family safe."

"I know, Scott. I know you will."

After dinner, Scott went to the desk in the bedroom, where he was preparing for the next day's work by reviewing medical literature. Ann was clearing the table. He could hear the clanking of dishes and the running of water.

Scott texted to Anton. "Meet me in the cafeteria, 6:00 a.m. for breakfast. Important thoughts to discuss."

Anton stood in front of the large window of his apartment. The sun was shining directly through it. His eyes were closed as he felt the sun warm his skin. He felt as if he could leave his body. Tilting his head up, he felt as if he could leave Earth entirely.

V. T. had left explicit instructions. There was no funeral or formal memorial service. He was buried in a quiet, private ceremony. Anton was one of a handful of invited guests. V. T. had even written his own eulogy. After the ceremony, Pat handed Anton a sealed envelope. The handwriting was V. T.'s: "To Anton Thresher in the event of my untimely death."

"I don't know what's in it," Pat said. "I've known about it for some time now. V. T. wanted me to hand this to you at this moment."

Anton took the envelope and put it in his pocket.

Later that day was a small reception at the Robertis' house. Pat served hot coffee and homemade croissants. If Anton closed his eyes, he could imagine hearing V. T. calling out to him. His presence was everywhere to be felt.

"Look at what he did," Pat said. "I wondered what he was so fervently planting. He would not let me help him. I thought he was up to something." She smiled.

V. T. had built the small garden up to a slight embankment. The hyacinths were in full bloom. From where Pat and Anton stood, the purple flowers spelled out the word *love* in capital letters. After that, the white hyacinths spelled out *vt*. Together, Pat and Anton wandered around the back yard. They stood, looking at the line of trees in the back that had so often been the focus of V. T.'s gaze. It felt like sacred ground. Neither wanted to leave, but the sun was setting. They walked back to the house.

CHAPTER 40

Anton was reflecting on that moment in V. T.'s garden as he stood in front of the window of his apartment. He had no clear path, as well as jumbled ambition and scattered hope. The beginning had been so clear. Now, the next step was uncertain.

His reflection was broken by the shuffling sound of Todd moving in the kitchen.

"It's best not to mourn on an empty stomach," Todd said as he brought some scrambled eggs and bacon into the living room. He and Anton had reclaimed their living space ever since Anton had moved the lab into a warehouse a few blocks away. The money that Mary had given them went to good use. They were capable of producing much more product more efficiently.

They ate in silence.

"You know that V. T. wants us to continue," said Todd.

"I know. I'm just not sure how."

"It might be time to blow it up."

"What do you mean?"

"Look, we have no legitimate path forward. We're so outside of the line that any attempt to crawl back in will expose us. Our enemies will pick our bones. We should hold a huge press conference. All our data, all our research—roll it right out there, full confession. We will be hated by everybody in medicine but loved by everybody on Facebook. We will lose our license but become famous. You promote the cure. Let the public deal with the consequences."

"Suppose they send us to jail."

"What, send two garage tinkerers to jail for curing cancer? It'll never happen. If it does, we will be in for only a few years. We'll come out more famous than ever. Besides that, chicks dig political prisoners. We'll be VIPs wherever we go for the rest of our lives!"

Anton smiled. "How in the world would you survive prison without women?"

"Two words: conjugal visits."

"You know, Todd, you might have something there." Anton looked pensively into the distance.

"What, the conjugal visits? I don't expect that to work well for you, Thresh. Despite your godlike attributes, you haven't had much success in the environment of abundant, free women."

Anton smiled. In all of Todd's irreverent ramblings, every now and then he came up with an idea of merit.

"I mean the press," Anton said. "I think you are right. When we're ready, we go to the press. We can't trust the corporations, they will sell us out. We need to get this directly to the people. We're so close. I just need to figure out the final steps. Make it better. Make it easier. So close. I need to get out of Portland for a few days."

Possessed by a new idea and endowed with sudden energy and direction, Anton stood up from the table, went to his room, and started to load up his backpack with clothes and supplies for several days.

"They won't miss me on the rotation. I'll text Dale and let him know I need some time to gather myself before I start up again."

"Where are you heading?" asked Todd.

"I'm not sure. Maybe Biddeford. I need to be alone for a while. So close. I can feel it; it's right there. I need to get out of here."

A light wind was at Anton's back. The late-morning sun had warmed the pavement, and he could feel the heat rising from the street. He churned faster on his bike, with his blood surging through his legs. Cruising at top speed, he was in his element. He liked to pedal so hard that his legs were on fire. He liked to imagine that no one else was capable of tolerating that degree of pain. Pushing harder, he could feel his mind being washed clean. Sweet pain purged every thought. So close. He knew that if he could empty his mind, his path would be made clear. Without a preconceived plan, he headed south on Route 1 toward Biddeford. He was drawn to the docks and knew this area well, for he would run by here frequently when he was in medical school. He liked to watch the sun coming up over the ocean as the clammers and lobstermen headed out in their small boats. It reminded him of his high school days back in East Greenwich when he had worked summers digging clams off a small skiff.

He stopped now and folded his arms as he stood on a ridge overlooking the docks. The clammers were beginning to return after a day's work. He could hear them yelling to one another, friendly profanity punctuated by laughter. Anton had never known a better job—no boss and no worries, other than the direction of the wind and the tide, the size of the waves, and the daily catch.

He was not sure how long he had been standing there. A cool breeze woke him from his trance, and he noticed he was hungry. He rode his bike over to the Biddeford Motel and checked in. He didn't want anybody to know he was here.

The next day, he awoke before sunrise because he knew the clammers liked to leave early. He paced about the docks, watching as they arrived. It was easy to convince one of them to rent his boat for the day. Anton offered triple the clammer's daily earnings in cash. The man whose skiff he was renting had a sturdy face that projected honesty.

"Never had anybody want to rent my boat before," he said. "Are you sure you know what you are doing?"

"Yes. I spent years on the water."

"I never heard of anybody digging clams for sport. You

ain't got no better way to spend your day?"

Anton smiled. He offered to give the man his wallet with his license and credit card as collateral, but the man declined.

A slight chop was on the water. When the boat was at full speed, it would bounce over the waves, kicking up water that would occasionally hit him in the face. It felt good. After about thirty minutes at full speed, he arrived at the clam beds. He turned off his engine, picked up his anchor, and tossed it off the portside. Anton needed only a few minutes to put together the long pole referred to as the "stale." With a mighty throw, he launched the rake into the water and watched as it drifted to the bottom. The handle was in a *T* shape and was attached to the stale so that he could grab the handle with both hands. With a couple of thrusts, he could feel the teeth digging into the bottom. The wind was light enough that he was able to control his drift with the rake alone.

He could feel the teeth of the rake hitting a thick area of clams. It made a distinct sound, unmistakable in its tone. The thrill of the catch surged his adrenaline as he pulled on the stale, bringing the rake to the surface. He could see it packed with clams. Success! How strange something so simple, so small should make him so happy. He grabbed the rope to the anchor, pulled his boat back over the same bed he had just harvested, and threw his rake into the water. Another big hit. Another quick pull of the rope. Pull, rake, lift, dump the catch, then repeat. He paused only to drink his water and wipe his sweat with a towel. As with riding his bike, the intensity of the activity cleansed his brain.

Now, his mind began to run over the details of his research. The chemical reactions, the treatments—what could be made better? In the monotony of his clam-harvesting work, his mind was released. The formulas floated in his brain and came together in new arrangements. His consciousness summoned techniques that he hadn't conceived before. So close. He knew where he wanted to go. Somehow, it begin to coalesce. Then, he saw it so clearly that he wondered what had taken so long.

"That's it!" he said outloud to no one.

He pulled out a notebook and pen, tied the rope off to the cleat so that his boat would not drift, and began writing furiously. When he was finished, he broke down his stale into its components, secured it to the boat, pulled up the anchor, and was off back to the docks.

He was back on his bicycle by 1:00 p.m. The ride to Portland would take only about an hour, which he thought was perfect. He took his old route back to the campus and felt like a ghost as he rode around. Where once he had known everybody, now they were all strangers. It all felt so long ago. He walked into the anatomy lab and looked at the spot where Dr. V. T. Roberti used to stand. Anton imagined him playing his trombone, and he smiled. He rode past the Robertis' house, just to look at it. He didn't even slow down. Next, he went to Mary's Country Store and Deli. He stopped just outside the building, guided his bike to the side of the road, got off the bike, and stood holding it. He could see shapes of people moving on the other side of the window. He could tell one of the shapes was Lisa; there was no mistaking her movements. After a while, he became self-conscious. Suppose someone saw him? How long had he been standing here anyhow? Suppose she looked out the window and directly at him? Would he be compelled to go to her? He knew that in his backpack he had written down notes that would change the world. The knowledge had been given to him, deposited in his brain as if out of nowhere, as if by the hand of God. His divine mission lay before him. He got on his bike and headed north.

CHAPTER 41

Dale Davis had ridden his bike over to Anton's laboratory. "Fuckin' A, would you look at this place. Fucking Superman's got it going on."

He was one of the few people Anton trusted. Of late, Dale had been rotating at another hospital and had returned to Portland only within the past week. The next phase of the study was nearing its conclusion. The early results were even better than the last phase. Just by their clinical appearance, patients were thriving. The hospital was buzzing with anticipation at the expected results. Anton had wanted to gather Dale and his other closest friends to help strategize the next step in the process. In addition to Dale, Ben Able, Todd Freeze, and Scott Antonelli were all at the laboratory that day. Todd had returned the past week after completing his rotation in Rhode Island.

The laboratory was set up in an old mill building. Brick walls, concrete floor, and arched windows that flooded the space with sunlight gave it the feel of the 1800s. Well-organized benches were set up throughout the room. A sterile hood for mixing intravenous ingredients dominated one end, and the constant whir of the fan's filter provided a soothing white noise backdrop. Anton insisted on doing all the work himself. He allowed Scott to help deliver the end product, but no one except Anton knew of the entire process. This was by design.

Anton had divided the group of patients into two cohorts. To one cohort, he allowed Scott to deliver intravenous product. To the other, Anton himself had delivered the oral capsules that he had recently made with the new formulation created after his return from Biddeford. No one knew there was an oral component to the protocol. In addition to delivering the formula, Scott and Anton took blood samples from patients that they would process themselves at Anton's lab. All the cancer markers in the blood had been declining back to normal. Just as importantly, there were no signs of any harm being done by either the intravenous therapy or the oral therapy.

The men sat around the table as Anton began the conversation.

"In a few weeks, the final round of imaging and lab testing will be performed. The results undoubtedly will be overwhelmingly positive."

"It's going to be a motherfucking frenzy," said Dale. "I can just see that pompous jackass Proctor, eyes glowing, standing in front of microphones, and announcing his brilliance to the world."

"This is going to be very tricky," said Ben. "We've got to get our message out before the official announcement. Once that happens, it's going to be difficult for us to attract attention. The hospital, the medical community, and OncogenX will attempt to discredit us. I have kept copious notes documenting every step of my process. They are all locked up in my greenhouse. When we get scrutinized, I will be able to validate our statements with detailed facts."

Scott had been nervously looking around the lab. He was under enormous pressure from Dr. Proctor. They were reaching the end of the research protocol, but Scott had yet to acquire the information needed. He had taken photographs of every square inch of the laboratory and recorded as much about the process as he could, but he had not acquired the detailed knowledge of the formulation and how to create it. In the early phases of the protocol, it was easy for him to forget what his ultimate mission was. He had enjoyed the sense of renewed friendship with Anton. He had witnessed the benefit coming to the patients as they regained energy. As the deadline was approaching, he became more distant, short tempered, and irritable at home and distracted on his rotations. His career, perhaps even his life, depended on his success.

"How about we just try to approach them?" Scott asked hopefully. "I mean, make a meeting with Proctor and the representatives from OncogenX. Tell them what we've done. I mean, they would be motivated to work with you, Anton, if they know that their protocol doesn't work but your treatment does. Wouldn't they want to make you part of the team?"

Todd snorted. "Sure, no doubt they would immediately promote him to head of research and give him full creative control over the process. There is nothing pharmaceutical companies like better than inexpensive treatments that completely cure a disease."

"Oh, Scott," Dale said. "Scott, my naive friend. They would quickly kick Anton to the curb and convert his research into a convoluted, chronic maintenance therapy to maximize profit. Nobody in the cancer industry actually has a sincere desire to obliterate cancer. They would all be out of work."

"I wish it were that simple," said Anton somberly. "But it only gets worse from the perspective of the pharmaceutical company."

"What do you mean?" asked Ben.

"Ben, the oral formulation actually worked. I've been using it throughout this protocol. Those capsules are working just as good as the intravenous treatment."

A silence fell over the room. Nobody moved. For a while, nobody spoke.

Anton continued. "I've even started to give it to other patients on the cancer ward who are not in the protocol. People with end-stage lung cancer or prostate cancer and people on hospice care have shown signs of improved vitality."

Another silent pause ensued.

"Fuckin' A," Dale said. "You mean to tell me that this plant is going to cure cancer, all of it?"

"It's too early to say that, but it just might," said Anton.

"You realize, gentleman, that as a natural substance, this

plant extract may not be patentable," said Ben.

"What difference does that make?" asked Scott. "Wouldn't OncogenX be happy to bring such a product to market? That would make billions."

"No, they would make nothing," Ben said. "The product would be available over the counter. People could buy it the way they buy vitamin C."

There was another round of silence.

"Can you imagine the unintended consequences?" asked Scott. "Think of all the hospitals, all the research, all the surgeons, and all the people put out of work. The economic effect could be devastating."

"Think of all the lives saved," Anton said. "No, Scott, there's no debate here. There's no uncertainty about how to move forward. We press on. That is why we need to control the process. There's no guarantee what they will do with it if they get their hands on it. Just like you said, Scott, it could destroy their wealth at the same time it cures cancer. I don't want to bet on the corporation doing the right thing if it means their financial ruin."

Todd spoke up. "I have an old girlfriend who is friends with a reporter, Stacy McCoy, from the *Boston Globe*. I've already reached out to her. Anton and I have a meeting set up with her this Saturday. Ben, I would like you to come with us. We need to be credible if we are going to get our story out."

"See, Freeze, I always knew your hose-bag ways would come to good someday," said Dale.

"Look, men, this is gut-check time," said Ben. "There's no telling what will happen next. Our reputations, our careers, and even our lives can be at risk when this news is released. Do not underestimate the potential that this disruption can have and the extent to which those who would be harmed by it will go to prevent us from succeeding. If anybody at this table is not prepared to pledge their reputation, their livelihood, and their life to this mission, it's better to leave now."

Ben paused and looked at each man individually. Nobody

moved.

"How about you, Scott?" Ben asked. "You have a family. Are you ready for this?"

"This work is too important to abandon. We have to complete the job," Scott said.

"Freeze?" Ben looked at Todd.

"Really, you have to ask?"

Ben and the others smiled.

"This is too much goddamned fun to get off the train now," said Dale. "I'm in."

Todd broke the tension. "Well, then, I think we should toast to our inevitable success." He got up, went over to one of the drawers beneath the bench, and pulled out a bottle of Southern Comfort along with glasses for everybody. He poured a round. "Alcohol alone moves the wheels of science!" He held his glass in the air. "No great innovation ever came from a clear-thinking man. To scrambled neurological pathways leading to brilliant insights!"

The glasses clinked. Everyone drank.

The evening unfolded into light banter until it was time for everyone to head out. Scott lingered as the others left before him. Todd had poured himself another round.

"You know, Anton," Scott said. "I've been thinking that it may be a good idea to share your formula with me and Todd. I mean, the whole thing depends on you. Suppose something happens. All your work and all your research could be lost. You know I will stand by you. I won't let any harm come to you. They will have to go through me to get at you. I'm not afraid to kill someone to protect you."

Anton knew that Scott was not speaking metaphorically.

"I know, Scott." He knew that his moment was at hand. Although he had prepared for it, it did not make it any easier. He had prepared two detailed folders and each one contained a paper file and an electronic file. He handed one folder to Scott and the other to Todd.

"If anything happens to me, this is everything that you

need to know to manufacture the treatment of the intravenous form. You need to swear to me that you will not compromise the work. You must keep it pure."

"Purity is my middle name," said Todd, smiling. Anton smiled, too. He had no doubts that Todd would never wobble.

"What about the oral form?" asked Scott.

"I haven't put all that info together yet, but once I do, I will pass it along. OK, let's continue our work and be prepared."

"Do you want me to come with you to speak with the reporter?" asked Scott.

"No, I will be all set with Todd and Ben."

"Well, I'm going to get back home. My wife will be waiting for me." Scott embraced Anton and kissed him on the cheek. "I think you are a great man. A great man. Everything will be OK, I promise." He clutched the folder and dashed out the door.

Todd and Anton sat at the table. Todd poured them each another glass.

"All it takes is a room full of committed people to change the world," said Anton. "I think we have the right team. I don't think anything can stop us. We have a great team, and we have truth on our side."

Todd nodded. "That reporter will be critical to our success. We need her to be like an investigator. Maybe I should seduce her—you know, make her knees buckle and have her do my bidding to gain sexual favors from me."

"I thought you said that alcohol turns the wheels of science."

"That is true, but sex turns the wheels of journalism. Come to think of it, alcohol and sex can lubricate just about any human endeavor."

Anton smiled. He could feel the end was coming and was glad to have Todd by his side.

CHAPTER 42

S tacy McCoy had been working at the *Boston Globe* for over twenty years. Despite her longevity, she had just turned forty. She began working for the paper right out of high school, first in customer service and then as a volunteer reporter. Currently, she was one of their leading investigative reporters. Nobody in the newsroom was more respected. Two Pulitzer Prizes and an untiring work ethic separated her from her peers. At one point, she was going to night school to get her degree, but she gave it up as her career took off and time vanished. She had given commencement addresses and been awarded honorary degrees. Somehow, though, they felt hollow. She intended to finish her academic work someday.

Her day began at 4:00 a.m. with three double espressos and an unfiltered European cigarette. She often said the best part of the day was the sunrise. Her favorite attire was a pinpoint oxford shirt with a contrasting tie. Every now and then, she would wear a dress just to keep everybody off balance.

When once asked what her sexual orientation was, she responded, "I prefer humans." When pressed, she turned to her inquisitor. "Why don't you fuck me and find out for yourself? It's none of your goddamned business." No one ever raised the issue again.

Before she agreed to take the meeting with Anton, she performed exhaustive research on him, Ben Able, Portland Medical Center, the research protocol, and anything else she could acquire relevant to the topic. She did not schedule meetings very lightly. She would spend time only on worthwhile people and topics.

Stacy had advised Todd Freeze to be at least five minutes early to the meeting. She had a reputation for being devastatingly on time, and if a person didn't reciprocate her punctuality, the meeting would be canceled before it began.

Now, Stacy looked directly at Anton. "OK, boys, you got about ten minutes. Tell me what you got." She spoke bluntly, as usual.

Anton regarded her silently, still not convinced that he could trust anybody. Todd broke the silence. "Well, about four years ago, Anton began studying a process—"

"Cut out the preliminaries. I know about you guys. I know about the study at Portland Medical. I know that OncogenX is about to announce a major breakthrough in cancer research and that somehow the three of you have something relevant to share with me. Please get to your point."

"We believe we have found a cure for cancer," said Anton. "We found a natural product that we've been giving to patients who are in the Portland study without their knowledge. It is the natural product that they have been getting from us that is leading to the great results reported in Portland. The outcomes have nothing to do with the drug the pharmaceutical company is giving them. We can prove this fact."

Stacy sighed. "Do you have any idea how many loony bats have claimed to have found a cure for cancer in the past month alone? You better have a lot of goddamned meat on the bones and share it with me right now, or this meeting is about to end."

Ben Able cleared his throat. "I have summarized the results from our study and our lab. Here is a summary of the cultivation process for the orange fern. I've included in this summary the extraction process that Anton has developed and the formula that we have been giving the patients. It includes the sequential lab results and the lab testing that can prove that the orange fern kills cancer. I've also included the outcomes from the other centers where the same cancer drug was being given to patients without the orange fern extract with no clinical benefit. This is real. The report that will come out of Portland has the potential to mislead the public and set cancer research back decades. We need your help to get out the truth."

"Let me get this straight." Stacy tapped a finger on the table. "You, Dr. Thresher, took it upon yourself to design a drug intended to cure cancer. And rather than go through the usual research process, you decided to take a shortcut and start giving it to patients without their knowledge or consent. And the other two of you aided and abetted this entire process." She looked at each man. Todd averted his eyes and shuffled his feet. Anton stared back at her.

"The protocol at Portland Medical would've killed them," he said. "If we had waited, people would've died unnecessarily. We cannot trust the pharmaceutical industry with this information. They would destroy it and sacrifice patient outcomes for profit."

"So, the three of you rebels decided that it was better to break every known ethical and legal boundary with regard to patient care to deliver this rogue product."

Anton could feel his anger rising. "No. We broke every business protocol and antiquated, petrified barrier to innovation in order to save patients from a toxic treatment and give them a chance to live in the face of an inevitably fatal illness. We are not the ones out of line. It is the medical establishment that sacrifices patients for profit."

"Are you suggesting, Dr. Thresher, that these good and noble men and women—researchers of the highest caliber—could be influenced by money?"

"What I know for sure is that you can always count on people to act in their own best financial interest. Anything else is uncertain. It is a rare man who would sacrifice himself for the good of others."

"And I suppose, Dr. Thresher, that you are that man—that you are a savior, and everybody else is corrupt. Is that about it? Is that what you think? Do you want me to run this story and risk my professional reputation so I can promote your orange fern product?"

"Yes, that is exactly what I would like you to do," Anton said sternly.

"The three of you realize, of course, that you'll be arrested and prosecuted and likely spend a long time in jail because of your transgressions once the story becomes public. There will be no parade and no celebration of your genius."

"Just because something is true doesn't mean it will be accepted," Anton said. "That, however, does not absolve us of the need to report what we have discovered."

"So, the three of you are all prepared to face the consequences of the story being reported?" Stacy looked at each of them slowly. "You realize that I am not your friend. I am not your marketing agent. I'm a goddamned investigative reporter, and I will tear through you to get down to the molecular structure of truth. I'm going to report what I find, all of it, without bias. I don't give a shit if the three of you rot in prison. The truth will be reported. I don't care who gets mud in his face, and I don't care who gets glory. You have your calling, gentlemen, and I have mine. I will demand full access to everything in your possession—every note, every detail. If I sense you are misleading me in any way, I will crush you with no remorse. You realize that at this point, you've already crossed the line. The story is now mine to do with as I please. You can cooperate or not cooperate; my path will not be altered."

"Good," Anton said with confidence. "That is exactly what we want."

Todd had sat upright at this point, inspired by Anton's confidence. "Prison, no prison, it doesn't matter to me. This must be reported."

Stacy looked up and Ben, who nodded.

Stacy leaned over to her intercom. "Tabatha, cancel the rest of my day. I'm gonna be with these gentlemen for a while. And send in Bubba Mohr. Tell him to bring his camera."

By the time Anton, Ben, and Todd had left, it was well toward evening. Stacy and Bubba Mohr sat across from one another in her office. They regarded each other in silence.

"Holy shit," said Bubba.

"Yeah."

Jeff Turner, their editor, walked into the room. "Tell me, was it worth killing your entire day for these three characters?"

"Jeff, I think I'm about to win my third Pulitzer Prize. We need to move fast. I need you to clear my schedule for the next two weeks and give me an open budget."

"That big?"

"Probably the biggest story our paper has ever done. We need to keep this very, very quiet. Nobody should know what I am doing except for the three of us. This is going to be explosive."

"Sounds like your kind of story," said Jeff with a smile.

CHAPTER 43

D
r. Tara Lidoffi began her Catholic confession. "Bless me, Father, for I have sinned…"

She and Father Bob Earps were sitting comfortably across from one another, as if having an afternoon chat over coffee. Some Catholics embraced this new format, whereas others were repelled. But it was the setting in which Dr. Lidoffi felt the most comfortable. After all, she had been meeting like this with her parish priest for many years. She no longer thought of him as an authoritarian figure but as a trusted friend. Father Bob had studied at Providence College and had a graduate degree from Boston College. He was the type of priest who led with his heart more than his doctrine. She knew she could trust him.

"Father, I'm facing a huge dilemma with my company."

Father Bob nodded. "What is it, Tara?"

"My company is on the verge of announcing a major advance in cancer research. The product we will bring to the market has the potential to save many thousands of lives."

"But?"

"But we have acquired some of the information through less-than-savory means. We discovered that a rogue medical resident was instilling our patients with a substance he had created. It turns out the substance is more likely responsible for their benefit than our drug. We know he is doing it, and we will acquire the formula for the drug that he is instilling in our patients. My company is planning to integrate his formula into our treatment. To avoid having to go through another ten years of FDA testing, we intend to do this without informing anyone of the alteration in the basic formula. We also plan to neutralize the physician who is performing the clandestine—and, I might add, illegal—activities."

"I see," said Father Bob. "There's a dilemma between a greater good to be served and the means used to get there. May I ask what exactly do you mean by *neutralize?*"

"Render him harmless by eliminating his capacity to report his findings."

"Oh, so you're not talking about having him killed?" Father Bob chuckled.

Dr. Lidoffi chuckled as well. "We are a company, not the Mafia. I'm just not sure that I'm doing the right thing. How can I be fair to my company and to the patients this product can help yet be fair with the doctor whose discovery we are using?"

"You know, Tara, the affairs of men are not the affairs of God. Sometimes, earthly law, virtue, and morality don't fully align with the will of God. It is not an accident that you find yourself in the position you are in. These affairs have been set into motion by the will of God. The ultimate outcome will be based on his will. He's not bound by earthly concepts of morality and righteousness. If you are not violating the Commandments, if you are acting in your best conscious, then you can feel confident that God will use you to perform his will. Perhaps going to this individual and trying to bring him into your process would help clarify your path. If you offer him a way out of the secretive box he has created for himself, you will have given him a chance to come clean. If he takes advantage of it, your dilemma will be solved. If he doesn't, your path will be clearer."

With Father Bob's words fresh in her mind, Dr. Lidoffi walked into the emergency meeting of her advisory group. Cliff Doherty and Javier Torres were there. Dr. Proctor was wired in on the speakerphone.

"Is everybody there?" Dr. Proctor asked after Dr. Lidoffi entered the room.

"We are all here, Proctor," said Cliff. "You called this meeting. Tell us what's going on."

"We've got it. We've got the formula, the entire production process, and everything that we need. Antonelli came through with flying colors."

Everybody around the table smiled broadly. "That's great news, Walter," said Dr. Lidoffi.

"Um, there is one slight hitch," Dr. Proctor said. "It turns out that Thresher has created an oral form of the drug. He's been using it on our patients in this latest phase of the study. It looks like it's working just as well as the IV formula."

"That should not matter," said Cliff. "We have the formula now, so we can do whatever we want with it."

"Well, Antonelli hasn't gotten the formula for the oral form."

Silence fell around the table. Then, Cliff shouted. "Well, tell him to get the goddamned formula tomorrow! These results are going to be reported in a couple of weeks. We don't have time to fuck around."

"He has tried. Thresher won't let go of it, certainly not in time for our needs."

"It doesn't matter," said Dr. Lidoffi. "We have the formula. We have all we need. It's time to close the books on Thresher and his misguided pack of criminals. We need to bring the study home and get this product to market."

"Yeah, but there is one more complication," said Dr. Proctor. "Thresher has been talking to Stacy McCoy from the *Boston Globe*. It looks like she's interested in reporting his story. His story will claim it's his supplement and not our drug that is helping patients."

Cliff slammed his fist on the table. "Fuck. We've got to move fast. We have people at the *Globe*. We should be able to take care of this."

"Yeah, we have people," said Dr. Lidoffi. "But Stacy McCoy is not one of them. We are not dealing with a piker. She has the potential to be a major adversary. This could unravel quickly. We need to contain the spread of information immediately and get our report out first. Thanks for the update, Walter. I want you to sit tight for now. Don't say or do anything. We will still plan our press conference after the results have been officially reviewed. We should have all these other details resolved by then."

Dr. Proctor signed off from the conference, and Dr. Lidoffi turned to Cliff and Javier. "I don't care how it happens, and I do not want to know the details, but you need to make a plan to eliminate the possibility of this information getting into the public domain. I'm going to make a trip up to Portland and have a conversation with Thresher."

"What?" Javier and Cliff asked simultaneously.

"At this point, we have nothing to lose. My conversation will be between Thresher and me and include no one else. If we can bring him in, all our problems will be solved. If we can't, then you will need to solve them. I'm leaving this afternoon. I want you to be prepared for action within forty-eight hours, but don't do anything until you get my word."

CHAPTER 44

Ann was concerned. "Scott? Scott, are you coming up to tuck in Scott Junior? He's waiting for you."

First, it had started with an occasional vodka while he was studying. Lately, Scott had retreated to his study immediately upon coming home from his rotation and told Ann he wasn't to be disturbed because he was busy studying. He would typically get in four or five glasses of vodka before going to bed.

"I can't, Ann. I've got too much to do. Tuck him in for me. Give him a kiss for me."

Scott had his books open in front of him. Somehow, it made him feel better as he stared into space. It had been only a couple of weeks since he had handed over the formula to Dr. Proctor. Scott had once again made him repeat his promise that he would not harm Anton. Dr. Proctor had given him verbal reassurance and congratulated him for doing the right thing.

"Your friend has lost control. He is on a dangerous path, Scott. You've done the right thing. What you've done will help him and millions of patients. Sometimes, doing the right thing means hurting people you love. You'll see. This is for his own good and the good of all mankind. Your act is one of courage."

If only Scott could believe him. The study protocol had been completed. All the patients looked robust, and lab testing and clinical observations all pointed toward a great outcome. All that was left was the final imaging, it's interpretation, and then the press conference to follow. Scott's name had been added to the primary investigators of the study. They were able to insert him retroactively into each phase of the research without raising any suspicion. They needed to create a linear story, a rational basis for him to be involved. He would be their link to the orange fern as an ingredient in the formula. OncogenX had already suspended all the other branches of the study to eliminate any perception of inconsistencies.

Scott came out from his room. His glass was empty. He walked over to the cabinet, opened the door, and prepared to pour himself another glass.

Ann sat at the kitchen table. Scott had not noticed her as he walked in.

"Scott, please stop. Just stop," she said in a weak voice, tears streaming down her face. "What's happening to you? What's happening to our family?"

"Nothing. Nothing's happening. This time, it's just...it's just very hard. I can stop whenever I want. It just helps calm me, helps me focus. I have so much on my mind."

Scott stopped before pouring the next glass, put the cap back on the bottle, and placed it in the cabinet. He took a deep breath and then sat at the table across from Ann. "What would you think if I decided not to be a doctor?"

"What? Don't be ridiculous, Scott. We haven't worked this hard to give it all up! What else would you do? How would we make any money? What about Scott Junior? What kind of life would he have?"

"I don't know. Sometimes, I wonder. It hasn't been what I expected. I thought it would be all good, helping people. Ann, I want to feel good every day I come home."

"Look around you, Scott You have a wife who loves you and a beautiful child, and you come home to a beautiful meal and a clean house every night. Your future is guaranteed. What more does a man need to be happy?"

"I don't know, Ann. I wish I knew. I'm trying to find it."

"You're not going to find it at the bottom of that glass."

"I know, I know." A pause ensued. "Ann, there is something I need to tell you."

Ann's thoughts raced ahead of Scott's words. Was it a

nurse at the hospital? Maybe it was a drug rep. How she had dreaded this moment!

"I've been deeply involved in a study at the hospital. The results are going to be released soon. My name will be mentioned prominently. I had to keep this from you because the study was top secret."

Ann sighed deeply. She didn't care what else he had to say, as long as it wasn't what she thought he was going to say. "Scott, that is fantastic!"

Scott sat up a bit straighter in the chair, getting a sense of purpose. "Yes. Yes, it is. In fact, I am one of the lead researchers in the study. My name will be featured as one of the primary investigators."

"Scott, that's great news! I had no idea you were so involved in research."

"I had to keep it from you. I hope you don't mind."

"Of course not. Your business is your business. I'll always support you, no matter what you're doing."

"Well, the company that commissioned the study wants me to be part of their board. And, if this drug performs the way we expect it to, this opportunity could represent millions to us."

The word reverberated in her brain. *Millions*. Every dream she ever had suddenly flooded her thoughts. She stood up, walked over to her husband, sat on his lap, wrapped her arms around his neck, and kissed him passionately on the lips.

"So, this is what's been troubling you so much, holding this information back from me?" She held his face between her hands and looked him in the eye. "Scott, you precious man. How I love you. I knew I could count on you to do the right thing for our family."

Ann got up and whispered in his ear. "I'm going to freshen up and change. I'll only be a minute. Come meet me in the bedroom." She kissed him on the temple and walked off.

Scott's moment of feeling good vanished the minute she left the room. The room fell silent and dark. His lie had taken on another dimension. Ann thought he was a hero. He stood up, walked over to the cabinet, opened the bottle, poured a drink, and drank it in one swallow. He held the empty glass in the air. "To you, Anton, you motherfucking genius." He poured another shot, drank it, and then went into the bedroom.

CHAPTER 45

L isa packed her bags full of her essential items, hopped in her car, and started to drive north toward Portland. Once on the highway, it occurred to her that she had no plan, only a desire to see Anton. Actually, the desire was more of a need. She had called Todd and asked for his help. He knew how to keep a secret.

"Anton goes to the lab every day after his rotation ends," Todd had told her. "You can count on him being there. I hope it works out. I always thought Anton was a fool for walking away from you. By the way, any chance you can bring a friend with you?"

Lisa smiled and shook her head as the conversation ended. It was nice to know that some things didn't change.

Her decision had formed the day after she talked with Mary. Joe was a fine catch, but why couldn't Lisa shake the feelings she had for Anton? Joe was good looking, had a good sense of humor, and was on a path toward a great career. He wanted to get much closer than she did, talking about things like commitments and the long term. When he did, Lisa would listen to him as if she were watching TV. She noted what he was saying but didn't think it applied to her.

"I don't know, Mary. The earth just doesn't move when Joe touches me. Does that make any sense? Nothing moves."

Mary sighed. "Oh, you poor darling. I remember that earth-moving feeling. It happened with my first husband. I never felt anything like it again. I guess you could say it ruined me for all other men. I never realized how important it was to me until it was no longer there. When the earth moves, it either horrifies you or entices you. Either you run away from it, or you can never leave it. The lucky ones never feel the earth move at all. Their life goes on without a ripple. The few of us who can't live without it are destined for a painful life."

"I would rather feel pain than nothing," said Lisa.

"I know. Then you have to abandon reason and go to Anton."

Lisa was now on the outskirts of Portland. She supposed that her life had come to following a man who offered her no chance of any material gain but made the earth move under her feet. She wanted that feeling more than life itself and was willing to risk anything to get it. After all, what had the world offered her besides a cold shoulder and an apron?

As usual, Anton entered the lab, thinking about the task at hand and with his head down. He looked up and stopped. Lisa was sitting on the floor in the middle of the lab. She had set up a blanket underneath her. The late-afternoon sun was streaming in through the large windows, striking her long hair and giving it multihued highlights. He froze.

"Lisa," he said. It was more a reflex than a question, akin to a probe to ensure he was not seeing an apparition.

"Sit down, Anton." Lisa gestured to a chair that was set up to one side of the blanket.

Her manner was so assertive, and Anton was so unsettled, that he followed her command without hesitation.

"Anton, do you trust me?"

"Yes," he said immediately, perhaps not knowing until that moment how thoroughly he believed his answer.

"There are some things I would like to say, but it is hard for me. This way works better for me." Lisa got up and walked over to him. She had a scarf with her that she wrapped around his eyes and tied behind his head. "I want you to hear me and feel me, but I cannot look at you," she said in his ear. She then unbuttoned his shirt and took it off him. Standing behind him, she began to massage his neck and shoulders. She could feel his sculpted body relax under her hands. She then took off his shoes and socks and began a deep massage to his feet.

"When I was with you in Hopedale, I felt more peace than at any point in my life," she said. "All I wanted was for that moment to never end. Then, the world fell on us. I tried to forget you. The more I tried, the more thoughts of you grew in my mind. We belong together. The world cannot hold us. The world does not understand us; it doesn't have to." She stood up and kissed his neck. The room was slowly darkening as the evening shadows grew long. Lisa sat on his lap and faced him while she took off her shirt and then her bra. She took his hand in hers and put it on her breasts. After doing this, she ran her hands over his back while kissing his chest. His perfect body was the way she remembered it.

She reached behind him and took off his blindfold. The room had darkened enough to give her comfort. "Anton, I love you." Before he could speak, she put her index finger to his lips. "Don't speak. I know you love me."

They kissed. She leaned back and looked directly in his eyes. They were burning with desire. Or was that her desire being reflected? Did it even matter? She was trembling. Anton wrapped his arms under her and stood up, holding her close to him as she wrapped her legs around his waist. Then, he lowered her to the blanket.

Somewhere in that moment, every cut they had ever felt, every doubt they had ever possessed, and every wound that had ever been opened within them became a point of connection. One thousand points touched as they entangled their bodies and their lives. They were complete.

The sun had set, plunging the room into darkness. Tomorrow, the sun would rise on a different world.

CHAPTER 46

S tacy McCoy met with Anton on the warm outdoor patio attached to the coffee shop. She was already in midday form at 6:00 a.m. "Thresher, it's a good thing I like you. Otherwise, I would've been gone. How dare you make me wait. You know how I hate that. Sit down, Galileo. We've got a lot to cover and not much time."

She had taken to calling Anton "Galileo" as a way to acknowledge his lonely pursuit of truth. The more she researched, the more she grew to admire the impressive work that he had performed. Everything about him was checking out. The laboratory results showed the death of cancer cells. She studied the clinical results in the patients who received his orange fern derivative and compared them with those who hadn't. She also noted the curious way the company had shut down the other arms of the study.

"This is about to get very public," she said. "I have submitted a Freedom of Information Act request to seek all the internal memos and notes from OncogenX. We will find something incriminating. Someone on the inside knows an awful lot and is feeling very bad about it right now. All we need is enough public pressure, and they will turn."

"Will your paper publish this story?" Anton asked.

"Hell yes! My editor has given me full support. However, we need a strong basis. We are trying to take down a king. If we swing and miss, we will be executed. I'm not sure I even mean that metaphorically. Certainly, they will try to assassinate our careers. Anton, you have to understand how things can go when billions of dollars are at stake. Your life and the lives of your friends are all in jeopardy."

"I have known that since I started. Everybody with me is in all the way."

"I wouldn't be so sure. Money and fear can make people do strange things, even people you thought you could trust."

"Not my people."

"Maybe not. Maybe I'm just an old, cynical reporter. I've seen it too many times to believe it's an isolated phenomenon."

"What about you, Stacy? What about your life and your risk?"

"You can't be great in my field without abandoning fear of consequence. I crossed that line a long time ago. I live for these kinds of moments. Besides, it's hard for them to get at me. I have so many connections that it would raise profound suspicion and likely backfire on them."

Stacy took a long, slow drag on her dark-brown cigarette, snuffed the base out in the ashtray, and then threw back the remnant of her third espresso. "They are planning a press conference for two weeks from today. I'm waiting on a few more documents, but so far, everything you said has checked out. We're planning on running our story next week, one week before their scheduled press conference. If everything works out, the topic of their conference will pivot from bragging about their study results to explaining what has happened. Anton, I admire you. But you have to understand that it is very likely you will be arrested. I suggest you and your friends contact an attorney and be prepared for criminal proceedings. I will do my best to advocate for you, but there's no telling how the public and the courts are going to react."

Anton sipped his coffee. Stacy wondered how he could be so calm. His world was about to unravel, and yet he seemed happy.

"This is what I've been looking forward to," said Anton. "This is what I have been living for. Our path is fixed. All that is left is for us to walk it."

People were already starting to call the treatment the "Portland Miracle." The final results wouldn't be released for another two weeks, just before the press conference, but patients and their families could tell. Dr. Proctor's office was flooded with letters of thanks and gratitude. The Internet was starting to heat up with testimonials. The switchboard at Portland[CE246] Medical Center was jammed every day with desperate patients looking for the next opportunity. Calls were starting to come in from newspapers around the country, wanting to know more about what was going on. Morning report was growing in attendance every day. The energy around the hospital was palpable.

"Fuckin' A, can you believe this place?" asked Dale. He was sitting at lunch with Anton, Todd, and Scott.

"Yeah, I can't wait for the reaction the day after Stacy's story hits the front page," said Todd.

"None of you have to make the final walk with me," Anton said. "You've all gone beyond what any friend could be expected to do. No one has to know that anybody other than me administered the substance to these patients. They have no way of knowing who administered the substance. I will take full blame."

"The hell you will," said Todd. "And steal all my status as an outlaw rebel? You're going to ruin my street cred."

"This is no joke, Todd," Scott said. "You could be facing some serious criminal charges, assault and battery among them."

"Well, if I'm facing them, aren't you, too?"

For a moment, Scott had forgotten to shield his immune status. He shot rapid glances at his friends. "Well, uh, of course I am. It's just that...well—"

Dale cut him off. "Damn it, Antonelli. We're all in this together. Remember that night at the lab? We pledged our reputations, our fortunes, and even our lives. Well, this is the moment of truth. If the motherfuckers want to take us down, let them take us down together. Let them try putting us in jail for curing cancer. We will win this fight eight days a week. Fuck you, Anton, if you think you're gonna cut me and Freeze out at this point. Blame, my ass. I fully intend the march back to Arkansas dipped in glory! My boys back home know truth when they see it and know bullshit when they smell it. After this all breaks, I might not have to buy another round of whiskey for the rest of my life."

Scott tried to save face. "No, no, I'm in it with you guys. Really. I was just thinking that maybe it would be safer to—"

"Hey, bro," Todd said. "We left 'safe' behind at the starting line a couple of years ago. The best thing to do now is to walk proud and talk loud about what we have done. All those people with cancer went home to their families thanks to what we've done. That has to count for something."

Anton was on a rotation in dermatology. After lunch, he returned to the clinic, where he was preparing to see patients. The secretary informed him that Dr. Proctor had asked him to report to his office. When Anton walked into the office, the doctor and a woman were sitting at the table across from the empty chair they offered to him.

"Anton, this is Dr. Tara Lidoffi. She is from OncogenX. Her company, as you may know, has been very involved with the study at Portland Medical."

Dr. Lidoffi stood up, smiled broadly, and shook Anton's hand with great enthusiasm. "I've heard so much about you, Anton. It's a pleasure to finally meet you. Walter, could you leave us alone, please?"

Dr. Proctor left quietly.

Anton sat in the chair. He hadn't responded to Dr. Lidoffi's laudatory greeting, and his expression was blank.

"Dr. Thresher, I respect your intelligence. I know you are far too insightful not to have surmised why I am here, so I will get right to the point. OncogenX has been aware of the infusions you have been doing to the patients at Portland Medical. We are also aware of your offsite laboratory, your cultivation center in Hopedale, your lab at the warehouse in Portland, and all the research that you have done with orange fern."

Anton did his best to remain impassive, but questions were building in his mind. How could they have so much information?

"Anton, we are very impressed with you, the quality of your work, and the commitment to your cause. Quite frankly, the fight against cancer needs brilliant minds like yours. Now, your techniques are a bit unconventional. Some people would say that the ethics and legality of your methods are in question. I am not here to debate that aspect of it. I am here on behalf of the patients whom we both can serve together by collaborating in the pursuit of a cure for cancer."

Dr. Lidoffi paused and did her best to read Anton's body language for a sign about the impact she was making. He seemed to relax ever so slightly. Perhaps she was having some success.

"How did you get so much information, and what do you have in mind?" he asked.

"With regard to your first question, I am not at liberty to disclose all the means by which we acquired our information. Suffice it to say that your results were remarkable enough to have generated a lot of attention. Of course, it's incumbent on us to be knowledgeable about every aspect of the patients in our cohort. We spared no expense in our scrutiny of what was happening here at Portland Medical. As to your second question, I am here to offer you a leadership role at OncogenX in the fight against cancer. You will be put in charge of your own division. You'll be given a budget that you'll have full control over —complete creative freedom. Anton, I respect your maverick nature and the creative impulses that go with it, but think of how much more you can do with all the power and resources of OncogenX behind you. You can devote your energy full time to this pursuit. No more running around trying to get raw materials and hiding your activities. You can have a full staff, with as many bench researchers as you need. It is amazing what you've done with scant resources. Imagine what you can do given all the resources of OncogenX."

"And what is it that OncogenX wants?"

"Control and stability. Anton, if we impose too radical a change on the medical establishment, who knows what could happen. Creative disruption is welcomed as long as it is not so seismic that it would rip apart the infrastructure that has taken generations to construct. Yes, we need to bring this research to the patients, but we need to do it in a controlled manner with proper research and development."

"With proper attention to long-term profitability," Anton said.

"Look, Anton, there's a right way and a wrong way to go about bringing innovation to market. Don't you see that I'm on your side? I don't need to be here right now. There are people back in New York who think I'm wasting my time. They want your head on a platter, and they have the means to do it. I think that would be a horrible waste. I admire you, Anton. I admire your work and your commitment. I think we can work together."

"And what if the research leads us to an inexpensive, widely available nutritional supplement that would have the power to prevent cancer? What if that supplement turned out not to be a drug?"

"Dr. Thresher, you've got to be realistic. Do you really think we can sprinkle paprika on our food and dance through life without disease? How would we ever control those results? How would we know what dose, frequency, or whatever was working?"

"We wouldn't care about any of that as long as the disease was resolved."

"Don't be a fool, Anton. Can't you see I'm trying to save you? Join us, and we can get this product to help patients right away. Who knows what will happen in the future. Things need to evolve."

"No, truth needs to be acknowledged. People dying from cancer don't have time to wait for evolution. The current system will swallow this research and corrupt it to satisfy their needs. The machine will win, and patients will lose. Nothing would change. We don't need evolution; we need a revolution. The system needs to be torn down."

"You realize the position you are in, don't you? I have the power to prevent you, Todd Freeze, Dale Davis, and even your girlfriend, Lisa, from living a life of misery. If you're simply reasonable, you'll be basking in wealth and glory. Hell, you could win a Nobel Prize! Damn it, Anton, there's nothing wrong with living well. Don't be so stubborn."

"Your definition of *misery* and my definition are quite different. Some of the most miserable people I have known live in wealth and glory. You think you have power, but you have none. Do with us what you will. We are the ones who will be at peace. Can you say the same about yourself?"

Anton stood up and walked toward the door. As he went to open it, Dr. Lidoffi made one last attempt.

"Dr. Thresher, if you walk out the door, your life as you know it will be over. You and your friends will be broken, imprisoned, and shamed. Is that how you imagined your life ending?"

Anton opened the door and walked out.

Dr. Lidoffi stared at the door. For a moment, she had thought she could get him. She sighed deeply, pulled out her phone, and called Cliff. "Anton rejected my offer. Take care of business."

CHAPTER 47

T he job had become more lucrative than Anthony Sam could ever have imagined. There was enough money to be made for him to retire. He had always dreamed of a place on the Pacific coast in Mexico. He could live like a king. Women there were cheap. He could have one each night. But doing this work was so much fun! What would replace the thrill? These thoughts ran through his head as he began the final sequence. He could feel his skin tingle in anticipation. A sense of power surged through him as he imagined what was to come next.

The greenhouse was so easy to enter. Security was non-existent. The foolish target operated under the illusion that no-body was watching. As Anthony inspected the premises, he concluded his target was a rank amateur. All the guy's notes were on paper! There would be no trace.

He heard a car arrive. "Right on schedule," Anthony said to himself. "Not only does the fool have no security, but he has a very predictable routine."

Ben Able entered the greenhouse, turned on the light, walked to his desk, and sat down, as was his usual routine. He had not noticed Anthony, who had positioned himself in the shadows behind the desk. Anthony thought this would be as easy as shooting fish in a barrel, although he would still enjoy administering the drug and watching him die.

He approached Ben from behind and slapped his neck with a substance that immediately created a burning sensation. Ben turned quickly to face Anthony, rubbing his neck,

"What the—"

Only then did he notice that Anthony was pointing a gun directly at him. Ben didn't move as Anthony walked toward the front of the desk, grabbed a chair, and set it directly across from Ben, maintaining eye contact and keeping the gun on him the whole time.

"I promise not to shoot you, as long as you don't move."

Ben sat forward, his hands folded in front of him. "Who are you? What do you want?"

"Consider me a friend to mankind. What I want is for you and your sick friends to stop fucking with people and ruining things. You all think you're so goddamned smart. How smart do you feel right now?"

Ben began to feel weak. "What did you put on my neck?"

"I'm sorry, but that is a trade secret. See, how does it feel to have somebody give you a drug you don't know about, didn't ask for, and didn't even want? How's it feel having a taste of your own medicine?"

Anthony needed a few more minutes for the drug to fully immobilize his victim. There would be that wonderful interval during which the victim would be incapable of movement but fully conscious and awake. Anthony watched him closely. He noted muscle twitching. He stood up and raised his hand as if to slap Ben in the face. Ben didn't move to defend himself. Anthony smiled, for he knew the drug was working.

"See how that feels? You can't move, you can't even speak, but you can hear me clearly. You can see me and watch what happens next." Anthony walked around the greenhouse with a spray bottle containing an accelerant that was impossible to detect. Amateurs used gasoline or lighter fluid. There was no way the fire department could accurately determine this accelerant. It would look like a natural fire, the result of Ben Able's experimentation gone wrong.

"In a few minutes, your entire greenhouse will be ashes. They will find you burnt within those ashes. But enough of you will remain to determine that you died of natural causes. A heart attack is about to occur within you, the result of the drug

I've given you. Genius, isn't it?" Anthony looked at Ben to make sure he was still weak.

"Now, look at what I'm doing." Anthony set up some of Ben's lab equipment. "I'm creating the basis for the fire. Your sloppy technique will have led to this fire and to your death. They will discover you were part of a meth ring. They will never know that I murdered you. Genius, isn't it? Yet I don't really consider this a murder. I'm doing this to protect mankind from your terrorism. I'm not a murderer; I am a superhero, a noble vigilante. Oh, by the way, did I mention how well I'm being paid? It might flatter you to know that you're miserable life is worth well over three million dollars."

Anthony saw Ben's eyes close and his head slump on the desk. Anthony felt sad. Somehow, this didn't satisfy him. He walked over to Ben's body, took out his gun, and pointed it right at his head. Ah! How he longed for the good old days. There was nothing quite like putting a bullet in somebody's head. Such power and satisfaction. He put his gun down. "I guess this fire will have to do," he thought aloud.

He opened the door to ensure his escape, struck a match, tossed it in, and watched the flames begin to build. He would be able to linger for a few minutes to watch his handiwork and be sure that everything worked according to his plan. He would want to leave before people started to arrive. He drove away, thinking about a place in Mexico. He could hear the sirens in the distance as his car left the scene.

"So far, so good," he thought. The first part of his mission had gone easier than he thought. The next would be more challenging. Silencing Stacy McCoy had been deemed so important to the mission's objective that Anthony was given full latitude to use "any means necessary."

What he knew was that he had permission to shoot her in the head. The mere thought of it sent ripples of excitement through his veins. "Anytime you get to shoot a liberal, lesbian bitch in the head is a good day," he thought. Although he had been given carte blanche to deal with Stacy as he saw fit, there was a premium placed on not killing her. Shooting her would net $1 million, but disabling her would be worth $5 million —far more money than he had ever made in the past. After he combined that money with the cash from Able and added the money owed to him after he took care of Thresher, this night would net him close to $12 million. He had already received a $1 million advance. "Who says hard work and dedication don't pay off anymore in America?" he thought.

As was her habit, Stacy stopped by Frank's Irish Pub for a pint or two after finishing her workday. Anthony had placed a tracking mechanism on her car so he could tell where she was. Cliff Doherty had supplied him with a drug that would have the desired effect. If Anthony could somehow get it into her, he would be able to collect his $5 million, but he would not get the joy of shooting her in the head. He liked to think about what other thrills $4 million could buy him. It made him feel better about bypassing the opportunity.

He positioned himself at a table within sight of Stacy. He ordered a beer and some potato skins and made himself look inconspicuous. Cliff had given him careful instructions not to let the toxic substance touch his skin in any amount. It was a slow-acting neurotoxin that could cause irreversible, catastrophic brain damage. Cliff didn't care if Stacy was dead, so long as she didn't speak again. The toxin would take hours to have its effect, giving Cliff and Anthony time to create a cover that would eliminate suspicion.

Stacy ordered another pint and was staring at her phone's screen while sipping her beer. It was a perfect opening for Anthony. He got up to approach her just as another woman walked up to her, put her arm around her shoulder, bent over, kissed her on the cheek, and sat next to her. "Disgusting lesbians," thought Anthony. "And that girlfriend of hers is so young! Disgusting predator. Maybe I can get them both."

It wasn't hard for him to get the valet to point out the new girl's car. Anthony was amazed what people would do for $100.

In no time, he popped the hood and manipulated the engine just enough. She would now need to get a ride home from somebody, probably from Stacy. "Buy one, get one free," he thought as he headed back into the pub.

By now, the place was filling up. This would make his job easier. People were standing directly behind Stacy and her girl-friend in the bar area. With one gloved hand, he reached into his pocket, took the cap off the substance, squeezed some out of the tube and on his gloved finger, and walked toward Stacy. He faked a stumble and reached out, rubbing the substance into her neck. "Excuse me, I'm so sorry," he said as he walked away.

He left the pub, got into his car, and waited. He could not leave until he had confirmation of success.

Back in the pub, Stacy was starting to feel tired. "I don't know what hit me, but I think I should be heading home soon."

"Aunt Stacy, why don't you let me drive you? You look awful. Really, it's on my way back to my apartment." Rita Cote was in her fourth year at Boston University. She had come to Boston from her home in New Jersey to study journalism. She always admired her aunt as a role model and made time to meet her on occasion in the city to get caught up. When Rita's car wouldn't start, they decided to take Stacy's.

Anthony sat watching from his vehicle. "Perfect," he thought as he watched the two women climb into the car. But then he noticed that it was the younger one who would be the driver, not his intended victim. "Fuck!" he yelled, and he started to run the options through his mind.

Without the car accident, there would be questions about what happened to Stacy McCoy. Why was her brain so damaged? He needed the accident to create cover. The plan had been to instill the drug to ensure the outcome. If the crash killed her, fine. If it didn't, her brain would be damaged beyond recovery, and she would never be able to speak coherently again. The plan was designed to be fail safe. "Well, I guess this is where I earn my money."

He knew the route that they would take to Stacy's house.

He knew the choke points. He planned to pull alongside the car, shoot the driver, and hope for the intended accident to occur. But what about the money? Suppose Cliff tried to screw him out of his money, claiming that he resorted to shooting? Technically, he would not have shot the target, but he didn't trust Cliff to be fair. Suddenly, another plan dawned on him. He smiled at his own cleverness.

He settled in behind the car and followed it to Stacy's apartment. He waited as the driver assisted her up the stairs and into the apartment building. In a few minutes, the driver reappeared, hopped in the car, and drove away. Anthony prided himself on being a professional. He came prepared for many contingencies. He grabbed a kit from the backseat of his car and went to let himself in the apartment. When he opened the door, he saw Stacy lying on her couch, asleep. He took out a needle and syringe and a vial of a clear substance.

He was an expert in dosing and administration. The right amount would leave a significant finding during the toxicology but wouldn't be enough to kill her. Cliff and the team had preferred Stacy to be in a persistent vegetative state rather than dead, for they thought it would eliminate any possibility of a murder investigation. Anthony's new plan was to inject heroin directly into her vein. It would be enough to explain the brain damage, especially when combined with alcohol, and perhaps expose her as a closet addict.

Anthony wrapped the tourniquet around her arm, found her vein, and easily pushed the drug and a small dose of the alcohol tincture. He then sat and monitored her vital signs for the next thirty minutes to ensure that she wouldn't die. He had a dose of Narcan ready in case things didn't go as he had planned. Professionals were always prepared.

When he was satisfied that his work was done, he left her apartment. She would spend the rest of her life hospitalized with a feeding tube, unable to speak until she finally died. "Serves her right," Anthony thought. "It's people like her who ruin the fabric of society."

CHAPTER 48

Anton was in the lab when he took the call from Todd, who was back at the apartment. Anton stood with the phone in his hand as he stared out the window.

"I spoke to Mr. Carlisle," Todd said from his end. "It's a total loss. They're saying it was triggered by sloppy laboratory practices. Anton, Ben Able died in the fire."

Anton closed his eyes for a moment. "They won't stop with Ben. Todd, they will come after us. We can't wait. We need to act now and get our story out before we no longer have the ability to do it."

"I'm ahead of you, boss. I sent Dale over to Stacy McCoy's. He'll head over to our apartment after he meets with her. Our plan is to have an emergency newsbreak tomorrow. Where's Lisa?"

"Back in Biddeford."

"Do you think she is safe?"

"I don't know. Maybe they'll be satisfied by just getting me. Maybe I should go to them. Perhaps that would put an end to this."

"Are you fucking crazy? I didn't follow you all this way to have your knees buckle. We knew they would come after us. Fuck them all. If you think of quitting now, you won't have to worry about them. I will be the one to put a bullet in your head."

Anton smiled. It was the response he had been hoping for.

Back at the apartment, Anton and Todd sat at the table, strategizing their next move.

Anton spoke out loud as if addressing himself, but Todd

listened. "We know they will not stop here. And we know they will act quickly. We have to consider their options. One, they could try to kill us all. A bit sloppy and difficult to execute, but it's something we must consider. Two, they could ignore us and plow forward with their own announcement. We would be left trying to react to it, looking like the lunatic fringe, screaming to the world that this was really our discovery that they stole from us. Of course, that runs the risk of them underestimating our abilities and us winning the public-relations war."

"Or they could just get us arrested and defrocked," Todd said. "Mr. Carlisle told me that the initial investigation of the fire site demonstrated evidence of a meth lab. They're framing us."

Without knocking, Dale burst into the room. "Fuckin' A, Stacy McCoy's in the hospital in a coma."

"Son of a bitch!" Todd said.

"I got as much information from the nurses I could. They're saying it's from a drug-and-alcohol overdose and that she has permanent brain damage."

"Bullshit. The motherfuckers got to her," Todd said.

Anton put his hands behind his head. "This means they're more likely to attempt framing us. They want to cut off our ability to respond. Stacy was working in such secrecy that there's nobody at the *Globe* who can corroborate our story."

The three men sat silently at the table, too stunned to feel emotion and too stressed to consider mourning, not sure what to do next.

"We need to call Lisa," said Anton.

As always, Lisa picked up the instant she saw Anton's name on her phone. She listened impassively as Anton described the series of events. Whereas some people developed anxiety after facing trauma, others became more resilient. Lisa fell into the latter category.

"We think you may be targeted next," Anton said. "We will be there in just over an hour."

"I'll leave the door open for you," said Lisa.

"Maybe you should go to Mary's place. It might be safer there."

"No, better not to entangle more people. I'll be fine here." Her voice was so confident and strong that Anton was not inclined to argue the point.

Anthony Sam headed north toward Biddeford. "This one will be the most fun," he thought. He had been given free license to do whatever he wanted. As long as his targets were silenced, his sponsors would be satisfied with his work. He had his kit with him. Lisa would be just another statistic, another youthful drug addict dying from an overdose. Nobody would care. Nobody would research her. He was thinking about how he could amuse himself with her. The thought of having her tied up, bound, and gagged while he raped her was especially enticing to him. He moved in his seat behind the steering wheel, adjusting his position to accommodate his erection.

He arrived at Lisa's apartment prepared for any contingency. He had tracked her and her friends all along and knew that she was in her apartment. He also knew that Anton and Todd were on their way to Biddeford. Based on his calculations, they were approximately one hour away. "Plenty of time to have some fun before they get here," he thought. He reflected on the convenience of having them come to him. How unfortunate it would be that they would have all succumbed to the same bad batch of heroin. Closet drug addicts and friends in life, their death would be a morality play of what not to do. By killing them all, Anthony was probably saving hundreds of lives. How many impressionable young minds would read about the tragedy and turn away from experimenting with drugs? If it could happen to people of such talent and potential, it would help break the stereotype of addiction being a disease strictly of the underclass. Anthony was feeling quite egalitarian.

He was mildly surprised that Lisa's door was open. Then again, she was a brazen whore. He silently entered the apartment. The front room was dimly lit. He could hear the shower running. He smiled and laid his kit on the table next to the couch. In his hand was a chloroform-doused rag that would render her unconscious in a matter of seconds. The rest would be easy.

He took off his shoes. Then, he removed his pants and folded them neatly on the couch. His pulse quickened as he became hard at the thought of violating his unconscious victim. "Right up the ass, she's going to take it. I might need to let her wake up a bit just so she can feel the pain," he thought as he crept toward the shower, the rag in one hand and his erection in the other. "And to think they actually pay me for this!" He reached the bathroom door. With one quick motion, he opened it and pulled back the shower curtain.

The shower was empty. He was momentarily confused, and then he heard a sound from behind him. He turned around. Before he could let go of his penis, Lisa fired two shots into his chest. He collapsed backward into the tub. The shower water ran over his face, washing the blood from his chest and down the drain.

Lisa felt nothing—not joy, not relief, nothing. She walked into the kitchen, poured herself a glass of water, and put the gun on the table, waiting for Anton to arrive.

Anton, Todd, and Dale rode in silence to Biddeford. Restraining the urge to travel at extraordinary speed, they were aware of the risk of being pulled over. That would only delay them further. When they arrived at Lisa's apartment, they noticed her car was parked in the usual spot. No other cars were in sight. They sprinted up the stairs and burst through the door. Lisa heard them but did not move from her spot in the kitchen. She waited for them to find her.

Anton spotted her first and saw the gun on the table. "Lisa, are you OK? I'm so glad we got here before anything happened."

Lisa smiled, jumped up, and fell into Anton's arms. They were locked in each other's grip, as if to prove they were both alive and present with each other.

Todd spotted the gun. "So, Lisa, when did you start packing heat?"

Dale picked it up and looked at it admiringly. "Hell, back where I come from, everybody carries an equalizer, especially women. I don't know what's up with you Yankees, but back home we don't take kindly to being passive victims." He then noticed the powder residue on the barrel. "This thing has been discharged recently."

Lisa loosened her grip on Anton and took a step back. "In the bathroom."

Todd was the first one to get there. "Holy shit!"

Anton and Dale followed.

"Fuckin' A, fuckin' A, Lisa. Way to go! Gave that son of a bitch what he had coming," Dale said.

Todd wiped his mouth with the back of his hand. "It is, of course, a bit of an uncomfortable dilemma for us. After all, what do we do with a dead body and massive bloodstains?"

"He is not our worry," Anton said. "They cannot acknowledge his existence, or else they compromise their identity. We can safely dispose of this body. Nobody will ever look for him or acknowledge he ever existed. We have to anticipate their next move."

"They could just hire somebody else to kill us," said Todd.

"Perhaps, but I expect they will want this trail to go cold. They framed Ben Able, and they could easily frame us, stick us in jail for a couple of decades."

"OK, time for an intense strategy session," Todd said. "Lisa, do you have any alcohol in this apartment?" Not waiting for an answer, he began opening cabinets in the kitchen. He grabbed a bottle of vodka, took out four glasses, and poured a portion in each. "I don't know about you guys, but I do not plan on going to jail sober."

"Ain't nobody going to jail," said Dale as he lifted his glass and offered a toast to his friends. "To overcoming adversity, surviving great odds, living the adventure of a lifetime, and bringing OncogenX and all their cronies to their knees."

"Bold statement for a guy facing twenty years to life for running a drug cartel," Todd said. "But I like your spirit. I'll drink to that!"

Anton looked at his friends and Lisa. "I would tell you that you don't need to follow me into this abyss. I'm prepared to insulate you from consequence and walk this path that I started alone."

They were all about to protest, but Anton held up his hand. "I know your hearts, and I know you're in this just like I am. I still believe we will find a way. I can call my father. We can get a great attorney and fight this."

Todd scoffed. "Look, Anton, the whole call-your-father thing didn't work out so great last time. You have a genius for certain things, but legal strategy doesn't appear to be one of them."

Dale nodded. "Freeze is right. This is not our moment. They have too much power, too many resources. We need to strategically redeploy and live to fight another day."

"What does 'strategically redeploy' mean?" asked Lisa.

"We gotta beat a motherfucking retreat and get the hell out of this country to safe haven," Dale said. "Cuba does not have an extradition treaty with the United States. Furthermore, they fancy themselves leaders in advanced medical research. We could be welcomed there as rebel researchers."

"Should I be concerned that you know so much about extradition?" Todd asked.

"Where I come from, we don't always look at the federal government as our friend. Let's just say I've had buddies take advantage of safe haven."

"It is warm in Havana," said Lisa. "Nice beaches for midnight swims." She squeezed Anton's hand. He blushed.

"Cut out the goddamned flirting, you two," Dale said. "We got serious business to focus on."

"*Quiero una mujer hermosa,*" Todd said. "I hear the women down there are hot."

Anton looked at the clock. "We have a few hours. Whoever sent him will expect a report back at some point. When they don't get that report, they will seek answers themselves. We have a small window of time."

Dr. Tara Lidoffi sat in her office sipping brandy as she stared out the window from her large conference table, listening to Cliff Doherty.

"So when we didn't hear from him, we did a follow-up and found his car parked in an alley near Lisa's apartment. No sign of him. No sign of Lisa. Thresher, Freeze, and Davis likewise all disappeared."

Dr. Lidoffi rolled the brandy in the glass, alternating sips with staring out the window.

"Should we go after them, Tara? I have other resources."

"They're running. As long as they're running, they present no threat. Do we have everything in place as we had discussed?"

"Yes, we have our contacts ready to act if needed."

"Good. Let's wait a few days. Let them flee. Then, call the police and get the warrants. Wherever they land, they will be trapped there, unable to move. If they are in the United States, we will put them in jail. If they are overseas, they will be irrelevant."

She sat up straighter in her chair. "Tomorrow will be an exciting day for OncogenX and for us. The press conference and the publicity storm to follow will send our stock skyrocketing. We stand on the threshold of a massive fortune. It was a tad sloppy, but in the end, things worked out for us, Cliff. Sometimes, God works in mysterious ways. Thresher may have been a genius, but he needed to be eliminated in order for his work to show its true value. Whatever we did to get to this point is justified by the good that will come of it." She drank the remainder of her brandy in one swift gulp.

CHAPTER 49

T he small package was postmarked "Hopedale, Maine, USA."
It flooded Lisa with warm memories. She brought it out to
Anton, who was sitting at his desk on the back porch overlooking Havana Harbor. Anton was writing, as usual. Ever since arriving in Cuba six months ago, he had spent his time reviewing
his research and working on new theories. Lisa had gotten a job
at El Gato Tuerto. She had immersed herself in the language and
culture of the country. She was already conversant in Spanish
and had become one of the most popular waitresses at the club.

Dale and Todd had purchased a fishing boat. When they
were not working the water themselves, they would take out
rental parties for fishing day trips.

Lisa handed the package to Anton. "It's addressed to you.
Open it. It's from Mr. Carlisle."

Anton opened the box and took out two carefully packed
coffee mugs with the Cambridge Inn's logo on them. He took out
the accompanying note and read it out loud.

"Never forget your time in Hopedale, the feelings you felt,
and the plans you made. Remember all the friends you made
and all the people who believe in you. Truth can only be buried but never killed. I know you will know what to do with the
small package. In the memory of my beloved wife, I've taken
up a new horticultural hobby. I hope this information pleases
you!"

The box had a false bottom. Upon opening it, Anton took
out a smaller package. It was orange fern. He held it up to show
Lisa.

"From Mr. Carlisle."

"Whoever thought he would possess the heart of a fearless rebel?" she said. "Well, what now?"

"Time to call in the fishermen from the sea and let them know their vacation is over. Looks like it's time for us to get back to work."

The limousine crawled through the streets of New York City. Scott and Ann Antonelli sat in the back.

"Really, Scott, don't you think you've had enough champagne? You'll need to be speaking in front of the entire board."

"They don't give a fuck what I say. I just need to show up."

"Scott, that's a terrible attitude. You're an important man. If not for you, none of this would be happening. You've earned it. You should be feeling proud of what you've done."

"Yeah, Ann, I am incredibly fucking proud."

Ever since the press release, the stock at OncogenX had tripled. Scott's name and likeness, along with those of Dr. Walter Proctor, were distributed throughout news outlets around the country. Dr. Proctor had been basking in all the glory. Scott was quiet or irritable, at times. His attitude baffled Ann.

The money was flowing in, as were the accolades. Scott was a medical hero. Ann could not have been more proud.

The drug trials were going so well that the FDA was planning on fast tracking the drug to market. With an estimated retail price of $5,000 per month for treatment, profits were projected into the billions. The results were so profound that the insurance companies would have no choice but to cover the expense. It was a medical gold mine.

Scott had yet to practice medicine—or, for that matter, actually pursue any work. His life revolved around giving interviews, delivering speeches, and showing up at his office at OncogenX just often enough to give him proper cover. He and Ann had bought one of the most expensive homes of the east side of

Providence, Rhode Island. They were immediately welcomed into the circles of the elite.

Ann had made it her business to screen all the mail they received. On occasion, she would recognize the handwriting on a letter that was postmarked from Havana, Cuba. She would never open such letters but destroyed them, even though they were addressed to Scott. They were part of Scott's past. They didn't belong in their new, beautiful life. Why couldn't his former friends leave them alone?

Ann had always thought that Anton's behavior was strange. After the arrest warrant for drug production, it all seemed to make sense to her. Of course he was a closet drug addict. Of course he was doing things illicitly. That explained so much—his distance, his failure to fit in. Ann wanted Scott to have nothing to do with him or the others. She wanted Scott to pick a new godfather for Scott Junior.

Periodically, there would be a repeat round of stories in the press describing the secret lives of Anton Thresher and his friends. Apparently, they had used their status as physicians to gain access to the laboratory equipment necessary to run their illegal drug operation.

So long as they remained invisible in Cuba, OncogenX could comfortably ignore them.

Scott continued his nightly habit of staying awake late, long after Ann and the baby were in bed. She was expecting their second child and became tired more quickly than ever. On this night, Scott was somewhere between his fourth and fifth round of vodka. He was shuffling through the papers on the desk and saw an envelope that Ann had missed. He recognized Todd Freeze's handwriting. He felt a strange joy as he tore the envelope open. In it was a photo of Todd, Dale, Lisa, and Anton sitting around a table with one empty chair. Scott could recognize the orange fern on the table.

Todd had scrawled a message at the bottom of the photo: "Truth never sleeps. There is a chair for you at our table. You can live a better life."

Scott stared at the photograph for perhaps a minute or an hour. He walked through his palatial home, slowly examining each room. They had been here only two months, but already Ann had filled it with the most elegant furnishings. In one hand, he held the vodka; in the other, he held the photo. He found himself in his bedroom looking at Ann in her contentment of sleep. He knew he had done the right thing. If he had not acted, what good could have come? Shame? Poverty? Had he not been a force to move things forward?

His wandering led him to his office. It was in an isolated wing of the house. His glass was empty. Fortunately, he had another bottle in his bottom drawer. He opened it and poured.

He held the glass up to the photo. "To you, Anton, you fucking genius. You saved the world and destroyed me all at once."

He took out a cigar, put a match to it, and took in a deep breath. He folded the photograph and stored it in his bottom drawer, underneath a box. He kept it with the other photographs that he had been able to save before Ann had a chance to purge them.

Scott sat on his desk and looked across the table to the opposite wall. He held his glass up toward the large crystal sculpture, the one that he had been awarded for "Medical Innovator of the Year."

"A toast to me, medical fraud of the year!" He drank the shot in one gulp, filled his glass, and sat behind his desk. His drunkenness was now at the peak of disinhibition and just before the rapid deterioration of motor function. He liked feeling this way, with no pain. The alcohol washed his mind clean. It seemed to clear his vision. What was he doing here? What purpose could he serve? He imagined his friends in Havana laughing and enjoying each other's company, thinking about what they would do next. What would he do next? He was alone in his lie, and he would take it to his grave.

He opened the drawer, took out the pictures, and began looking through them again. One of them was his favorite. It had been taken around the dinner table at his father's house. All his friends were there. That had been a great night, the best ever.

A thought came to him, and with that he felt his mood lift. He stood up and noted he was still capable of walking, as long as he concentrated. He went to the kitchen, grabbed the keys, and headed for the garage. Once there, he took the cover off his baby. He ran his hand over the motorcycle's gas tank and then the seat. He stood back to admire its beauty. He put the key in the ignition, turned it on, and straddled his machine.

With one swift kick-start, the engine roared to life. He suddenly felt clear headed and sober as the adrenaline surged through him. He opened the throttle, felt the vibration, and reveled in the sound.

"Son of a bitch, you beautiful son of a bitch!" he yelled at a level equal to the roar of the engine. "Remember that night, Anton? Do you remember it like I do? Motherfucker. Fuck you. Fuck me. Fuck everybody!" He was overwhelmed with the urge to take his motorcycle out to the street and race at the highest-possible speed. He opened the garage door.

It was then he noticed movement out of the corner of his eye. Ann was holding Scott Junior in her arms.

Scott let the engine quiet down enough so he could hear her.

"What are you doing, Scott? You woke up the baby, and now he's crying! What is wrong with you? Have you gone mad? Why are you doing this to me? Why can't you just be happy?" The tears were streaming down her face as she clutched Scott Junior, who was crying as well. "You have everything, Scott. You have everything."

Scott looked at her and the baby, and then looked out toward the night. He pushed the motorcycle off the kickstand and balanced it while revving the engine.

"Where are you going, Scott? You can't drive in that condition. Get back in here this instant. I'm telling you for the last time, Scott, get off that motorcycle. It's the last time I ever want to see that thing."

Scott pulled in the clutch and put the motorcycle into gear.

"I'm warning you, Scott. What do you think you're doing? Where do you think you're going?"

"Havana, Lisa. I'm going to Havana."

He was not quite sure how he did it, but somehow, despite his inebriation, Scott was able to pilot his motorcycle from Providence all the way down to Galilee, a beach about forty-five minutes from his home. He found himself lying on a bench, facing out toward the ocean. He must have fallen asleep because he could see the early dawn light streaking through the dark sky. In a short time, the sun would be up. He sat up on the bench, put his feet on the ground, and rested his elbows on his knees as he looked out over the water, waiting for the sun. He looked at his phone. There were four texts from Lisa. Then, he noticed one that he hadn't expected. It was from his father.

It was simple: "Please come home."

This sun had now risen. Scott closed his eyes and felt its orange warmth on his eyelids. He imagined dying a noble death. How nice it would be not to have to look at his reflection in the mirror anymore.

He felt his pocket. Salvation! He had a small bottle with him. He opened it and drank it like a thirsty man drinking water. He instantly felt revived. Energy and purpose came to him.

"Looks like it's just me and you," he said to his motorcycle. "What do you say we play motorcycle roulette? Let's let the Fates determine what comes next."

He hopped on his motorcycle and headed for the highway. At this early hour, it was nearly empty. Seventy, eighty, ninety— the speedometer kept rising as he kept the throttle wide open. When it hit one hundred twenty, he yelled. "Fuckin' A! Take me home! Take me home!"

Hello friend, and thank you for reading my book. I hope you enjoyed reading it as much as I loved writing it. The first chapter was started when I was 25 years old. One of the things I find remarkable is that the social, financial, and emotional truths in the book have stood up over time. This fiction is informed by true life motives. The story comes frighteningly close to reality.

Now that you have read the story, I would like to ask a favor. If you could please write an honest review telling others what you think of the book, and hopefully giving it a robust five star rating, that would help raise its profile and spread the message to others that would enjoy hearing about it. Please also include if you would like to see a sequel to this novel. I already have the process happening in my head, with a little nudge it will become my second book. Hopefully I can write in less than 25 years.

Please leave your review on Amazon.com

spetterutiwriter@gmail.com

www.ingramcontent.com/pod-product-compliance
Lightning Source LLC
Chambersburg PA
CBHW020243180626
46810CB00006B/2339